UNDER THE STRETCHER

MAX LEVIN

PRAISE FOR MAX LEVIN

"A gripping account of American Jewish youth's service in an elite unit of the Israeli paratroopers. A must read for young people who are considering serving as a Lone Soldier in the IDF or making aliya to Israel."

~ Michael Oren—Former Ambassador to the United States of America

---

Under the Stretcher is the journey of Max Levin from St. Louis to Los Angeles, to summers in Israel, to a battlefield, to being an instructor.

It is more than a journey of time, it is a journey of strength, determination, passion, compassion and loss. Max Levin's, Under the Stretcher, gives us life lessons of perseverance in situations no one could be prepared for, until the moment in which they happen. At that defining moment, his thoughts would go back to his family, his training, friends, team and officers, all who gave him honor, dignity and the ability to act. A boy who dreamed, acted on those dreams, worked hard, and became more than a solider. He became a better human being, helping others to become better than themselves and wishing for a world of peace.

Under the Stretcher tells the story of Max Levin, yet it motivates all of us. To be carrying a stretcher with the goal of saving a life. Max Levin carrying the stretcher helps us see our choices and the legacy we can make.

~ Russell Robinson—CEO Jewish National Fund

Max's story exemplifies what it means to be a good soldier and the morals that we instill in our young men and women. He goes above and beyond and shows a new side of being an Israeli soldier, one that not only faced difficult decisions but also shows the vulnerabilities and strength our young men and women endure. I recommend this book to all that support Israel, it's army, and those that want to better understand on the ground situations here in the Middle East. Max's story has shown the reality of being an IDF soldier today and his continued commitment to the reserves (miluim).

~ Brigadier General Rami Zur—Second Division Commander of the Paratrooper Reserves Units 55 and 5535

I am enormously proud of Max and all that he has accomplished. His story exemplifies what it means to be a true Zionist, one that is willing to learn, feel, and support our great nation even at great risk to his own life. He shows that Israel is not just a land for Israeli's but for all Jews, one that we must defend and protect at all costs.

~ Naty Saidoff—Founder and principal owner of Capital Foresight & Chairman of the Board of Israel American Council (IAC).

Max's story is riveting. I have the pleasure of knowing Max personally. He is a leader. He is a zionist. He does not quit. This book is a testament to all of his wonderful qualities. I can undoubtedly say—Under the Stretcher is a MUST read.

~ Natalie Elisha Gold, CEO Goldberg LLP, Media personality and 4x bestselling author

---

Max,

I started reading your book today and simply could not put it down.

I finished the entire book in one sitting.

You forgot to tell me to have some kleenex nearby.

Max Levin takes us on a journey of dedication, will power, and ultimately triumph. For anyone who wants to know the real path to protecting the State of Israel, Max takes us through unforgiving 'sands' and endless tribulations toward creating one of the finest fighting forces in the world. He also details for us the intense emotions in the midst of battle, and the loss of beloved 'brothers' who fell in the defense of their Jewish homeland. Under the Stretcher is a must read for those who care about Israel, and for all of us to understand what it really takes to defend a nation.

~ Dr. Bruce Powell—Former Head of DeToledo High School and Milken High School

---

As a former teammate of Max's and now the current commander of the Palchan Tzanhanim Unit, I am very proud to see that Max has shed light on many of the difficult situations and decisions our IDF soldiers have to make every day. His story and our team's story will shake you to the core of what it means to be an IDF soldier and make difficult decisions in dire circumstances. I highly recommend this book to any who aspire to one day become a special forces combat soldier or simply want to learn more about what it really means to be an IDF soldier today.

~ Major Ofir Tuchterman—Current head of the Special Forces Unit—Palchan Tzanhanim

---

Max Levin is an extraordinary individual. While still in his 20s he has already lived, seen, experienced, suffered and survived enough to fill a book, the one before you. It is a story of ordeal and adventure, of idealism put into practice, devotion, unyielding will and true grit. The book is written in a simple but engaging style, clear-eyed and with utter honesty. But one feels that Max's tale has only just begun ...

~ Joey Price—Head of Languages Department at Tel Aviv University

חבלה מוצנחת

"Under the Stretcher"

Published by Red Penguin Books

Bellerose Village, New York

Library of Congress Control Number: 2020916702

ISBN

Print 978-1-63777-046-7 | 978-1-63777-034-4

Digital 978-1-952859-30-4

Although all the stories in this book are true, many of the names and places have been changed in order to protect people's identities, as many of them are still actively defending the state of Israel and the Jewish people against those who wish to do us harm.

CONTENTS

MAPS

ISRAEL
LEBANON
UNDOF
SYRIA
GOLAN
MEDITERRANEAN
SEA
Nahariya
Acre
Karmiel
Sea of Galilee
Haifa
Tiberias
Nazareth
Afula
Hadera
Netanya
Tulkarm
Nabulus
Tel Aviv-Yafo
Petah Tikva
Holon
Rishon LeZion
WEST BANK
Ramla
Jericho
AMMAN
Ashdod
JERUSALEM
Beit Shemesh
Ashkelon
Bethlehem
Gaza
Kiryat Gat
Hebron
Dead Sea
JORDAN
GAZA STRIP
Rahat
Khan Yunis
Ofakim
Beersheba
Ar'arat an-Naqab
Dimona
EGYPT
Eilat
Gulf of Aqaba

Kfar
Qaddum
Kedumim
Nablus
Jinsafut
Ariel
WEST
BANK
ISRAEL
Jerusalem
East Jerusalem
Maale Adumim
Gillo
Um Tuba
Har Homa
Al-Khas
Nu'aman
Betar Illit
Nahalin
Bethlehem
Nahal Gevaot
Neve Daniel

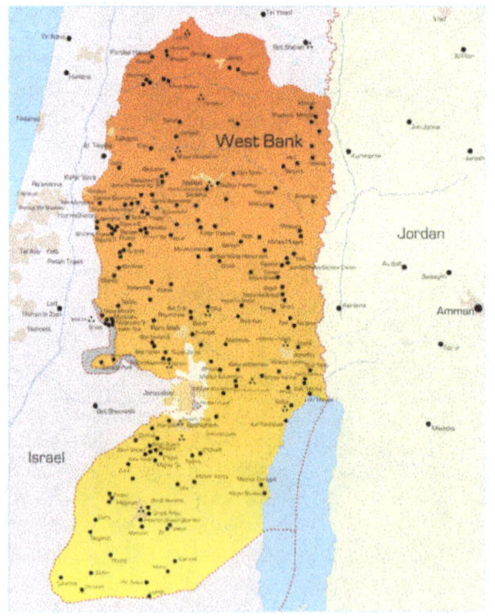

West Bank
Jordan
Amman
Israel

MEDITERRANEAN
SEA
Yad Mordehai
Netiv Ha-Asara
Erez
Erez/
Beit Lahia
Beit Hanoun
Jabalia
GAZA
Wahsh
Mefalsim
Kfar Aza
Karni
Nahal Oz
Sa'ad
Alumim
Shuva
Tushiya
Nuseirat
Bureij
Deir al-Balah
Mughazi
Be'eri
Shokeda
Re'im
ISRAEL
(Kissufim)
Kissufim
Jarara
Ein Hashlosha
Bani Suheila
Khan Yunis
Nirim
Abasan al-Saghira
Abasan alkabir
Nir Oz
Magen
Rafah
al-Buyuk
al Fukhari
Ein Habsor
EGYPT
Sufa
Ami'oz
Rafah
Yesha
Sufa
Nir Yitzhak
Mivtahim
Kerem Shalom
Kerem Shalom
Holit
Sdej Avraham
Pri Gan

PROLOGUE

Members from my team practicing entering tunnels

I had just returned from a drill with my team. We'd been under the scorching sun all day and were exhausted. The team and I had been preparing for a mission to enter Gaza to destroy two terrorists' tunnels. Long hours were spent going over the details of the mission, what everyone's job was, the maps, what to expect, as well as the "what if" scenarios. This was what I had signed up for, to be able to protect my country, my family, and my friends, and maybe for some sense of duty, honor, and glory, but days like these were draining. Now all I wanted was to get back and collapse on my cot to rest.

Finally, reaching the opened green tent, I laid down my gun, put my bag in a chet formation, which is like a square with one side missing, with the rest of my team and collapsed onto my cot. However, before I had a chance to close my eyes, Paz, my commander, came through and ordered us to clean our guns, restock ammunition, repack our bags and make sure we'd be ready at a moment's notice.

I sighed and grudgingly went outside, exchanging glances with Noah and Dover, two of my teammates, wondering if this exercise was really necessary. As I started to clean my gun, shouts of "Hakpatzah! Hakpatzah!" came from one of the boys from Team 20 as he ran through the camp. This was what our commanders would yell during training when there was an emergency. But we'd been through over a year of training and had finished our most recent drill.

I felt paralyzed watching that guy run through camp. I looked over at Noah and Dover, and muttered, "I hope this isn't for real."

That's when Paz exclaimed that it was the real deal. "Something's happened. We need to respond. Immediately!"

That's when the team and I went into a frenzy, everyone grabbing their bags, vests and, of course, guns. I sprinted back and forth, tossing equipment onto the green Egged bus, which is the largest transit bus company in Israel. Soon, eighteen of us had gotten all our gear onto that bus and were leaving camp.

As we drove out from the base, I studied Paz who was the only one with any information, getting it from the walkie talkie in his vest. Just then, he turned toward me. "Do you know the way to Kibbutz Nir Yitzhak?"

Of course, I knew! It's where my friends and I used to go and party at their bar on Saturdays. I said, "That's a five-minute drive from my own kibbutz, Nir Oz."

Paz then announced to us that a group of Hamas terrorists had infiltrated into Israel through a tunnel under the Gaza border. As far as he knew, this was the first time an incident like this had occurred. Our mission was to defend the kibbutz from a possible attack. I gazed out the window, at the arid countryside, not a person in sight, the bus kicking up dust and the sun was setting as we traveled into what would be an unknown situation. Right then, my stomach began to turn, the gravity of what could be was becoming clear to me: I was going to my neighbor's kibbutz, a five minute drive from my own, to defend friends and family.

With little time to think, I opened the Google map on my phone, making sure we followed the quickest route. I stood next to the driver, giving him directions.

Just then, Paz yelled, "Wait! We now must go to Kibbutz Nir Am!"

I looked over at Paz. "Not Nir Yitzhak?"

When Paz confirmed as much, I changed the route on my phone and redirected the driver. Moments later, we'd arrived at the edge of the kibbutz. The sounds of rocket fire were in the distance. This *was* the real deal. I grabbed my bag and helped my team with their things. We hurriedly formed a chet formation around Paz.

He looked at me and instructed that I was to go out with a group of eight soldiers, along with our sergeant, Tamir, to patrol the southwest border of the kibbutz. I ran to the head of the line, next to Tamir, and we rushed to the area where rockets and mortars from within Gaza were pounding the neighboring kibbutzim. Israeli planes and helicopters were retaliating with their own rocket fire.

As we patrolled, the earth shook from the persistent explosions. After eight hours, the sun rose. But we didn't have any updates. I switched my night vision goggles for binoculars and continued searching for any suspicious movements outside of the kibbutz's security fence. The mortars and rockets had slowed but would it stay that way? Camouflaged, Matt, another American-Israeli soldier from my team, and I climbed on top of some hay bales for a better view. Still, no movement could be detected.

Once another four hours had gone by, Tamir returned from his patrol. He explained that Maglan, another Special Forces unit that was also charged with searching for terrorists, had found and captured the enemy a few miles north of us. The kibbutzim wanted us to stay put and continue guarding for the next couple of days. I walked back to the center of the kibbutz to regroup with my team, reminded of how I got from St. Louis to here.

1

JOURNEYS

"You can be cut from the same cloth and still make different garments." ~ *Baylor Barbee*

I was raised in St. Louis but visited Israel every summer with my family. My father worked for United Jewish Appeal, a philanthropic organization, but we traveled there mainly because my parents were ardent Zionists. They believed in supporting Israel, the homeland for all Jews. They went on many missions supported by the Jewish National Fund (JNF) of which both my parents were volunteers and served on local and national boards.

During one of these annual trips, when I was eight years old, we visited a close family friend, Udi, who was a commander in the Israeli Defense Forces (IDF) at the time. My mom insisted that we visit him during our trip. Before leaving the States, we visited a Sam's Club so that she could load up on American candy to bring him and the other soldiers. She literally stuffed an entire suitcase full of M&M's, Twizzlers, Hershey bars, Nestle's Crunch, and other candies.

At the time, Udi was stationed near the West Bank. This was not a safe place to travel by car, but we were determined to see him. The signs were all in Arabic, and we got lost along the way. We were circling for hours before we finally made it to Udi's base. He greeted us warmly at the perimeter of the base and escorted us in.

The sights and sounds on the base were enthralling to me as a child. The guns, the men in uniform and the guard posts rising into the sky. The military atmosphere was mystifying, like something out of a movie, only it was real and in front of my very eyes.

Udi gave me a tour of the base. I asked a million questions about everything. We passed by an observation tower with a tall ladder running up to a platform where armed men were patrolling. Udi explained that it was a sniper lookout point. He told me that the week before, they had needed to disperse protesters by firing rubber bullets from the tower. They also had real bullets, of course, in case of an actual attack and not just a protest getting out of hand.

The scene played out in my head like an action movie. In my mind, Udi transformed into a real live war hero. I was in awe of all the soldiers. I wanted to be like them—brave and defiant and ready to defend our nation from attack. I began making plans right then and there to join the IDF when I turned eighteen. I told Udi my plans. He seemed pleased. He gave me a big hug before we left at the end of the day. He even let me try on a vest and hold his gun. I promised right then and there, at the ripe old age of eight years old, I would come back one day and help protect Israel, too.

My parents continued taking me to Israel every summer. My love for the place only deepened as I grew older and established more ties with Israel. My first true Israeli friend was a boy named Aharon, whom I met at summer camp in Jerusalem. We became very close and met up every summer when I came back. We spent days in the pool at the King David Hotel, where my parents stayed. We played soccer at parks and in the streets with his friends. I visited him at his home in Jerusalem every summer.

In the eighth grade, my family moved from St. Louis to Los Angeles. I started attending a Jewish high school. This is when my love of Israel really flourished. As a child, I had great affection for the place. As a teenager, I began to understand what it meant to the Jewish people. In the tenth grade, I joined fifteen classmates for a three-month exchange program to Israel. I did not want to come home at the end of the three months. I actually hid inside my host family's laundry in an attempt to stay. Of course, they found me, and I had to go back to California.

By this time, I felt firm in the conviction that had started all those years ago as an eight-year-old boy. I wanted to go to Israel and serve in the IDF. I started to research the different combat units of the IDF. One of my favorite books was Aaron Cohen's *Brotherhood of Warriors*, which told the story of an American from Los Angeles who served in the prestigious Duvdevan unit. By chance, a family friend, Arik Poremba, had been a captain and commander in that unit. He served nine years in total. These personal connections made serving in the IDF seem more plausible, despite the great distance.

Arik lived in St. Louis and I would have lunch with him when we went back to visit for the holidays. The last time we had lunch, before I moved, I was a senior in high school then and nearing graduation. The idea of going to Israel to serve in the IDF loomed larger than ever in my mind. Over lunch, Arik and I talked about his service. I confessed my desire to join the IDF and asked if he had any advice. He was very encouraging and gave me a workout routine to follow. He even suggested that I might be a good fit for the paratrooper Special Forces, known as Gadsar Tzanhanim, which consisted of three special units—the Palsar, the Palchan, and the Palnat or nicknamed "Orev" after the missal the Palnat carried. Taking his advice to heart, I decided I would attempt to join one of these three units.

I had one more opportunity to visit Israel before graduating. My high school offered a "March of The Living" program during my senior year, which consisted of accompanying a group of holocaust survivors living in Los Angeles on a trip. We would spend one week in Poland and another in Israel. This was an opportunity I couldn't miss. I was fortunate enough that my parents allowed me to go on such a trip, one that was inspiring. I was already sure of my decision to join the IDF. That trip only cemented my desire.

However, I still had to get my parents on board with the idea. I broached the subject when I came home from the trip. They were not pleased. They both wanted me to enroll in college. My mom was so against the idea that she applied to a dozen colleges on my behalf! I was angry but tried to reason with her. I was eighteen now and capable of making my own decisions. My decision, I explained to her, was to go to Israel. This did not go as smoothly as I hoped, but after much yelling, she agreed to come with me to see the college guidance counselors at my school.

At the counselor's office, we came to a compromise. I would not join the IDF on a whim nor would I go straight to college. Instead, I would spend a gap year in Israel as part of a program called Young Judea. This would allow me to live as an Israeli for a year before committing to join the IDF. We both agreed, but with different motives. She wanted to keep me from making a hasty decision to enlist. I saw the program as an opportunity to live in Israel and strengthen my Hebrew before enlisting.

During my year abroad in Israel, I spent four months in Jerusalem, three in Bat Yam, and the final three in Arad. I took classes during this time, largely to appease my mother, who didn't want the year to be a "waste" if I changed my mind, though many of the classes were also helpful. They helped me practice my Hebrew so I could try to become fluent before joining the army. I took courses to become a medic as part of a joint program between Young Judea and an Israeli ambulance company, Magen David Adom. While in Jerusalem, I spent a total of five weeks training to work on an ambulance as a medic before being issued my medic's uniform. I was proud to be already wearing a uniform, even if it wasn't an IDF uniform. I knew the training would be useful later as a soldier.

During my time in Bat Yam, I volunteered as a medic with the ambulance division. I was pumped. This was a chance to further improve my Hebrew while getting hands-on experience responding to emergencies. I expected to be plunged straight into the kinds of harrowing situations I had seen on television. But most emergency calls were not 'real' emergencies. On my first day, I was dispatched to help an old lady who had fallen out of bed and couldn't get up. By the time we arrived, her son had already helped her back into bed. I took her vitals. She was frazzled but ultimately fine. When we were done, the ambulance driver announced that this was my very first call. I turned red from embarrassment while everyone clapped.

Not all dispatch calls were so positive, of course. We often were called in for emergencies. During my three months working as a medic in Bat Yam, I had thirteen patients who could not be saved. I performed CPR on seven people and not one of them survived. The movies had taught me that CPR would bring people springing back to life, but the truth is that it only works 10 percent of the time at best. I knew there was nothing more I could have done, but that didn't make me feel better when someone died on what I considered my watch. I would feel sick to my stomach and get angry when there was nothing more I could do. These times were hard but were balanced out when we were able to save a life or otherwise come to someone's aid in a time of need.

When my time in Bat Yam was over, I went to Arad. Instead of working as a medic, I enrolled in Marva, a three-month army course designed to give Americans a feel for life as a soldier in the IDF. This was just what I needed to decide if I was on the right path. In my second week in Arad, they put all the Marva participants on a bus and transported us to a base in Sde Boker in the Negev Desert.

At the base, we were each issued army boots, a green uniform, and an M16 with cement poured into the barrel to make it inoperable. We were supposed to keep our "rifles" at our side at all times, just like real soldiers, but we weren't real recruits, just a bunch of kids, and they didn't trust us with working rifles. We did do a lot of "real" basic training, though. This is where I learned how to stand in *chet* formation, which meant standing abreast in three lines to form a boxy U-shape around the commander. This allowed the commander to issue orders to everyone at once, which he did almost all day from sunup till sundown. I was both exhausted and exhilarated. We focused on something different each week. We spent a week learning navigation. We spent a week learning to shoot. We even spent a week in the field, known as the *shetach*, where we camped in tents and practiced basic army maneuvers.

During the shetach week, Marva held a simulated *gibush*, or tryout, which was a mock Special Forces tryout. They called the tryout Sayarot Marva. Sayarot was the title given to Israeli Special Forces units. I was excited about the tryout and knew I wanted to join the Israeli Special Forces. So, this would be my chance to prepare for the real test.

This tryout lasted for four grueling hours. We spent the whole-time sprinting, crawling, lugging heavy sandbags, and digging holes. Only the most motivated and determined succeeded. I was proud to be one of the few among the finalists when the whistle was blown at the end of the hole-digging session. We only had one task left: to hold our guns over our heads for thirty minutes straight. This sounds much easier than it actually is. By the time the half-hour was over, my arms were not only exhausted but in actual pain.

The tryout wasn't real and didn't mean anything, but I was proud to have finished and passed. By the time I graduated a month later, I was recognized by my commander as the best soldier on my team. I felt accomplished and sure of my decision to join the IDF. I was secure in the knowledge that one day I would try out for Special Forces for real.

After finishing the Marva program, I joined Garin Tzabar, an organization that helps foreigners interested in joining the IDF get settled in Israel. I was assigned to a kibbutz, Nir Oz, located a mere two kilometers from the Gaza border. This was not the safest location, but Nir Oz felt like an oasis in the desert. I was happy there and it quickly came to feel like home.

I was not alone in this sentiment. I was one of nineteen "lone soldiers," who had come to support Israel by serving in the military, stationed in Nir Oz as part of the Garin Tzabar program. We were called Garin Nir Oz, and together the nineteen of us would be joining the IDF. These people were my "Garin" or community, and without their support on the days I was coming home, this journey would have been much harder and lonelier. "Lone Soldier" is a term for any soldier in the IDF who does not have their direct family in Israel to support them. Although this is not always the case, it is generally a term for those who come from abroad to serve. We were eleven men and eight women, and we all loved the kibbutz and came to see it as home. We were all united through our love of Israel and passion to serve.

These men and women became my brothers and sisters. We trained together daily. We went on long runs. We hit the gym hard. We did laps in the pool and scrambled up dunes together. We carried stretchers weighed down with sandbags around the kibbutz. We trained hard day in and day out. Every one of us wanted the same thing: to get into the best unit we could. Most of the men, myself included, wanted to join either Special Forces or one of the Infantry combat units, such as Tzanhanim aka the paratroopers, or the Golani Brigade. I had never felt so driven in my life, even though I had no idea what the future would hold for me.

My Garin

The Garin at a family Dinner – with our collective father Eli on the right

Swimming pool party with some of the boys

Chocolate eating party (we were not allowed chocolate so don't tell my commander)

2

MY FIRST GIBUSH

"If the plan doesn't work, change the plan but never the goal."
~ Unknown

Doing well on the Sayarot Marva felt good, but ultimately it meant nothing beyond what it did for my confidence. To join the most elite units of the IDF, such as the Special Forces units, I would have to undergo a true *gibush*. This was a serious matter. New recruits are only given one chance to try out for a specific unit. This is where dreams either come true or get laid to rest. There are no do-overs. There are no excuses. Being sick or injured is no excuse. You only get one gibush, period.

The gibush is different from many military tryouts. It doesn't just measure speed, strength, or agility. You are also judged on heart and spirit. The IDF wants to select recruits who will persevere or die trying.

My first gibush was on *Yom Sayarot*, or Special Forces Testing Day. I was bursting with excitement on the day of my tryout. I rose early and left the kibbutz with many of the boys in my garin who were also trying out. We carried our bags and chatted along the way. We were anxious and even giddy with the excitement, unsure of what to expect, but full of hope and aspiration.

The gibush was being held at Wingate Institute, a huge facility where Israeli athletes come to train and that also houses a military base. We arrived four hours early. It took us half an hour to make our way to the back of the facility where we were to convene in a sandy ravine. Several green tents and soldiers were waiting for us at the bottom of the ravine. We confirmed that we were in the right place and checked in.

With three hours to kill before the tryouts, I tried to relax. I listened to music and napped in one of the tents until more people trickled in and the tryouts began. We then formed lines so that they could check our invitations, ID's, and administer a quick medical checkup.

Bureaucratic necessities finally out of the way, the physical test, or *barur*, began. We were split into four groups. Each group underwent the test together. We ran a two-kilometer lap around a field and did sets of pushups and sit-ups. Like typical Israelis, we pushed against each other to get to the front of the lines so we could test first. For the two-kilometer run, I managed to get to the front of the starting line, where two men squeezed in against me on both sides. We were packed together like sardines. Suddenly, the instructor counted down from three and shouted "*Tzeh*!" or Go! We all took off in a sprint. I pushed forward with everyone else, afraid of being trampled by those behind me.

Keeping my wits about me, I remembered to pace myself and conserve my energy. I waited until the last two hundred meters to really push myself, suddenly sprinting ahead of the five men in front of me. Only a certain percentage of us would pass this test. Those who could not finish the run in under ten minutes would be cut and not even get to finish the gibush. I was determined not to be one of those who were cut. I pushed my body forward over the finish line, coming in at a respectable seven and a half minutes.

After the run, we started stretching and waited for the next test. I was trying to rest and gather my strength. Around this time, the soldiers served dinner, rice and vegetables, and we crowded around the food to refuel. After the meal, they started calling out names. Everyone who stood was bigger and huskier. It became clear that these men had failed the running test and were being dismissed. Running and speed are important for Special Forces. They didn't cut anyone for doing poorly on the sit-ups or push-ups but passing the running test was non-negotiable. Thankfully, they did not call my name, nor did they call any of my friends. We had all passed the first part.

We were given sleeping bags and told to get some shuteye. We would be waking up early in the morning. We each undid our sleeping bags and slept on the floor. I tried hard to sleep, but the floor was uncomfortable, and bright fluorescent lights were shining down on us from above. I struggled to get any sleep at all. Before I knew it, they were waking us up at three o'clock in the morning.

The previous day had only been the preliminary tests. The gibush really got started the second day. We began with a short run and light stretching to warm up. We were then taken to an area with equipment lined up in rows. There were stretchers, sandbags, jerry cans, shovels, and everything else we would be working with for the next few hours.

Equipment for the Gibush

I heard my name called over a loudspeaker along with my assigned number. I was teamed up with about twenty others. Each group formed a *chet* formation around our commander. The commanders looked imposing in their black fleeces and big dark sunglasses. When they spoke, we listened. They gave commands in Hebrew. My Hebrew was still not the best, but the commands were simple, and I followed along well enough. We carried out their orders to a T with all of our effort.

The commanders ordered us to pick up the equipment and follow behind them. Each man scrambled to fill his arms in an effort to impress the commanders. At their order, we filed into lines behind one of the commanders and hiked up the sand dunes with the gear in our arms. They climbed high up onto a large central dune before they ordered us to stop. "*Azore*!" the commanders shouted, and we stopped immediately and fell into *chet* formation again.

They had us run drills up on the dunes. We started by sprinting down the dune and back up again. The sand gave beneath our boots, making it hard to run, and grains of sand blew into our eyes and mouths. We stumbled down the dune together and then, spun around and came trudging back up to where we began. We were pushing and shoving each other to be the first to finish. I hoped my days drilling for the high school football team would give me an edge. I came in third.

We trudged up and down the hill over and over. The commanders would call out our numbers and jot them down. They were ranking us against each other. We had no idea when this would end. We just did as we were told and continued to run the best we could. We weren't given a moment of rest before being ordered down the dune again.

By the time they let us break, after an hour of running up and down the dune, the group had begun to dwindle. Some of the men had dropped out, or simply stopped sprinting, deciding that this wasn't for them after all. These men were dismissed. The rest of us were told to form another *chet*. There were only about twenty men remaining. Six had already quit. We were instructed to drink water to rehydrate. The instructors watched as we helped each other pour water from the jerry can into our little plastic cups.

However, the water tasted funny. There were little bubbles of oil floating at the top. The jerry can must have been used to hold oil and probably had not been cleaned properly. The water started to make everyone sick and the men began vomiting over the sand. I struggled against the urge to vomit, knowing it might weaken me, so I held it all in. Realizing that something was wrong with the water, the commanders opened another jerry can and passed out clean water. This time, the water tasted better, but it was too late for me. I was already sick. My stomach was churning.

After having more water, we were ordered to fill sandbags with sand and load them onto the stretchers. We were also told to place two full jerry cans by each stretcher. We then resumed our drills. This time, we would sprint down and up the hill as before, but the first eight men to finish would do another lap while carrying the stretcher. The next two men would carry the jerry cans down and up the dune. The rest of the men would have to run the next lap empty-handed, which was easier. Essentially, if you were one of the first ten, your life would be harder.

I scrambled as hard and as fast as I could. I didn't get back in time to get the stretcher, but I was able to grab one of the jerry cans. The second time around, I dove for a stretcher and managed to grab hold of one end. We hoisted it up onto our shoulders and carried it down the dune and back up again.

Carrying the loaded stretchers was difficult and tiring, but we fought over the right to help carry the sandbags. The point of the drill was to test our determination. The commanders wanted to see who was the strongest and who tried the hardest. It wasn't just about strength—it was about having heart and determination.

My stomach was really starting to bother me at this point. I became very nauseous and realized that I should have thrown up when I had the chance. The sun was beating down on me and my head was spinning. My performance started to suffer. I started to get discouraged and began questioning my own abilities. The negative thoughts were getting the best of me, so I forced them out of my mind. I promised myself that I would finish, no matter what, even if I didn't make the cut.

We were given another water break and I took the opportunity to move off to the side and vomit into the sand. This helped me feel a little better. I felt a renewed strength to match my determination and ready for anything. I needed this optimism when people were dropping out left and right. When we formed another *chet* to receive our next orders, another four men had dropped out. There were only sixteen of us left standing.

Our next test involved hole digging. We were instructed to dig a meter-wide hole as deep as possible. We were not told how much time we had. They just wanted to see us dig as fast and hard as possible. I grabbed my shovel and began to dig. No one had ever taught me how to dig a hole properly. I didn't even know if there was a proper way. I simply drove my shovel into the ground as fast as possible. Eventually, the hole was deep enough to sit in it. I sat on the side and kept shoveling deeper.

Unfortunately, this position caused my legs to start cramping. I kept shoveling through the pain, but eventually my legs locked up and wouldn't move. I took a few minutes to stretch, making a mental note to stretch between tasks in the future. I went back to shoveling as soon as I possibly could. Reminding myself that this was my best shot of getting in. Every second counted.

We must have been shoveling for an hour straight before the commanders told us to stop. Every muscle in my body ached. The commanders walked around and asked us about our holes. Everyone's holes were more or less the same, except for one man who had dug a hole twice as deep as he was tall! Fortunately for him, he was pretty short.

When we were done, the commanders told us to shovel the sand back into our holes. I couldn't believe the request, after all that, just to undo the work was infuriating. But they seemed very serious and gave us five minutes to finish the job. For some reason, the act of filling in the hole felt demoralizing. I was erasing what had taken an hour of backbreaking labor to create. Closing the hole underscored the meaninglessness of having to dig it in the first place. Still, I did as I was told, determined to finish the gibush.

Our last physical test involved running laps up and down the sand dune as before, except this time we had to carry a full sandbag over our shoulders. We were, once again, given no time limit. We were simply supposed to do as many laps as possible, keeping track as we went. I counted off another lap every time I rounded the last jerry can we had set out as markers. I moved up and down the sand dune with a brisk clip, but the sandbag was heavy, and I was careful to pace myself. Not knowing how long we would be drilling I didn't want to collapse in exhaustion under the weight of the sandbag.

Time plays with your mind during these tests. When you don't know how long you will have to do a task, time starts to become meaningless. Ten minutes can seem like two hours. Pacing yourself is difficult in these conditions. Push too hard, and you may not finish. Go too slow, and the others will beat you. This really messes with your mind, which is the whole point. They push your mind as far as possible, not just your body. I was eventually grateful for these exercises when it came to real war.

My considerable stature and long legs gave me an advantage over the men who were not as tall. I could take fewer steps and still keep pace with the others. One of my friends, Nick, a Chilean guy from my Garin, moved even faster, despite being shorter than me. I felt both proud and envious of him. We did laps on the sand dune, the bag up over our heads, for another hour or so as the sun came up and started beating down. I was sweating so hard I could barely see. The heat and exhaustion were taking a toll on both my body and mind. I couldn't think straight. My whole body was in pain by the time the commanders told us to stop.

The commanders asked each of us how many laps we had run. I had done twenty-two laps, a respectable number, though not the best. I had come in fourth, which made me proud. Once we gave them our numbers, they nodded and told us to pack up the equipment. Aiming to impress, we had everything packed up and were ready to march down the sand dune in two single-file lines within two minutes.

When we reached the bottom of the sand dune, the commanders told us to form a large circle. They removed their sunglasses and congratulated us for having finished the physical part of the gibush. I hadn't realized we were already done. A huge weight lifted off my shoulders then.

"This is no simple task, you should all feel proud," the commander said.

They finally introduced themselves to us and told us what units they were from. Now that we had passed the physical test, they treated us more like people and less like numbers. We were asked to say something about ourselves. I was shy, unconfident with my Hebrew, and thus unable to give a proper introduction.

They had one more task before letting us go. The commanders handed out slips of paper and asked us to write down the names of the three participants who had performed the best, as well as the three who performed the worst. We were not allowed to choose ourselves, only others. Most of my friends were in other groups, so my rankings weren't influenced by personal loyalties. I quickly chose those who had done the best and the worst. The decision was easy. We all had eyes and had clearly seen who had done well and who had not.

After we handed in our slips of paper, the commanders congratulated us once more and escorted us back to the tents down in the ravine. We sat in a large crowd with all the other groups. Eventually, a representative for each of the units we were trying out for came to read off a list of names. When called, the recruit rose and went to receive an invitation to another gibush, in which he would compete to join one of three top tier-Special Forces teams—Shayetet, Matkal, Sheldog, 669 and Chovlim. You see, Yom Sayarot, although a gibush, is like a pre-gibush. Once you finish, you are not accepted into any units. Instead, if your name is called, you are given the opportunity to participate in the next round of tryouts for these tier 1 Sayarot units, which were the best of the best.

One by one, men rose and left to receive their invitation to the next gibush. I waited anxiously as the ranks thinned until they were done calling names. My name wasn't called. I was devastated. The handful of us left behind were those who had not passed the tryout. I strained to temper my disappointment by reminding myself that I had at least finished the gibush. Just finishing the Yom Sayarot was an honor in itself.

Despite feeling deflated, I joined my friends to celebrate. The eight of us from my kibbutz all had finished the tryout.

Many of them had passed and were given the opportunity to go in and test for the next round of tryouts.

Once we all grabbed our stuff, we took a bus to nearby Tel-Aviv to celebrate at a burger joint. This was a nicer establishment and we were not dressed for the occasion. We were covered from head to toe in sand. We stank of sweat and probably looked ready to keel over in exhaustion. The proprietor took one look at our party and insisted that we sit outside. We broke out laughing but happily acceded to his demand. We were ravenous and spent. We ordered hamburgers and big glasses of ice-cold lemonade. Food had never ever tasted so good!

I was happy to celebrate with my friends, and truly happy for their good fortune, but my disappointment was immense. The silver lining is that there were other ways into Israel's Special Forces. While I had not passed this gibush and would not be allowed to try again, I was still eligible for other tryouts. Next time, I would have the knowledge and experience from that day to help me succeed. From carrying those sandbags, jerry cans, stretchers, and dealing with the elements, I was being prepared for the real test of protecting human life. So, I may have been disappointed, but I was still hopeful.

3

SWIMMING IN SAND

"Success is not final; failure is not fatal: it is the courage to continue that counts" ~ *Winston Churchill*

My second gibush was a tryout for the paratrooper unit. Once again, I headed over early with friends from my Garin. Not wanting to wait around for hours like last time, we aimed to get there only an hour early. The tryouts were being held at the *bakum*, the general enlistment base, which is a shit show of a place with so many things going on and is so large that unlike many other bases, it is common to use a car to get around. We were still plenty early, though, and had thirty minutes of downtime before we started filling out paperwork. One of the women soldiers, who was administering the paperwork, had to help me fill it out because my Hebrew was still not strong enough to do it on my own. After a quick medical check, I was ready to go.

I was feeling good about my prospects. I had done this once before. My mind was in the right place and I knew what to expect. My second gibush wasn't exactly the same as my first, but they both started in a similar manner. They broke us into small groups. There were far more people than last time and thus more groups. We again started with a two-kilometer run test to weed out those not prepared. I did the run satisfactorily. We then returned to our groups to be assigned commanders. The commanders were far less intimidating than the commanders at Yom Sayarot with their dark sunglasses and stern faces. This time, the commanders were younger and more relatable. We were given cots and tents to sleep in and told to get some rest. This was already a huge improvement compared to Yom Sayarot where we slept on the cement floor with bright lights in our faces all night. However, the real test would begin the next day.

Similar to Yom Sayarot, we got into teams, everyone grabbed some equipment and we made our way out into the sand fields. The next morning, we rose before the sun. I joined my team of twenty-eight men. We gathered equipment and carried it to the same area where we had run laps the day before. It quickly became clear that this gibush would be similar in form to Yom Sayarot.

We started out with sprints, barreling back and forth around a jerry can. We were supposed to keep to some kind of lanes, but with so many men vying for the front, pushing and shoving were inevitable. We were practically falling all over each other. This time I was ready for the competition. I steeled myself against other bodies and ran as hard as I could. Those who came in first at the end of a lap were moved into the outer lanes, which was a disadvantage because those further out had farther to go when rounding corners. I came in near the front after the first lap and was moved further out. The better I did, the harder it was to keep up the next time around. This created a perverse incentive to do well even though doing well meant working harder. That was fine by me. I was doing well. I was pushing hard. I stayed in the top six the whole time.

The commanders started opening up the *alunkot*, or stretchers, before we were even done sprinting. Once again, the second exam involved racing down a hill and around a jerry can and back up in time to grab one of the available loaded-down stretchers so that we could do another lap with it. Of course, there were not enough stretchers for everyone, so we had to compete for the right to carry the stretcher in a perverse game of musical chairs!

This had been one of the hardest tests last time, but I was prepared now. I knew what to do and how hard to push myself. I made it under the stretcher every single time. We drilled for ninety minutes straight, alternating between unencumbered sprints and another lap with the stretcher. We received no break aside from the couple of seconds it took for someone to write down our numbers. This time I was number twenty-one. I reported my number proudly each time.

Our next activity was public speaking. This was new to me. The paratroopers are the only regular battalion in the IDF that requires a tryout. Many great military leaders come from the Tzanhanim (paratroopers) and the battalion places an emphasis on communication and leadership skills. They look for these talents in new recruits. We took turns speaking in front of the group for a minute straight. Having been on the debate team in high school, I was accustomed to speaking in public, but, as I mentioned, my Hebrew was not very good. I spoke carefully as not to embarrass myself by saying the wrong word. We were not allowed to speak about ourselves or other people. I talked about trees for a minute straight, trying to sound confident and assured despite my dodgy Hebrew, before returning to the audience. Afterward, we broke into smaller groups and engaged in subject debates and group discussion. We had to come up with our own argument as a group and elect representatives to give a small presentation.

Because the speaking exercises were difficult for me, I may have been one of the few people relieved to return to the physical trials. Our next activity was to hold sandbags over our heads for as long as we could. I had never had much upper body strength and worried I would not do well. The bags were heavy, weighing in at around five to ten kilos each. After holding the bag for some time, I realized it was not a matter of strength but of endurance and sheer willpower. People started out strong, but I could see their arms beginning to tremble and sag as the minutes ticked by and soon people began to drop the bags and fall out of the test. I did not want that to happen to me. My arms were cramping. Shooting pains ran from my shoulders through my forearms. I distracted myself by singing songs in my head. Eventually the commander told us we could put our arms down. I hesitated first, wondering if this was a trick. I only lowered my sandbag after everyone else had already begun to do so.

For our next activity, we would be crawling in sand. The commander lined us up in front of a big square sandpit. We had to crawl across the sandpit to the other side, then circle back around by foot to get back in line so that we could repeat the process incessantly. My friend, Aharon, had given me advice about crawling in sand. He said to dive straight into the sand and then swim across as if it were water. I took his advice literally and flopped in on my belly. The impact was painful, but the dive gave me a head start, and I was able to push through the sand quicker by paddling through it. I was swimming on sand! I ignored the pain and paddled as hard as I could.

This worked so well that I was the first across the sandpit, which had two benefits. First, there was no pushing or shoving. I had left everyone in the dust, or the sand, as it were. Second, I made it back in line so quickly that I had time to rest while other people struggled to get across the pit. This gave me so much time to rest that the commanders took note and made me cut ahead to the front of the line and go twice in a row a few times. We crawled for thirty or forty minutes, but I must have gotten more rest than anyone else in the entire gibush. I was also pleased to have done so well. Who knew crawling on sand was my forte?

Swimming in the sand

The next test was a complex group activity that involved long ropes spun around and around two poles like a spider web. The rope web left narrow gaps between the poles. The team was tasked with getting from one side of the poles to the other without anyone touching the rope or passing through the same gap. If anyone brushed the rope or passed through the same gap, the entire team would have to stop, sprint to a distant fence and back, and then reconvene to try again.

I had seen a similar game when I was at Camp Taum Sauk, the summer camp where I had grown up in and eventually was a counselor. This gave me a little familiarity with the task ahead. I took charge of the group and directed people. I instructed team members on where and when to cross. This worked well, but there was still human error to account for. Someone would inevitably slip or flinch and touch the rope, forcing us all to sprint to the fence and start over. I was not the fastest sprinter, but I pushed myself to be the first back every time so that I could be there to direct the others.

Having to keep starting over slowed us down. On our last try we managed to get all but two men through the rope and past the poles when time was called. We then abandoned the activity and formed a *chet* in front of the commander to receive our next orders. We were told to get out the stretchers and load four sandbags on each one. The final physical test was a *masa*, or as it is literally translated to, a pilgrimage, but would, in this context, be more like a march or hike in which we would hoist the loaded-down stretcher up onto our shoulders and carry them to some undisclosed location. I knew by then that it was important to be under the *alunkah*, so I made sure to stand next to it before we began. As soon as the commanders shouted "*Tzeh!*" I helped to hoist up the stretcher, and we started marching.

Carrying a stretcher for a masa *with my team in my unit*

This was not my first time under a stretcher. I had carried them while training with the boys from my Garin many times. I tried to steel my mind so that my body would not feel the pain and would just do the work, but I eventually had to ask for a replacement. I followed close by, ready for someone to tag me back in under the stretcher.

We carried the stretcher two kilometers back to the concrete square where we had begun our first run. The team formed a *chet* around the commander. The eight of us carrying the *alunkah* set it down in the middle of the *chet*. The commander congratulated the whole team on finishing the physical exam. The gibush was not over, but we had survived the grueling physical challenges. The only thing left was an interview. We joined the other groups who were already there waiting. Food was being passed around, so I helped myself to a plate.

I looked around for my garin mates who had been assigned to different teams. To my disappointment, I couldn't find them. A commander instructed me not to leave the area until they called my name for an interview. I gave up on looking for my friends, hoping that they, too, had finished the gibush and were somewhere waiting for their interviews.

Almost an hour passed before they called my name. I shot to my feet reflexively and answered the call. I was taken to where they were conducting the interviews. Interviewees were lined up on rows of benches with the commanders around them asking questions. There was little privacy because it was so crowded. The whole thing seemed informal and disorganized.

I was told to sit on a bench across from two older gentlemen. They had been paratroopers in their early days but were now part of the Reserves. They asked me personal questions about my background and how I got there. I talked about growing up in the United States and visiting Israel over the summers. I talked about going to a Jewish high school.

"How do you think the tryout has gone so far?" one of the men asked.

"I thought I did very well," I said honestly, careful to sound confident but not boastful.

"Why do you want to be a paratrooper?" they asked.

This question was to be expected. Most people give vague answers about the honor of serving as a paratrooper, while some talked about family members who had been paratroopers. Whether it is true or not, many play up having always wanted to be a paratrooper. This simply wasn't true for me, and while I certainly could have lied, I decided to be honest and admit that I had not particularly wanted to be a paratrooper until that very day. I *had* wanted to be in Special Forces. I had been hoping to join the Givati Brigade, which on Wikipedia is compared to the U.S. Marines. They are generally known for working in the south around Gaza and Egypt. I admitted to having found the paratroopers seemingly pompous and conceited until that very day when this gibush changed my mind. I was extremely impressed by the men I had stood by that day and with whom I had undertaken all of the extreme physical trials. Anyone who could withstand such grueling mental and physical strains deserved respect, and I was proud to stand among them. I liked and respected everyone I had met that day, which had convinced me that going into the paratroopers and not some other unit was the right move for me.

The interviewers smiled at my candidness. It was probably not every day that someone said that they had not really been sure about the unit until the day of the tryout. I think this honesty and sincerity impressed them.

After a little small talk, the interview concluded. I returned to the tents to retrieve my belongings, where I finally found my friends. We were pleased to find that every single one of us had finished the gibush. We went out for burgers to celebrate, though we would still have to wait several weeks to find out if we had passed and would be accepted into the paratroopers.

A few days later, I boarded a plane to visit my parents in the States. I had a few weeks before being formally drafted into the IDF and wanted to spend the time with family. I was at home when I got a call from the Garin. My mother had answered the phone and yelled for me to pick up the line. She stood behind me while I spoke with Ela, a soldier who had been assigned to help our Garin prepare for the army. She was excited to relay the good news: I had been accepted into the paratroopers, perhaps the most prestigious regular combat brigade in the IDF. She congratulated me.

I took a deep breath, relieved, though not overly excited. This was a dream realized, and a great accomplishment, but it was also only the beginning. Being accepted into the paratroopers was not the goal, but the beginning of a great journey on which I was embarking. This was a first step, a reason to be proud, but only a first step.

answered the phone and waited for me to pick up the line. She stood behind me while I spoke with the [illegible] both [illegible] help our [illegible] prepare [illegible] was excited to relay the good news: I had been accepted into the [illegible], perhaps the most prestigious [illegible] [illegible] dated me.

I took a deep breath, [illegible] though not overly excited. This was [illegible] and a great accomplishment, but it [illegible] not [illegible] the beginning of a [illegible] journey, [illegible] which [illegible] The [illegible]

4

CLASS IS IN SESSION

"The journey of a thousand miles begins with a single step."
~ Lao Tzu

December 12th, 2012, I said goodbye to my new adopted family in my kibbutz and my Garin, hopped on a green egged bus and went to the bakoom, or recruitment center, and officially joined the IDF.

The IDF requires new recruits who lack sufficient Hebrew to attend a short assimilation program before being assigned their first real jobs. This program is either three weeks or three months, depending on how well one speaks Hebrew. I was tested by a woman at the *bakoom*. On a scale of one to twelve, I scored a five, just one point short of testing out of the Hebrew course. While they say that you have to score over a seven to enlist as an officer, I later learned that these scores become irrelevant once you are assigned an actual job and begin actual service. But, at the time, I was very concerned.

I reported to the bakoom early on a Wednesday morning to begin my assimilation program at the base Mikveh Alon. They bused us several hours away to an army base where I would spend the next three months learning Hebrew, learning about Israeli culture, and getting my first taste of life in the IDF.

We started out with a relaxed pace the first week. We were shown around the base and issued equipment—canteens, or *mimmiot*, sleeping bags, mattresses, work pants and work shirts, also known as our "*bet* uniform." Early on, we took a Hebrew exam and, based on our scores, were divided into *tzvatim*, or teams. The exam took almost two hours to complete. I was placed on team 1, in Plugot (company) Carmel, and met my instructors, all of whom were women. Since, the IDF has a mandatory draft, there are just as many girls as boys who join. Although girls cannot perform all the same military positions as the boys, they are able to join combat units and become commanders and officers. Becoming a pilot is considered the most prestigious unit in the army and it is coed. However, even though women can join combat units, many choose to take on crucial instructor, logistical and commanding roles, all of which support the combat soldiers. Therefore, even though I was going to eventually join a combat unit with male commanders, most of my instructors, like shooting instructors, were women. My main commander and Hebrew teacher were Tamar and Chayah, respectively, we were never allowed to refer to them by their first names. They were only to be referred to as *mefakedet*, or commander. "Yes, mefakedet!" "Attention, mefakedet!" "Please excuse me, mefakedet!"

We started out forming *chets* and two lines in different situations, which we had all done before, but now they were timing us. We had mere seconds to get into position and formation. They timed us with a stopwatch for everything, giving us ten seconds to run fifty meters and form two lines. Then they would start the timer again and we would go another fifty meters before reforming. We moved like this, in and out of formation, all around the base, forming and reforming as we went. It took forever to get anywhere.

At the end of each day, we were allowed *shatash*, an hour to relax, shower, make phone calls or write letters, and generally unwind. We only got the single hour each day, so each minute was precious. Many of us, myself included, did not use the shatash to unwind. We wanted to make it into one of the elite units, so we spent the hour training for the *gibushim*. We were spending most of our time in the classroom, which was terrible for staying in shape. That hour of rest was crucial for those of us that wanted to train and stay in top physical shape. We came up with different exercises each day, sometimes sprinting on the basketball court or up a hill the whole hour. We practiced our two-kilometer runs to improve our times. We did pushups and sit-ups and all kinds of other exercises. I used every free minute to train. We were given short fifteen-minute breaks throughout the day to eat a snack, have a smoke, or rest. I never rested. I would find a corner to do sit-ups and push-ups until they called us back together.

I put a pair of paratrooper wings in front of me while exercising. They were given to me by my family friend, Arik Poremba. Arik was proud I had stuck to his workout routine and gave me his wings upon hearing about my acceptance into the paratroopers. He was aware of my ambitions. It wasn't enough for me to be in such a great battalion, such as the paratroopers. I wanted to make it to the sayarot (Special Forces units), such as Duvdevan, just like him. Arik's wings were a reminder of my ambition and that someone believed in me. They helped me stay focused on my goals.

The army base is on a mountain and can only be accessed by a towering set of stairs that looked like they went up to heaven. Every Sunday, I reported to the base and scaled the stairs up the mountain. Dragging gear up the stairs was exhausting. I treated it like another physical challenge and a reminder that nothing about being a soldier would be easy. With my mentality on preparing for the special forces, I made sure I never walked up those endless stairs—I ran up them.

Shetach week, which began field training, was the first

time I ever shot in the dark. We weren't actually out in the field, there wasn't an appropriate space, so they had us sleep in sleeping bags on the ground by the shooting ranges. We took turns shooting on the range. There were 300 of us, and only space for sixteen men to shoot at a time, so there was a lot of down time waiting for your turn.

As I said, I had never fired a gun at night before and didn't know how to aim in the dark. I was taught by the officer of our plugot (company), also known as a Mem-Pay. She was an energetic woman that, despite her petite stature, commanded authority. Though she had little interaction with the new recruits, mostly dealing directly with our commanders, she somehow knew us all by name.

She had a funny way of teaching people how to shoot at night. This is very difficult at range, but we were shooting at human-sized targets that were only fifteen meters downrange. She told us to locate the two iron prongs sticking out at the end of the iron sights at the far end of the barrel on the end of our M16s, which she called the bunny ears, and line them up with a line at the front of the gun, which she called the carrot. I had no idea what she was talking about but tried anyway. I fired fifteen shots from a prone position and landed each one in the target, which wasn't that difficult given the close range. To this day, I *still* have no idea what she meant by the bunny ears and the carrots, but I have since learned to aim properly at night, even with iron sights.

When we weren't shooting, we practiced military maneuvers. My favorite was a military variation on the "capture the flag" game. We had to sneak up a big rocky hill and try to steal the flag. Everyone was on one team while the commanders patrolled the hill with flashlights, looking for us. Anyone caught in the spotlight had to go back down to the bottom and start over.

I crawled up the steep side of the hill with a few other guys. Most of the commanders were on the other side of the hill with their flashlights. We stalked up the hill, hiding behind grass, but were quickly spotted due to the size of the group. I went back to the bottom and tried again, this time taking an even steeper path to the top. I crawled over sharp rocks that pressed into my skin. My new path was so difficult that there were fewer commanders in the area. Each time I saw a flashlight come near, I put my head down and waited for them to pass.

It got harder to hide the higher up I went. The rocks near the top were much smaller, too small to hide behind effectively. As I neared the flag, I used a small rock the size of my head as camouflage, resting it directly in front of my face. In the daylight, this would have looked ridiculous, but whatever I was doing was working. I had made it within twenty meters of the flag.

Three commanders at the top were guarding the flag. I laid there behind my rock for ten minutes trying to figure out my next move. I needed to create a distraction, or I would never be able to reach the flag unseen. I picked up a small rock and hurled it in another direction, hoping to lure them away. It didn't work. They heard the noise but came directly toward me. They flashed their lights all around me.

"Chiyal! Chiyal!!" a commander shouted. "I see you! Come down!"

I didn't give up my location at first, hoping the commander was mistaken, or that they had spotted someone else nearby. Unfortunately, this was not the case. I turned my head slightly only to be blinded by her flashlight. I had been spotted. I rose to my feet and all the commanders at the top spotlighted me at once, surprised to find me so close to the flag.

Though I had failed, I was undeterred. I went to the bottom to try again, but just as I got to the bottom, there was a commotion at the top of the hill. Someone was screaming and yelling. Someone had captured the flag! Later that night I heard how they did it. Several soldiers had made it up and past the flag, doubling back in a group. The soldier who had captured the flag was in the middle, using the others to hide himself from the flashlights for long enough to capture the flag. It was a bold move that had paid off. If only I had had any teammates when I was at the top near the flag, but everyone else who started with me had been spotted already and sent back down the hill.

I enjoyed my time at Mikveh Alon, but it was not without incident. Mikveh is known for having a lot of fights break out between the recruits. We were new Israeli immigrants who came from all around the world. None of us were Israeli. We were American, Russian, German, French, Canadian, and from places even further afield. Cultural differences often led to misunderstandings, which, in turn, led to fights. The place is notorious for having fights break out between the Russians and the Americans, though during my time we both got along fairly well.

Things started to get more contentious when a company of Druze soldiers joined us on the base. The Druze are an Arabic-speaking ethnic and religious minority in Israel, mostly live around northern Israel and neighboring states that splintered off from Islam long ago. There are many Druze Zionists that have pledged allegiance to the State of Israel, and many serve in the IDF. However, they do have cultural differences, and this sometimes causes tension. With enough tension all it takes is a small match to ignite the flames.

In our case, the match was a wad of saliva. An American soldier spit on the ground near a Druze soldier after a meal break. A fight broke out between the two soldiers. Other people started piling into the fight, taking sides along whichever plugot they were in and within minutes a brawl broke out between the Druze *plugot* and our *plugot* consisting of Americans and Russians. There were maybe seventy or eighty recruits on each side of the fight. It was chaos. We were all armed to the teeth, M16s on our persons, though not a single shot was fired. Some people used their rifles as clubs, but most people just fought with their fists.

I tried to stay out of the fight but got pulled into the fray when one of my friends came under attack. I jumped into the fight and pushed his assailant away. The brawl went on around me. I shoved two more men away. I watched on as these supposed brothers in arms clobbered each other. This went on for another twenty minutes or so before the fight was broken up. It became known as one of the biggest and most intense fights in the history of Mikveh Alon, though there would be others.

Several of the Druze soldiers were arrested and taken to military jail, as well as two soldiers from our *plugot*. Technically, everyone who had participated in the fight should have been arrested, but they couldn't send us all to jail, so they made an example of a few instigators and anyone with a big mouth that was bragging about the fight. Most of us denied being directly involved. We were all reprimanded severely and ordered to stay away from each other, but we weren't arrested. This was the second of two fights between the Druze and the Americans, though I wasn't involved in the first, the commanders took strict precautions to separate the plugot's on all occasions, they had had enough and did not want a third incident.

Throughout training, we would often leave base to go back home to our kibbutz for Shabbat, the Jewish day of rest, which meant we were always going back and forth on buses. We couldn't let our guard down even when off base, not out in public, because the Meshtarat Tzfiet, Israel's military police, would patrol the bus stations and ticket soldiers that were improperly dressed. We had to show those tickets to our commanders. The usual punishment was to spend Shabbat on the base rather than having the weekend off to go home, which really sucked. Because of this, everyone hated the Military Police.

One day, two months into my time with the army, I was

stopped by the Meshtarat Tzfiet at the Beer Sheva bus station. I was on the way back to my base, Mikveh Alon, after spending a relaxing weekend at home. My beret had fallen from my shoulder and caught the attention of one of the military policemen. She asked for my ID. I knew that handing it over would result in a ticket and missing out on Shabbat that week. I played dumb and pretended not to understand Hebrew.

"Excuse me," I said in broken Hebrew, stumbling over my words intentionally. "I speak no Hebrew."

Once again, she asked to see my ID.

"Excuse me," I said. "I am a pencil." It was the first thing that came to mind, perfectly nonsensical, and I hoped to confuse her so that she would leave me alone.

She laughed, but insisted on seeing my ID. She pointed to my shoulder where my beret should be and said that it was missing.

I looked at my shoulder, as if confused and repeated, "But I am a pencil! I am a pencil!"

She looked annoyed now. She told me to go find my beret and come show it to her.

"Pencil," I said. "Thank you. Thank you."

I could not find my beret, so I took another route to avoid the military police and went home. Later, I would tell my teammates about this story. They never let me forget it.

Celebrating Purim on Base with one of the boys from my Team

Even in the army we were still able to have a lot of fun in the program. We were a bunch of young guys, some of us in our teens, which meant a lot of pranks and goofing off, especially when we were off the army's clock. One time, on the train back to Mikveh Alon, another soldier found his commander on Facebook. He literally jumped for joy on the train. This was big news! The commanders ruled our lives, but we knew precious little about them. We were hungry for more information.

I didn't know the soldier or his *mefakedet* very well, since they were in a different plugot, but I was able to use her profile to find my own commanders. I found Chayah first, and through her I located Tamar's profile. I forwarded the information to everyone on our team. Seeing their profiles was surreal. We had never seen them out of uniform, and there they were in plain clothes, smiling (not shouting!), and chatting with friends online. Suddenly, they became real people to us in a way they hadn't before.

Our commanders were normally stoic and distant. This was by design. In fact, it was in their job description. They were not supposed to laugh or smile in front of us at all. If they needed to laugh or break character, they were supposed to cover their mouths or leave so that we couldn't see. Some of the commanders were better at suppressing laughter and emotions than others. We sometimes tried to get them to laugh as a prank, the same way people try to make the Buckingham Palace guards laugh or break form.

At times, this required going to great lengths. One day, a few guys were able to get the commanders to bust out laughing while we were cleaning up the classrooms. At the end of each day we would clean our classrooms. In the army, you clean up the floors by dumping out water and squeegeeing it up, the way you would mop a deck, except we "cleaned" everything this way. Normally, we used as little water as possible to make cleanup faster. The more water you use, the longer it takes, but this didn't deter a couple of wise guys from filling a trashcan to the brim with water from a hose and dumping it out in the classroom. The water sloshed everywhere, but we were squeegeeing futilely like everything was normal. The commanders burst out laughing so hard that they had to excuse themselves so that we wouldn't see.

As soon as the commanders left, two guys came in with another trashcan full of water and dumped it out, too, turning the classroom into a swamp. We started splashing each other with water in a little water fight right there on base and what was supposed to be a quick twenty-minute job turned into a two-hour ordeal. The whole thing was ridiculous, but seeing the instructors burst into laughter had been worth it. Everyone needs a little bit of levity, even soldiers, from time to time. We might have been soldiers, and we took this seriously, but we were still young guys, too.

5

SPECIAL FORCES

"Crawling is acceptable. Falling is acceptable. Puking is acceptable. Crying is acceptable. Blood is acceptable. Pain is acceptable. QUITTING IS NOT." ~ *Unknown*

After my time at Mikveh Alon was up, I again found myself back at the bakoom. They issued me my *aleph*, or dress uniform, along with a pair of red combat boots. My aleph was different from everyone else's though because I was going into the paratroopers. Now that I was finally getting my paratroopers uniform, I took thirty minutes to get dressed, fussing over every detail. A soldier in the doorway started laughing at me for taking so long, saying that we were going to have to suit up faster in training. I shrugged it off. This was my first time putting on my aleph. I wanted to do it right, no matter how long it took. (Little did I know that in a few short weeks, I would find myself running around like a maniac every morning, throwing on my aleph or bet uniforms in under two minutes flat.)

After filling out paperwork, I had officially graduated from Mikvey and was now going into the paratroopers. I was even met by a paratrooper who would be personally taking me to my new base. He was a lean man that stood tall in his red boots and red beret. He moved with an easy confidence.

"You're the guy I need to pick up?" he asked.

"Yes!" I exclaimed, not bothering to conceal my pride and excitement.

We made our way to the paratroopers' training base. On the way, he looked over at me, gave me the up and down, and said, "Look, man, your belt is way too high up. You look totally *tzier*." Tzier meant young. In the army, you did not want to look tzier. He explained how no one wore their belt that way. It was considered "cool" to wear the outside belt down low. Embarrassed, I pulled my belt down as far as it would go and thanked him for the advice.

I was dropped off at the base, officially named Bach Tzanhanim, but known colloquially as Lunah Bach, which is a play on words from the only amusement park in Israel being called Lunah Park because the base was so much cleaner and nicer looking than the others; Israelis assumed it must be a very "fun" place to be, very much like an amusement park. .

During my first week there, we did *avodah rasar*, which best translates to logistical work, consisting of picking weeds, moving boxes and painting buildings. We worked all day, from sunup till past sundown. At 10 p.m. every night we were allowed our *shatash*, a one-hour break to relax. As with my breaks at Mikveh, I used this time to train for the gibush. This would be my final gibush, the Gibush Yechatiot, and would determine whether or not I would be admitted into the Special Forces units within the paratroopers.

Unlike the Special Forces mentioned earlier (Matkal, Sheldog, Shayetet, and 669) that were considered the tier 1 Special Forces units, there was another group of over 20 other Special Forces units throughout the army. These were considered lesser and tier-2, yet still extremely difficult and a great place to be. In America, I have learned it would be like comparing Delta Force or Seal Team 6 to the Green Beret, Army Rangers or the other Seal Teams.

I undertook the gibush during my second week. Early in the morning on a Sunday, we woke and got ready for the tryout. There were more than 500 of us in the gibush. We filled out our paperwork and legal forms as usual. One form was a contract in which I preemptively agreed to at least three years of service, if one of the units accepted me. There was no turning back now, not if I succeeded. Of course, I would never have turned back. This was what I had wanted since I stepped onto Udi's base in The West Bank over 10 years ago.

With our paperwork completed, we could relax for the rest of the day. I had butterflies in my stomach all day, giddy with excitement, but also anxious. I went to bed early because I would be woken up at two o'clock in the morning to start the tryout.

When the clock struck two, a commander opened the door and shouted. We all jumped from bed and put on our uniforms. I put on my most comfortable socks and cinched my new army boots as tight as they would go. We filed outside and formed two lines in the courtyard to meet the commanders. They split us off into groups. My group was made up of about thirty other men, all of us looking excited and a little bit nervous.

The commanders did a quick roll check, and once everyone was accounted for, we got started. My instructor, a man in a black jacket, black hiking boots, and green army pants, stood before us. He was also wearing those familiar dark sunglasses that gave the instructors an air of mystery, just like at Yom Sayarot. He had blonde hair and spoke Hebrew with just a hint of a Russian accent that made him sound tough like a mobster or a tough guy from a crime movie. This man embodied everything about the Special Forces and the soldiers it molds men into; initially perceived as weak and undisciplined, but eager, and transformed into hard-as-steel soldiers that acknowledge no fear and know no weakness. This was what I aspired to become.

He started issuing commands in that tough-as-nails voice,

and when he spoke, we jumped to obey. We were operating under the tick of the stopwatch, and he always reminded us of that fact. We had ten seconds to form two parallel lines.

"*Tzeh*!" he shouted with every order, a word I had come to know well from doing this so many times before.

He moved quickly and assuredly, and we had to jog to be able to keep up with his quick walk, while we followed him to a different area of the base. We formed a chet around the equipment we would be using. Some of us strapped on backpacks loaded down with a heavy sandbag. Others carried the stretchers or jerry cans, familiar pieces of simple equipment that would soon be used to test the limits of our bodies, hearts, and minds.

We were issued numbered shoulder tags, and numbered hats for identification purposes. I was number seventeen. We then formed two lines again and followed him up a hill, where we made a chet and dropped our bags at the instructor's command. Other groups were lined up around the hill, too, in formation around their own instructors; six groups in all. I spotted the instructors easily, wearing the same black jackets and dark sunglasses, standing at the head of the chet with men lined up around them. They held pads of paper in one hand and a pen in the other, ready to document our performance.

My instructor spoke: "Now, everyone, do you all see that jerry can?" He motioned toward a jerry can sitting on the ground about thirty meters up the hill.

"Yes, commander!" we shouted.

"Good, when I say *tzeh*, you are all going to sprint around the jerry can, from right side to left, come down to where I am and make a line, standing from left to right. The ones who come back first on the very left and so on. Does everyone understand?"

"Yes, commander!" we shouted in unison.

With barely a moment's notice, the instructor shouted, "*Tzeh*! And off to the races we went, sprinting up the hill as quickly as possible. The terrain was rough, full of rocks and thorny brush, and slightly treacherous. I didn't care. I pushed as hard as possible and came in third. This wasn't too bad, but of course I wanted to do better.

The commanders swept by, jotting down our numbers and place in line. They were so fast that I barely had time to catch my breath before we were ordered up the hill again, and then again and again and again. Each time, they took our number and order. Some of the other soldiers shouted out their number and place. Not me. I wanted to conserve my energy. I spoke calmly. This was likely a good approach, as the commanders themselves were not shouting. They spoke authoritatively, but softly. They were so quick and quiet that it was easy to forget their presence, even though they were watching us like hawks and recording our performance on paper.

The next activity was the *alunkah sosiometry*, where we would again sprint around the jerry can, come back to the starting line and grab a corner of a stretcher, hoist it up to our shoulders and run another lap. Like before the first 8 got a corner of one of the two stretchers (each weighing 200 pounds) and then 9 and 10 got a jerrycan (40-pound water-cooler) to run with. Again, we had to fight for the right to work harder and carry something. Of the 20 men who were not fast enough to get a spot they would drop and do ten pushups and then run another lap empty-handed.

Tzeh!

And we were off!

I sprinted up the hill, as I had done so many times before, and back down. As I finished the first lap, I dove for the stretcher and grabbed a handle. With three other guys, I hefted the stretcher up to my knee and then up on my shoulder. We went back up the hill with the stretcher this time, but unlike my previous times doing this test, each of the two groups under the stretcher continued to race. We were sprinting *while* carrying this 200-pound stretcher!

The competition now was among the four of us and the guys carrying the other stretcher. We were slower than everyone else who had to do pushups and another sprint. I pitied the guys doing pushups, not for the workouts, but for not being under the stretcher, which was insane given how much harder carrying the stretcher was. But this was the kind of mind game these tryouts played with you. They were tests meant to see if we would break. The tasks, as always, were repetitive and difficult, meant to do nothing more than try our will power and endurance. They would have been funny were we not all so caught up in the struggle.

I was able to get a spot under the stretcher the first few times around, until they took away one of the stretchers, leaving only six coveted positions rather than ten. I was no longer able to get a stretcher every time, though I realized, even if I came in seven or eight, I could grab a jerry can by not fighting for a spot under the stretcher. The stretcher was best, but the jerry can was better than nothing, so I sometimes went for the can rather than the stretcher. This tactical move paid off and consistently kept me out of the group doing pushups. After all, the instructors didn't care about who was the fastest or strongest. They wanted to know who wanted this the most. I didn't have to be the fastest as long as I had enough ingenuity and craft to stay in the game. Staying in the game was what mattered. Proving my determination was the whole point. We were free to drop out at any time, which they made sure to remind us. They wanted us to drop out. If we were going to quit, better to do so now than in the heat of battle.

Eventually, the sun came up. This was my only sense of the passage of time. The minutes and hours melted into one another during the tryout. Now that it was getting hot out, they let us break for water. It had never tasted so good. My strength started to come back, and I was feeling good about my performance so far.

Next, we did crawling. I smiled when they gave the orders, having done so well on that part in gibush tzanhanim (paratrooper tryout). However, this time we wouldn't be crawling on soft sand, but hard ground filled with sharp rocks and thorns. They also didn't let us wait for everyone to finish this time before sending us out again. This meant that I was crawling the whole time, no breaks, no matter how well I did.

The commanders tried to keep us on our toes by mixing up the exercises. We would sprint and then crawl. Crawl, then sprint. Sprint, sprint, crawl, crawl, and so forth. They didn't want us to get too comfortable with any one thing. It was stressful, but I just gave it my all no matter what we were doing and focused on what was in front of us.

It was all very confusing though. At one point, I sprinted when I was supposed to crawl. I looked back to see everyone left in the dust—literally. They were down on the ground crawling. They looked funny on the ground, flopping around like fish, but not as funny as me having run out ahead by myself. I doubled back, dropped to my knees, and started crawling. I was way behind but pushed hard and managed to catch up and come in fifth place. I didn't know if I should be proud or embarrassed. It was nearly impossible to tell what the commanders were thinking from behind their dark sunglasses.

We took a break for breakfast, which was nothing but *manat krav,* or food rations. The rations were made up of *chalva* bars, canned tuna, canned fruit, canned corn, canned beans, canned chocolate spread, and bread. I'm sure if they could have canned the bread, they would have. This was my first time having manat krav, but it would not be my last. We would be eating the exact same thing for the next three days, the length of this tryout. The commanders kept watching us, even as we ate, and so we were all careful about our manners, as if we were at a formal dinner and not eating army rations in the field on the dirt with our bare hands.

After breakfast, we took turns speaking. We each had to speak for a minute, saying a little something about ourselves. I ended up talking about American football, since I loved the sport and it was something most Israelis knew little about.

Next, we went on a masa with the stretchers and the jerry cans. Once again, the goal was to be *metachat ha-alunkah*, or under the stretcher, for as long as possible. Those who weren't under the stretcher had a jerry can, but everyone wanted to be under the stretcher. We marched quickly to keep up with the commanders, who were, of course, not so encumbered, except by the notepads where they recorded our participation. We marched up a small mountain range, through tall grass and thorny bushes, at such a fast pace that it was practically a jog, until we reached the top.

Once at the top, we continued to march around in circles, until the weight of the stretcher was almost unbearable. I had to trade off every ten minutes or so, not because I wanted to, but because the weight was too much and my shoulders and arms burned with pain. The weight was backbreaking. The pole dug into my skin. But still, I did not want to give up the stretcher. This was a competition, one in which you did not want to take turns. Failing to be under the stretcher was no real break anyway, since you would still have to carry a jerry can or shoulder a sandbag on your back, along with the shame of not being under the stretcher. Everyone who wasn't under, all circled the stretchers like vultures, looking for a man that might give up his spot in a moment of weakness.

The further we went up and down the mountain range, the more tired our bodies became. I could no longer do ten-minutes under the stretcher. They shrank to five-minute shifts, then two, until I could barely hold it any longer at all. We winced with unbearable pain all the way up the mountain, until we finally reached the top of the highest mountain on the range. Looking down, the view was beautiful, and it felt particularly earned, though our bodies were battered and bruised.

We only had a moment to enjoy the view though before they were sending us back down the mountain. This time, we did not keep to the dirt path, but instead created our own. We moved down a steep hilly path through the forest, the rocks and branches impeding our movement.

The terrain was so steep that we practically had to move on our hands and knees with the stretcher up on our shoulders. Though not under the stretcher at this point, I helped steady the men by holding on to their backpacks to keep them from tumbling down the mountain. Those of us not under the stretcher used our bodies to brace those who were. In this way, we lumbered down the hillside without dropping the stretcher, though there were several close calls.

When we got to the bottom of one of the larger hills on this mountain, the commander ordered us to turn around and go back up. We were all in disbelief, but there was nothing to do but comply and prove our mettle. We spent the next twenty minutes forcing our way back up the treacherously steep hillside we had just come down.

As we wound our way back toward where we started, we began to see other groups carrying their own stretchers, too. The commanders let us stop for a minute to have a drink of water in the shade, but even during the break we were instructed not to let the stretcher touch the ground. We had to take turns drinking water while others continued to shoulder the stretcher.

I would like to say that I had a moment to think of how much harder this tryout was than the previous two, but I didn't have such a moment. All I could think about was drink water, work harder, stretch so I don't get cramps, and do whatever the commander said.

When the "break" was over, the commander pointed at a tree trunk in the distance and asked how long it would take us to carry the stretcher around it and back.

"Four minutes?" one person said.

"No, three minutes!" another person boasted.

Neither of these answers was good enough. The commander said we had ninety seconds, and then shouted, "*Tzeh*!"

We gave it our all, but it took two minutes to make it around the tree and back, so they sent us back around it again. We tried again, coming in a few seconds faster, but still not good enough. We continued to sprint back and forth, at one point, the commanders asked if we needed help, which was a huge slap in the face and, of course, a hollow gesture. We wouldn't have dared ask for help. Around twenty or thirty sprints later, completely drenched in sweat and every muscle aching to stop, we finally made it around the tree in less than ninety seconds.

The sun was high in the sky and we soon took a break for lunch, which was more rations, the exact same as we had for breakfast. I was physically exhausted and needed food, but I was also afraid to put too much food in my stomach before going back to sprinting. I ate only what I absolutely needed and no more. After eating, I offered to help with cleanup while the others were still eating.

After lunch, we marched to the field. We no longer had to fight our way up and down a hill, but the terrain, while flat, was still rocky and full of thorny brush and tall brown grass. The commanders had us sprint and even crawl through the thorns and sharp rocks. We had been given knee and elbow pads, but they were of little use crawling in terrain that rough. We were all bruised and bloodied. I was happy to have eaten so little. Many of the other men were clutching their stomachs in pain. Some vomited up their whole lunch.

We crawled for what seemed like an eternity, the descending sun the only marker of time as it dipped toward the horizon. Now that darkness was descending, they marched us back the way we had come. I hoped that we were done for the day. My bag felt much heavier than it had that morning, but I knew better than to get my hopes up. They were always trying to play with your mind, and there was no way to know what came next.

We marched to a small, lush field right outside Bach Tzanhanim. We were instructed to partner up and build tents. My partner and I collected our equipment—a few stakes, a green tarp, some string, and hollow poles. I had built tents while a Boy Scout in St. Louis, so we finished quickly. While we waited, another soldier keeled over and hit the ground with a loud thud. By the time I realized he was suffering from heat-stroke, two medics were already pouring water from a jerry can over his body to cool him down.

I was suddenly reminded how dangerous the gibush really was. We were pushing ourselves to the max all day long in the hot sun. For some people, some bodies, the toll was too much. Eight months ago, another man had died at the gibush yahalom. Once the guy in my team dropped, the medics were handling the situation, so all we could do was continue like nothing happened.

We were then given dinner, more *manat krav*, and then slept. We had to stay on guard the whole night, so everyone took fifteen-minute shifts to patrol the camp throughout the night. We still had at least two more days of the physical tryout left to go. It was crucial that we get sleep, though my body was in such pain that it was difficult. I slept in my clothes because I had heard rumors that they sometimes woke people in the night to go marching. I wanted to be ready, so I only removed my boots so that I could stretch my feet. They were especially cramping and causing me severe pain. I massaged them until the pain subsided a little and then tried to roll over and go to sleep on the hard ground. Our tents were so small that I had to crawl in. I could barely sit up straight before my head hit the ceiling. I wouldn't have been able to sleep under normal circumstances, but my body was so dead that I managed to get a little shuteye throughout the night.

They woke us up at 2:00 a.m. to start the next day. The commanders walked between our tents, shouting for us to rise. I shot up so fast that the tent almost collapsed. I laced up my boots with my heart practically beating out of my chest. We only had three minutes to get into a chet outside of our tents.

Having slept in my clothes, I was one of the first people ready to go, so I helped other people with their things.

Everyone had grim expressions. They looked tired and beaten down, not at all like the day before. The excited faces were gone. We had bags under our eyes. We were cut and bruised from head to toe. We must have looked under-slept, overworked, and generally exhausted, which we were. I felt suddenly discouraged but tried to shirk off the feeling by telling myself that it would be okay and that my friends and I would make it through, no matter what happened. I wasn't sure I believed it, a boy had literally almost died a few hours earlier, but I told myself that anyway.

We gathered our bags and went on the day's first march. The sun would not be up for another few hours, but we were. Not for long though. We were only out for ten minutes before they led us back to the tents and told us to go to sleep. I didn't even know if I should go back to sleep. Were they just going to come by again in a few minutes and tell us to get our clothes back on? I crawled back into my tent, but this time I left my boots on.

They woke us up for the second time right at the crack of dawn. This was clearly a twisted mind game. We had four minutes to be out and in a chet formation again. Once again, they marched us out on the same path and took us up to the base of another hill. There was the familiar jerry can up on the hill. We did many of the same exercises as last time, starting out with sprints and then moving on to crawling. When it came time to speak, I talked about baseball. I told them about how I grew up watching the St. Louis Cardinals, which was easier than the day before because talking about baseball allowed me to use a lot of English words.

I was much slower than the previous day, but so was everyone else, and I managed to come in near the top, most of the time. My body felt strange and disconnected from weariness, but I made it a point to stand up straight and look strong while they recorded my scores.

After running, they took us to a hill and told us to find a spot, no more than a hundred meters away, and dig a hole and camouflage ourselves so that we could see them, but they couldn't see us. I went up the hill and found a place where a tree had fallen over so that I could dig my hole down where the tree stump had pulled away from the earth. There were spiders and spider webs down in the hole, but I was too tired to care. I didn’t want to have to dig more than was necessary. The preexisting hole was knee-deep and almost long enough to lie down in. That was an ample head start, so I chose the spot and started digging deeper.

I finished quickly, thanks to mother nature giving me a head start, which gave me time to chop some grass and weeds to cover myself with until my whole body was covered, except for a small hole with which to see down the mountain.

When the commanders called for us to stop working on our hiding places, they came up to inspect us. They knew where we were because they had watched us dig the holes.

When the commanders came to my hole, they asked why I had chosen that spot. I explained that the hollowed-out spot was natural, which gave me more time to improve on its camouflage. They asked if I was comfortable in there. I said yes, though after the last day, I was not sure what comfortable meant anymore. I hadn’t realized that this was a major concern because soldiers in the field might have to hunker down in a hole for hours or days at a time.

They gave no sign of whether my answers were sufficient or had done a good job. With their black sunglasses, boots and fleeces they just nodded and moved along. When they were done inspecting everyone’s hole, they gave us three minutes to destroy our spots and meet them back at the bottom of the hill.

We then went back to crawling. This time we were in a field that, while it had fewer rocks, had even more thorns. I stretched out my legs and pawed at my kneepads in anticipation of the pain. We spent the next few hours crawling, then sprinting, then crawling more, until it was time for lunch. Afterward, we carried sandbags up and down a hill. The commanders told us there was water set up, if we wanted to break for a drink, but we knew that this too was a mind game. Stopping for water meant less time to do more rounds. So I avoided the water, even after the sun beating down on my back had left me parched. I was afraid of coming down with heatstroke, like the man from the other day, but I dared not go for the water. I was second in place most of the time and definitely wanted to stay there. Instead, I conserved my energy by taking long strides down the hill on the descent rather than jogging hard the whole way.

Then I heard Azore! (Stop)

We then all came down, made another chet and told the commander how many laps we did. We were always honest, but they were also keeping count. Then once we finished the task, the Commander asked how we were? If we needed water or were able to continue? Even though all of us were very dehydrated we of course said we could continue. And then just like that he said great! Now go again! Tzeh! I thought this was a sick joke, but it was real. Again for an unknown amount of time we would be running up and down the hill, with a heavy sandbag and no break.

Walking up and down the hill during the try-out while holding a sandbag

This was perhaps the hardest trial of the gibush. I was dehydrated and exhausted. I needed water, rest and sleep. For a moment, I started to question myself. I wasn't sure why I was there or why I wanted to continue with this insanity—this torture. To steel my own resolve, I thought of Talia and Adir. Talia was a girl I had a crush on back in the States. I wanted to impress her. Adir was a dear friend of mine from high school. He and I used to talk about joining the IDF together in chemistry class, but unfortunately, Adir passed away in a car accident in 11th grade. While undergoing this difficult gibush, I thought of Adir and wanted to make him proud. Their images in my mind helped me push through and keep moving even as my vision started to go dark, my mind blank, and my body shifted over to autopilot.

When that exercise was over, they finally gave us a real break so that we could drink water. They realized no one was drinking because they didn't want to look weak. Maybe they were scared of someone having heat stroke again. I didn't care or think much. I just drank and was happy for the rest. Afterward, we did more sprints and crawls until finally the day was over. My body felt barely operational by the time we got back to our tents for dinner. I couldn't see straight. Everything hurt, all over, everywhere.

After dinner, we returned to base to do evaluations. We had to evaluate our own performance, as well as our teammates'. We were then taken to see the medics, who did little beyond asking if we were okay and applying iodine to our cuts and abrasions. When it came my time to see the medic, he looked me up and down and saw a boy covered in blood from head to toe. He said, "Yafah, hetzlachtah," which translates to "beautiful, you won" and threw the whole bottle of iodine at me. (I kept the bottle as a keepsake and still have it in my bedroom to this day.) We then returned to our tents for sleep. Anticipating another short night and abrupt awakening, I slept with my clothes on.

To my surprise, they did not wake us until it was already seven o'clock in the morning, which is late by army standards, certainly at a gibush. The commanders told us to pack up the tents and gather our equipment. We carried all this stuff back to the base, where we were informed that we had completed the physical portion of the tryout.

Next, we had what they call "break distance" with our commanders. It was called this because during the time with a commander, there is this invisible wall between the two of you. The commander is not supposed to be or act like a normal person, but more like a machine, kind of like the infamous "drill sergeants" in the American army, but with a lot less yelling. But once "distance" is broken then they can go back to their normal selves around you. It was funny that these introductions only came at the end of our time with them. They had previously seemed as "gods among men." They had put us through the most grueling and trying event of our lives, my life for sure, and we had seen them as greater than human. Now they were sitting with us, talking to us like real people, and it was almost surreal to have the spell broken. I was still in awe of them, but they now seemed more human. They told us about their lives in the army and in the units they served.

The final part of the gibush was the interview. We had to wait for what seemed like an eternity as they called us three at a time for our turn. I jumped to attention when they called my number and raced into position, because I knew they were still noting everything we did until the gibush was truly over.

They took me to another room where I waited longer until being called again. I was very nervous when they finally took me to the commanders that would be interviewing me. To my surprise, they greeted me warmly by name. There were six commanders before me, none of whom I had met before. They had on their same intimidating uniforms, complete with the black jackets and dark shades, but now they spoke much warmer and generously. They cracked jokes. They laughed. They were having a good time.

They already knew a lot about my life and background from my files, but I talked for thirty minutes anyway. I told them why I wanted to be in the army and serve Israel. I told them what an honor it was to undertake the tryout. We talked for thirty minutes, mostly me, while they asked questions. Afterward, I was done. I had officially finished Gibush Yachatiot.

I returned to the court where we all waited to hear if we had been selected by any of the units. A representative with a list of names and numbers for each unit came to announce who had made the cut for their unit. The Special Forces unit - Maglan was first. My name was not called, which was worrisome, though they were not my first choice anyway. In fact, I had specifically listed them as my last choice in my paperwork because I had met someone from the unit that I thought was a douchebag. I found out later that he did not survive the training process and was kicked out.

Next, was Palsar, which had been my second choice. Again, I was not called. This time it hurt more, and I was starting to get anxious I would not be called at all.

Next came the representative of Duvdevan. I had seen them trying out alongside us. I knew that they would not call my name, which allowed me to relax and be happy for the soldiers that had tried out as their names were called and they jumped for joy.

Next up was Gdude 202. 'Gdud' or as it translates to battalion, is a term used to indicate a regular infantry unit. Its counter is 'Yechida,' which translates to "unit," generally used to describe the Special Forces units. I prayed not to be called that time. Thankfully, my name never came up.

Finally, the commander of the Palchan, the last of the Special Forces that were in that try out, stepped up with his list. He was a short man, but bulky and all brawn, nothing but muscle. He began to read from his list. My heart started to sink as his group began to fill up and my name was not called. This was the last list for the "chosen units," as translated from Hebrew, or more generally known as the Special Forces units for the tryout I was a part of. I kept thinking I performed well in the gibush, without any doubt, but perhaps they had deemed my Hebrew too poor. I had been told that you needed a six or seven ranking in Hebrew to make those units, but after all my time in Israel and three months studying at Mikveh Alon, the best I had ever done was a five. I started to feel devastated that the language barrier was going to be the thing that held me back in the IDF, after all my training, all my effort, all those difficult tryouts.

And, then, I heard *Max Levin* the commander read off his list. I was in such shock, such elation, that I failed to respond to my name being called. He called my name a second time before I responded. I jumped up and sprinted toward him. I was beyond overjoyed to have finally made it into an Israeli Special Forces Unit. This was the beginning of a long journey, I knew that, but for a few moments I took stock of my fortune and felt proud of the work I had done. All of those hellish tryouts, ridiculous at times, the running up and down hills without reason, the crawling through sand, the flopping in thorny bushes like a fish out of water, the sand inside my dry mouth and nothing to slake my thirst—all of that suddenly felt worth it and more.

I formed a line behind my new commander with the rest of the men being called into the unit. We marched together to our plugot where we made a chet in front of my first special forces commander. I was still in awe of him, which I suppose was what they wanted. He introduced himself as Commander Natan and told us about his service in the Special Forces. Then we all introduced ourselves to each other. I made it a point to remember my teammates' names as best I could, now that we were on the same team and would undergo training for the next year and two months.

The rest of the day should have been uneventful, but everything in the world seemed renewed with purpose now that, finally, I had met my goal. There was a lot of bureaucracy to contend with. We filled out paperwork. I met my team's officer and sergeant. We were given instructions about rules and decorum. They taught us to salute officers whenever we entered the same room until the officer saluted back. We had much to do that day, none of it terribly exciting, and yet I had never been so excited in my life.

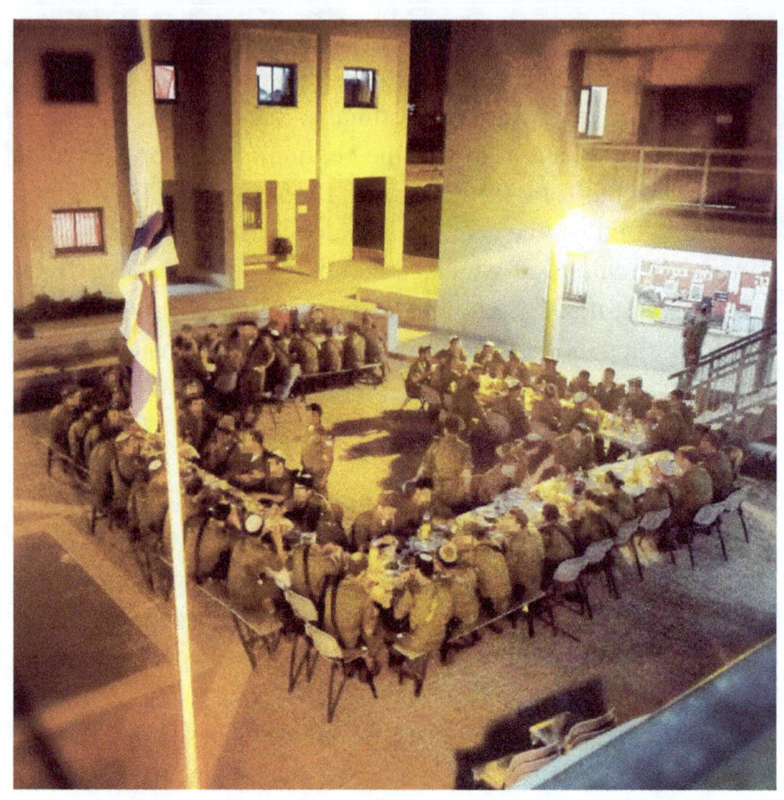

Spending Shabbat with my plugot on the paratropper's base while in basic training. It's not as nice as being home, but it's not so bad on Lunah Bach.

6

"NAGA NAGA NAGA"

Messenger: This is madness!
King Leonidas: Madness? This is Sparta! ~*300*

While my last gibush was behind me, my journey in the armed forces was just beginning. I was hardly even a soldier yet. I still had to complete *tironoot*, or basic training, a four-month program that all new soldiers in the IDF must undergo. I was not just training to join the infantry, though, but the Special Forces. I was still at the Bach Tzanhanim, where we went through basic training, as well as advanced infantry training.

Basic training is an all-day affair. We started each morning with a seven-minute drill. The commanders came in to wake us, giving us only seven minutes to be downstairs, lined up in perfect rows of three, ready to go with our uniform and boots on. We were always scrambling and sprinting throughout the entirety of basic training. Everything was timed, and I do mean everything, whether it was a march, getting our clothes on, brushing our teeth or even showering. While scrambling to get ready in the morning, I often thought of my civilian friends back home in the United States. They were away at college, partying on the weekends and even weeknights, sleeping in late, sometimes missing classes, having fun and being free. My life couldn't have been more opposite. I woke early, at the crack of dawn or before, and started training hard. There was no missing training. Whether tired or sick, we had to be downstairs ready to go, in under 7 min every morning. Being absent or tardy was not allowed and would result in severe and, at times, sadistic punishments. I slept seven hours a night at best, often less, and sometimes not at all.

And we did train hard, every minute except for our seven hours of sleep and our one hour of shatash. Every other second of the day was dedicated to training. They set seemingly impossible benchmarks that took us weeks of repetition to meet. When we finally did hit our target times, they raised expectations. The seven-minute drill every morning had started out as seven-minutes which then morphed into five-minutes before working their way down to two-minutes of precise and efficient movement. I learned to move faster and more efficiently than I ever dreamed possible.

This is what it means to become a soldier. You repeat the same functions over and over until they are etched into muscle memory and you can do them rapidly without thinking. This takes practice of which I have never experienced anything similar. You drill and drill and drill again. The four months of basic training were designed to remold us from civilians into soldiers. They were breaking us down and rebuilding us from the ground up. We didn't just shoot like soldiers. We moved like soldiers. We reacted like soldiers. We thought like soldiers. We tackled every problem as a team and learned to work together, not as a collection of men, but as a cohesive unit working as one. We were well-greased cogs in a machine.

Basic training was full of drills and marches and practice. We went on weekly marches, or *masaot*, which were similar to the one in gibush tzanhanim, but longer. These marches were arduous, especially when weighted down with equipment, weapons, gear, and ammo. We marched in our vests, helmets, and heavy boots. Our vests were loaded down with canteens, fully loaded magazine clips, various tourniquet and first-aid kits, and other equipment. And, of course, we carried our guns. Being in Special Forces, they issued us M4 assault carbines rifles. Most of the paratroopers were issued M16 rifles at first, but Special Forces units often got M4 carbines, which are better for close-quarters combat. (The M4s distinguished us from the more rank-and-file troops, which sometimes made me feel proud and other times isolated.) We also carried specialty backpacks and vests, loaded down with gear. In short, right off the bat, we were given better equipment, which made us stand out from the rest of the soldiers at base.

There was also shared gear to be carried. These were pieces of equipment that would be used by the team as a whole. For example, one person carried a stretcher on their back and another a jerry can. These big heavy items made the *masa* harder, though it was considered an honor to carry the extra weight. The rest of the team helped out by pushing these people up hills or giving them a helping hand. What wasn't allowed was offering to carry their extra gear, which they had to have on them at all times during the masa.

One of our weekly Masa's while in training

Our masa when we finished the paratroopers training and marched to our new base where we began the Special Forces Training

Carrying a Stretcher during a Masa in Training

These marches were very difficult because we moved quickly and steadily. There were twelve of us on the team and we marched in two lines. We started by marching for four kilometers (at a pace of 6 kilometers per hour) and then coming back. Over time, we went further and further afield as our bodies acclimated to the heavy loads. Eventually, we were marching ten kilometers with all our gear. After that, the marches would get longer with the additional component that for the last few kilometers they made us start carrying a stretcher weighted down with sandbags to simulate if one of our team members was injured.

Carrying a stretcher while on a march

While basic training was mostly just that, training, we did have occasional downtime. We still had *shatash*, an hour a day to use the phone, shower and relax. One day, during shatash, I received a disturbing text from Lia, one of the girls in my garin, that read: "Max, Batman ate your door!" Batman was what we called one of the cats that hung around the kibbutz. We called him that because he was all black and full of energy, always jumping off walls, running around, and bouncing to and fro. Given his energetic nature, I wasn't too shocked by the message. Of course, Batman had eaten my door. If any cat were able to gnaw through a wooden door, it was going to be Batman.

I told Commander Natan what had happened and asked for a day off to fix the door. Natan stared at me in disbelief. He said that he would need to get permission from our commanding officer. Worried about the situation, I confided in my team members. To my surprise, they burst out laughing. Only then did it hit me how ridiculous the situation really was. A cat had eaten my door! How was this even possible?

The officers apparently didn't believe it was possible. They denied my request. They clearly thought I was making it up to get a day off. They told me to have a friend fix the door. I didn't have anyone to call since all my friends were also in the army. So, I had to wait until one of our weekends off to go back to the kibbutz and check on the door. Thankfully, I found that Batman had not actually eaten my door, as cats don't actually eat doors, but simply broken through the screen.

In addition, during our time off and finally able to have our phones, we would often put on music for everyone to listen to. Believe it or not, but one of our favorite songs to play was Mulan's "I'll make a man out of you!" It was such a classic that resonated and fit the situation so well that once that song came on, the entire plugah, 90 Israeli soldiers, would start shouting the lyrics. From the balconies soldiers would jump up singing "let's get down to business… to defeat the huns!.." often we would go through the entire song multiple times a week as we laughed, sang, and enjoyed our precious hour off at the end of the day.

After the first few weeks of basic training, where we worked in teams and practiced the basics of being a soldier, we were assigned specific roles. At this point, they broke up the teams and put us into groups based on our specific roles. We would spend one week learning our roles.

Myself and three others from my team were picked to be Negevists, which meant that we would be trained to use the Israeli Negev gun. The Negev is a true machine gun, a fully automatic rifle that can fire armor piercing 5.56mm ammo. They weigh twice as much as the M4's that we had been using so far and required the operator to carry "a shit ton" more ammo. When all was said and done, the Negevist may generally carry about a hundred pounds, due to all of the ammo they need to carry along with the heavier gun and the rest of the soldier's basic equipment. This kind of weight requires the Negevists to be in tiptop physical shape. Normally only the biggest, bulkiest, strongest men are trained to use the Negev.

To be honest, despite feeling honored to be chosen as a Negavist, I thought my commanders had made a mistake selecting me for the role. There were other men on the team that were bigger and better candidates for the job, such as Rotem, who we called *Jonjote* or *Gingi*, due to his ginger-like complexion. Rotem had a silky, beefy build that was suited to carrying and shooting such a large gun. My body was nothing like his. I was lanky and wiry, in shape, but hardly bulky. I doubted myself in the role so much that I confronted my commanders about the matter.

I voiced my concern to David, a commander that had also been a Negevist and had the right build for the job. He was big and bulky, built like a refrigerator. David told me that not all Negevists were built like him. He pointed out that Tzvika, the officer for the other Palchan Team was also a lanky and wiry man, but he, too, had been a Negevist and one of the best. The most important part of lugging the Negev around, he explained, wasn't being able to physically carry the gun. The most important part was having the mental fortitude to carry all the weight and keep up, this required "rabak" or gusto. Rabak is a word used to describe someone who... is like an energizer bunny, they simply don't stop. They didn't just pick the biggest men for the job, but those that had the rabakist mindset. You had to be strong, yes, but you also had to be motivated and a little crazy. You had to be the kind of person that would push and push without ever giving up. Or, as David put it: "Max, you're fucked in the head. That's good. That's what you need. You'll do fine."

Though not totally convinced, I thanked David and promised to give it everything I had.

In order to become a Negevist, we had to go through a weeklong training course, the *Shavua Negev*. There were twelve people in my group, four of us from my team. They issued each of us two Negev rifles from the armory, one for shooting and another with a strip of white paint around the end of the barrel that was for everything else. We learned how to handle and care for them, going over every inch and every last piece of the rifles, inside and out.

Practice, practice, practice was the only way we were going to master the gun. We had to learn the subtle nuances of using the Negev; not only learning them, but incorporating them into our muscle memory so that setting up and shooting the Negev was as natural as extending our arms.

We started out doing dry drills (a drill without firing) with the white Negev. This was to get us accustomed to handling the Negev before we used live ammo. We would shout, "Naga, naga, naga!" as we pretended to fire. We must have looked ridiculous to casual observers, but we were far too engrossed in the drills to laugh at ourselves.

They tried to keep us on our toes by changing up the drills regularly. One commander, a stout but pudgy man named Segal, would blow a whistle periodically. This was a signal to drop what we were doing, run to a nearby dumpster, and spin it around a full 360 degrees. These were heavy dumpsters, roughly the size of a car, that could hold a month of trash. Moving them was not easy, even for twelve men working together, but we found a way. But Segal loved to blow his whistle, continuously pushing us to what we thought were our limits.

One day, while we were out doing dry drills, Commander David jumped on top of the dumpster and blew his whistle. We rushed over to spin the dumpster around while he was still on top. David was carrying a long piece of wood in his hand, which he used to beat at the top of the bin, shouting, "Negavists! Carry this bin to the sharpshooters at the other end of the shooting range and show them how strong we are!" He made us carry the bin half a kilometer (a quarter of a mile)to the shooting range, where the sharpshooters were practicing, with him standing on top the whole time. The bin wouldn't budge at first, but we figured out how to rock the bin back and forth so that we could shuffle it over the ground. We put all our strength and weight into the bin and inched toward the firing range. The whole time, David stood atop the bin, shouting at us. At one point, quoting the movie *300*, David started shouting, "What is your profession? What is your profession?" Each time he asked, we shouted, in unison, "Ahoo, ahoo, ahoo!"

It took us five minutes of backbreaking toil to get the bin to the shooting range where the sharpshooters were gathered. They looked shocked to see us. We left the bin in the middle of their range, blocking their practice, and shouted, "Ahoo, ahoo, ahoo!" before sprinting back to our own drilling area.

We went back to drilling until we heard the same shouts, "Ahoo! Ahoo! Ahoo!" coming toward our location. We looked up to see the sharpshooters coming back with the trash bin. They dumped it right in the middle of the area where we were drilling. We weren't that mad about this, it was part of the game, but we were upset that they had beaten our time. It had taken us five minutes to move the trash bin 500 meters. They had been able to carry it back in four minutes. There were eighteen of them and only twelve of us, so they had the clear advantage, but we still felt ashamed. We were the Negavists! We were supposed to be strong, wild, crazy, determined. Outnumbered or not, we should not have been beaten by the weak and nimble sharpshooters.

Training with the Negav

There were two major drills that we would have to complete before Shavua Nagev week was over. The first was to crawl 300 meters through the range with our Negevs. We knew this event was coming, and had prepared while doing dry drills, but we were not told exactly when we would do the 300-meter crawl, only that we would have to do so.

One day, toward the end of the week, we went on a six-kilometer run. I did very poorly. My body was tired and sore from carrying the Negev all week. I came in last and ended up puking in the field when we were done. We were allowed a minute to stretch and drink some water, but I was still practically wiping the vomit from my mouth when they told us that we would now be doing the 300-meter crawl.

They had set up a box of snacks and soda at the end of the range. The first person to reach the box would get to keep the whole thing. It is hard to convey how much we wanted those sodas and snacks. You don't get these luxuries in the army very often, so having them then, while so hot, hungry, and overworked, was like a little bit of heaven in a box. I will always remember the absurdity of my friend, Elazar, who lined up with the rest of us even though he had a broken toe and had been forced to sit out many of the activities. Elazar knew how to make everyone laugh and could've been a standup comedian. But, when it was time to get down to work, he meant business. Still, even with a broken toe, there was no way he was going to pass up his shot at the box.

I fancied myself a good crawler, one of the best on my team, but I was not used to crawling with the Negev and my body was already exhausted. Despite being a good crawler, I fell behind. In the end, one of the boys from the Palsar, Rubin, who trained with us, who was insanely filled with *rabak,* finished the crawl in fifteen minutes, very close to an all-time bach tzanhanim record.

The other major event of the week was a four-kilometer nighttime march with our *shachars*, which were night-vision goggles that fit onto our helmets. Most operations are often at night and the Negevist is usually at the front of the team, leading the way, aided by night-vision goggles, called a shachar, and laser sights. Learning to use these to move quickly in the dark is difficult and takes practice. The goggles are heavy and cause neck-strain and actually make it difficult to see close up. We needed to drill with them so we would be ready to use them in the field for real.

One night, also toward the end of the week, we were woken by our commanders, who told us to get ready for the march. We put on our uniform, boots, vest, as well as our helmet with the shachar, grabbed our Negevs, and headed outside. We lined up outside in front of Commander David. He looked at us disapprovingly. We were one man short. In our haste, we hadn't realized that we were missing a person.

David instructed us to look in our room where we found the missing man gagged and tied to a chair with glow sticks coming off the chair. It seemed preposterous that no one had seen him at the back of the room, but that is what had happened. Eleven of us had scrambled so fast to get ready and, in a state of myopic tunnel vision, somehow never noticed him. We felt embarrassed. Our commanders had pulled a fast one on us and no one had noticed. They did this regularly to keep us on our toes. Sometimes they snuck into our rooms and tried to steal our guns. If they were successful, we were punished. We were supposed to have one eye on our rifles at all times. This time, they hadn't only succeeded in stealing a rifle; they had succeeded in stealing a man. And not one of us had noticed.

We knew we were in trouble, but before we could think of what was going to happen, David called out for us to start the masa. We filed out of the base in two side-by-side lines and marched out into the darkness of the fields. Unfortunately for me, about 300 meters into the darkness, my shachar's battery broke and I could barely see out into the dark. There was nothing to be done though. It was too late to turn back for another pair of goggles, so I continued in the dark with the broken goggles blocking the vision in my right eye.

The only reason I was able to continue like that is because, while the shachar allows you to see into the distance at night, it actually makes it harder to see things in one's near field of vision. While I was blinded in my right eye, my left eye was able to adjust to the dark and see the ground better. While others stumbled over rocks and tripped on branches, I was able to move more swiftly thanks to my broken goggles.

Unfortunately, this was the only thing I was able to do well. We spent the next few hours crawling through the dark and hunting for sticks that emitted infrared light, a task that absolutely required night-vision goggles. I wasn't able to find any of the sticks, but I was able to crawl around in the grass with my teammates, so I more or less blended in. Luckily, this wasn't a gibush, but actual training, so no one was scoring my performance.

When we were done, we had completed Shavua Nagev and were ready to return to our teams and continue with our basic training. However, because someone from another team was late to god knows what, to end the week the entire plugot spent the next few hours crawling and holding pushing position over sharp rocks, at the back of our base.

7

JUMP COURSE

"Yippy Ki-Yay Mother Fucker!" ~ *Die Hard*

Our last week in Basic Training was to go to jump school. It is a two-week course, and generally known as one of the more relaxing courses; that is, for most people. But we were still in Basic Training so, as one could say, there was no chill. Just like the rest of Basic Training, when we weren't doing the jump course itself, we were either sprinting around, doing exercises or seven minute "shamnashim."

Two days into our course, we were given that new exercise, the shamnashim. Our sergeant, Uri, came up to us and said, "Okay, guys, in seven minutes you take all of your personal and the teams' equipment, lay it out nicely like it is about to be inspected, count all the bullets and make sure everything is in tip top shape."

Uri calmly and quietly explained everything, then said, "Seven-minute shamnashim 200 meters by the fence, Tzeh(go)!" And like cockroaches scattering when the light comes on, we started grabbing all our stuff and rushed over to the fence.

Seven minutes went by. Sergeant Uri came around to see

that we weren't even close to finished. He looked at us disappointed, and said, "How much longer do you need?"

Adam, one of the boys on my team, said, "Five minutes." Uri laughed and said "you have three, Tzeh!"

Surprisingly, we were able to finish in the three minutes, but that was the last time we were ever given extra time to complete the task. Aside from making us run around like crazy people, taking all of our equipment from one side of the fence to the other, the goal was for us to be able to have all of our equipment laid out, checked, and in order within an incredibly short amount of time; all important tools we would need to be good soldiers, tools that I had to use later when it really counted. In order to instill such discipline, about three times a day every day, we would run across the camp and do another shamnashim and, of course, once we were able to complete it the first time, one of Uris most important rules was added: to do it without speaking.

On one of our shamnashim, I saw this guy, lean, black hair, buzzcut like everyone else, and with a small beard, but he looked oddly familiar. I walked over to him, and to my amazement it was my longtime friend, Aharon! We were both in shock as we greeted each other. Although we had stayed in touch, who would have thought that when we were eight-years-old, we would be meeting up again, not only in the army together but the next week we would be jumping out of planes together. Unlike me, Aharon was not in Tironoot. He had already finished a year of his training in the combat engineering Special Forces unit "Yahalom." Since he had already finished most of his training, his commanders were much more lenient to them, allowing them to relax during the times they were not training on the jump course.

The course itself was very different from anything else I had or will ever experience in the army. We would leave our commanders behind and go out with our jump instructors all day and work on falling on the ground. Standing in the sand, we all bent our knees and fell down, first letting our shins, then thighs and then the rest of our body hit the ground. By doing so, we would do a 360-degree roll, also known as the 'Paratrooper's Roll.' We worked on this and learned how to operate the parachutes and all the commands we would be given while in the plane. We went over all the equipment at the course repeatedly for a week. Then every time we weren't with our instructors, we went back to our commanders, and it was back to our workouts and shamnashim.

On the little off time we had, usually before bed, having all those different special units around, brought about an air of competition, but not any physical competition, since everyone was exhausted from the day. So, we had our "Osim," which was like our version of a rap battle.

At night, we got into our sleeping bags, keeping the tents open to allow the cool air to breeze through, and then suddenly, I would hear the guys in the Oketz unit, a Special Forces unit that worked with dogs "Os! Palchan Tzanhanim the honorable, Os! You have a long training and tryout, Os! Only to put on a Kerami (body armor) and to stand on the border all day."

Leor from our team would yell back: "Os! Okets the honorable, Os! To guard it, isn't nice, Os! But it's better than cleaning up dog shit all day, Os!"

Then Oketz would yell, "Os! Yahalom the honorable, Os! You play with explosives, Os! In a few years you won't be able to give a thumbs up! Os!"

Back and forth we went, laughing and cheering until everyone fell asleep. I must add, those chants all rhymed and sounded much better in Hebrew.

After our training week was over, it was finally time for our first jump. All the falling on the ground and simulator training was going to be nothing like the real thing. Nothing ever is. But like everything in life, you take it one step at a time and continue to push forward. We got all our gear ready the night before so there was nothing to worry about. Our guns, vest, ammunition and all the other army equipment was wrapped in a leather bag with a long cord attached to it. I woke up that morning at five a.m. extremely nervous. My group got together, and we all got on a bus to the airfield. There we put on our parachutes and strapped our bag filled with our equipment to our belt. Once we jumped, we would have to let go of the cord, allowing the bag to drop four meters below us, still attached to our belt but not strapped to our legs. If we didn't let go of the cord, there was the risk of landing on the heavy bag and breaking our legs. Once everything was ready, we sat down and waited. They told us we could eat a small breakfast while we waited for the planes to come. I was too nervous to eat anything. We sat there for about thirty minutes until three huge planes came flying in. It was the famous Hercules aircraft, by far the largest plane I had ever seen. As it came in, we all grudgingly got to our feet. It was very hard to move around with the parachute on my back and all my equipment strapped to my leg. Yet I hobbled over and got in line, waving goodbye to Aharon as we boarded different planes. From there we all sat down, almost on top of each other. I made my way to the back of the plane. I would be one of the last to jump. As we all sat down and got "comfortable," a bell went off, the doors closed and the plane began to move. I was already feeling the adrenaline rush in and we hadn't even taken off yet. As the plane took off, we started to yell, "Ya up, Ya up, Ya up," a tradition stolen from the British. We would be going 1200 feet up with the plane traveling between 400-500 km/h. Once we made it to the right altitude, another bell (like a school bell) went off, telling everyone to be alert and get ready, as if I was not already super alert the entire ten minutes we were flying. Then suddenly, two of our instructors standing by the doors in the back of the plane, heaved them open. A gust of wind blasted through us, making it almost impossible to hear anyone without yelling in their ear. Another bell went off. The eight guys closest to the door on my side stood up, and the eight guys closest to the door on the other side stood up. They all lined up and attached the yellow cord that they had been holding to a metal cable running through the plane. This is because when you jump out, the yellow cable, attached to the plane, will apply pressure on the parachute and pull it open. Once this is done, as commanded, we pat the guy in front of us and yell out our number. "One ready! Two ready! Three ready!" until they get to the end and the last guy closest to the door yells at the top of his lungs, "Eight ready!" Then he swings his yellow cord over to the instructor, and slowly walks closer to the open door with me in the back looking at the soldier leaning outside of that huge monster of a plane in continuous disbelief that it was really happening. Thirty seconds went by and a bell went off, along with a green light next to the door, signaling the paratrooper to jump. And just like that, he jumps! Or what looks more like a fall rather than a jump, outside of the door and into the white abyss. Just as he goes, the paratrooper behind him swings the cord and cautiously walks up to the entrance and jumps out, too. It went on like that until the last one was out. Then the plane makes a U-turn and we began again. To me the first eight guys looked as if they had just disappeared. One minute they were here, the next gone, as if never to be seen again.

As the plane came back to where it started, the next eight guys got up and the process was repeated. And, again, another U-turn. Then it was my turn. I was the last in my group, so there was no one behind me inching forward, almost pushing me to go. No, I was all on my own. I had to make the crazy decision to jump out of the plane without anyone egging me forward.

As we finished our third and final U-turn, the bell went off, I stood up and yelled, "One ready!" Then the guy in front of me yelled, "Two ready!" until we got to number eight. Number eight approached the door. I couldn't even see what was outside yet, but could only imagine. Then again that green light came on, and he's off. I inched forward, lightly tapping the guy in front of me. The guys in the front continued to throw their cables and jump out. Within seconds, I was the second to last guy. I saw the outside! Everything was so small and the wind so strong! The butterflies in my stomach felt as if they were exploding. Then without even thinking, I threw my cable and crept forward to the front and leapt. As I went down, I screamed my head off. Then suddenly, I was yanked upward. I looked up. My parachute was open and full! I completely forgot that I was supposed to count to three and check to make sure my parachute was okay. Lucky for me the yellow cord opened the parachute and there were no issues. Next on my mind was the sack attached to my leg. No time to enjoy the view, I had to pull that cord. I reached under my reserve parachute attached to my chest, and with all my strength, lifted the lock to the cord up. Then in a swoosh, the cord came falling down, and I felt a jolt pull me down. I had about ten seconds to enjoy the view before my next stressful endeavor: preparing myself to land. The view of Israel is breathtaking, and I felt incredibly lucky to be able to be there. At that moment I was filled with Zionistic pride and happy to be going through all those hardships if it meant I would be one of the soldiers guarding our amazing country.

As quickly as the thoughts and feelings entered my head they left and were filled with the stress of getting ready to land. I noticed that I was going forward and to my right, so I needed to turn my feet and legs to my left. I bent my knees and pressed my legs as hard as I could together. Like putting invisible glue on them, I wanted them to be stuck together. That way my whole body took the impact from the landing, not just one leg. As I got closer, I pressed harder and harder, gritting my teeth, then BAM! I smacked onto the ground and rolled over, getting the wind knocked out of me from landing on some rocks and bushes. I was on my stomach, in shock, unable to breath or move. Just at that moment, a gust of wind took my parachute up, which then began to drag me across the shrubs and rocks. I grabbed my parachute and released the buckle on my shoulder, detaching the parachute to my harness. The parachute released and I stopped getting pulled across the desert floor. In pain and anguish, I lay in the desert. My tooth felt loose… I hoped it wasn't chipped. I learned a lesson from my first jump: It's better to land on your feet than to land on your face! After taking a few deep breaths, I started to get my stuff together and began my march to the landing strip. From there, I met up with the rest of my team and Aharon, who had a much nicer landing than myself and together we all headed back to base with jump one down, there were three more-day jumps and one night jump to go.

The view as I prepare to land – Get those feet stuck together like glue

One of my friends jumping

8

NAVIGATION

"Sometimes when you lose your way, you find yourself" ~ ***Mandy Hale***

We concluded our training at Bach Tzanhanim with our final masa. It is a 70km hike with all of our gear, ending in Jerusalem at Givat Hatachmoshet (Ammunition Hill). For the paratroopers, this was the pinnacle of their training. They had finished basic training, which taught them to become a soldier. They then went on to advanced training, teaching them how to become a paratrooper and combat-ready soldier. All of this took about seven to eight months and ended with receiving the coveted red beret on top of Givat Hatachmoshet. We, too, did the 70km march and received the beret; however, for us this was not the pinnacle of our training. It was the halfway point. Until this point, we were taught how to become paratroopers. Until one fateful day a group of soldiers came in with black shirts that said lochama (warrior) on the back. They had on black sunglasses and were wearing the coveted Special Forces hiking boots, of which we would receive at the end of our training. These men were the lochama and were going to be our new instructors in Krav Maga, Navigations, Camouflage, and generally anything extra that we needed to learn that would separate us from the regular paratroopers. We soon realized that every time we saw one of their black shirts, we would associate it with pain. As we were introduced to Ivan, one of the lochama, he first told us to "forget everything you have learned at this place." It was time for us to undergo another rebuilding phase. This time not from civilian to paratrooper, but from paratrooper to Gadsar.

A camera crew capturing us as we finish Masa Kumtah with the Paratroopers

Justly, the next part of training was navigations, in which we learned how to maneuver in the deserts, forests, and urban environments of Israel. We started navigation training on a small four-kilometer track in order to get our feet wet. They broke us into groups of four, gave us a map, and set us free to find the target destinations on our own. The map was soon taken and, instead, we would have to create a path on a map, memorize it and be given only a compass to find the target locations.

We often navigated at night because we operated under the cover of darkness. Flashlights were frowned upon and if spotted could be met with punishment. Maps were forbidden at this point, as were phones. We actually did have a map and phone in our backpacks, but it was only for emergency purposes. The map and phone were sealed inside an envelope so that they could check to see if we had cheated by sneaking a peek.

Navigation teaches self-reliance. You learn to put trust in yourself because there is no one else to depend on but you and you alone. I often found myself lost in empty terrain and forced to radio in and admit that I was lost. My commanders on the radio would never offer any help. They just told me to keep moving my legs and eventually I would get there. This may seem callous, but what they were really saying was that they believed in me and I needed to believe in myself. Their advice, while not helpful in the moment, taught me to trust in myself and my abilities. They were right, too. I kept moving and eventually found my way.

Learning navigation resulted in some of my most trying times, but they were also fun times.

One of my first times out, I was with a friend, Mekonnen, who happened to be one of the best navigators in my team. He had experience navigating in high school, so was ahead of the game. We began our journey in Dimona and headed into the mountains just outside the city. The terrain was steep and hard to traverse. We avoided anything that looked like a path as we were instructed, and instead moved from peak to peak, following the topography. We created our own paths as we did in our gibush. Paths can change. Topography does not.

We were looking for codes that had been painted onto rocks or trees. Once we were able to locate our codes we could then proceed to the final destination where the team all met up again. There was no room for error. We would draw our paths around finding the first code and move from there to the second and, finally, the end. We therefore could not get lost or else we would not know how to get to the end. After some time of walking, we made it to our first point. There was a code, and all was well. Mekonnen and I then picked up the pace, as more hours of us hiking up and down the mountains outside of Damona, covered in the darkness went by. We made it to what seemed to be our next point. Yet something did not add up. There was no code where there should have been. I started to search frantically all around. I worried that we had missed the code and suggested turning back and retracing our steps. Mekonnen said no, that we must believe in ourselves and keep moving forward. He said that if we had passed the code, we would have seen it and that it must still be ahead of us. I reluctantly agreed to keep moving forward and we eventually came to a hillside where the secret code was sitting on top. I realized then how dangerous self-doubt can be and promised to trust myself in the future.

Similarly, to Mikvey Alone, our commanders also put on the same act and were not supposed to laugh or smile in front of us. One day, later during my training, or in Hebrew known as Maslool, we returned to base sweaty and exhausted from a long week of navigating. Our commander gave us only ten minutes to clean our equipment, shower, change into a fresh uniform, and line up in a chet before him. I sprinted to the showers, put my gun somewhere safe, and bathed with my soiled sweaty uniform and equipment still on so that I could wash my body and the uniform at the same time. I rubbed a handful of shampoo into my hair and over my vest and helmet. I hung up my uniform to dry and went to put on a fresh one. Unfortunately, I couldn't find a clean shirt. Running out of time, I put my wet shirt back on and lined up in the chet formation right before time ran out.

The sergeant took one look at me in my wet shirt and burst out laughing. After almost a year of training under him, he had never broken, I had never seen him laugh or smile before, so this was saying something. The rest of the group looked at me and started laughing as well. When I looked down at myself, I started laughing too. Not only was my untucked shirt wet and dripping, so was my hat. My boots were untied. My pants were disheveled. I looked like a wet dog.

Normally, this would mean certain punishment, either sprints for thirty minutes or Matzav shtiyeem (waiting in push-up position) for thirty minutes. But since even our sergeant laughed, he took mercy on me and gave me one minute to go back to my room, change and get fixed up before we headed out again.

Matzav shtiyeem

One of the painted codes

Israel has lots of varied terrain, which means learning to navigate in different conditions. No one thinks of Israel as a tropical country with jungles, but Israel does in fact have jungle terrain, or *tzfach*, in the north. I learned this the hard way one week during what was supposed to be a simple navigation exercise. I thought that the mission was going to be easy, typical mountainous terrain, but found that the map was wrong. My path was blocked by a twenty-foot-tall wall of vines. Unfortunately, this was the only path I had studied and planned, and it was too late to find another way.

I decided that I would cut my way through the vines. I used my gun and a pocketknife to hack through the vines. It took an hour to make it fifty feet into the jungle. I turned to my partner to say that it was not working, and we would never make it to the destination in time. Nonetheless, we continued hacking away for another hour, but the vegetation continued to get thicker and thicker. At that point, we decided it was better to chart a new course on the fly and try to circumvent the jungle. *Charting a new course on the fly, with no map, is a terrible idea.*

We followed a river around the jungle. Along the way, we passed other teams that were also attempting the same thing.

We weren't supposed to collaborate with other teams, but we decided to walk together regardless. We followed the river for hours and it took us much longer to reach the destination point than the commanders anticipated. Our mefaked got worried that no one had arrived on time. Eventually, we were ordered to unseal the maps in our backpacks in order to figure out where we were. We had completely disregarded all the waypoints and headed straight to the end point. Still, I was two hours late. The last straggler to make it to the meeting point was six hours late. We were glad to have all made it, but the venture was mostly a failure, and we felt ashamed. The *svach,* or jungle, had beaten us.

As time went on, Navigations evolved and instead of going in twos, we would go out alone. New Year's came and went during one of our navigation weeks. On New Year's Eve, we were out scaling the mountains around the city of Dimona. The sky was clear, and the night stars were on full display, though I hardly noticed them. I was too busy trying to navigate.

I had done this many times before, but that night was different. I felt bothered by the fact that it was New Year's Eve. Another year was starting, a basic milestone for most people, and there I was wandering in the desert. My mind kept drifting to thoughts of New Year's in America and how I had always spent the night with family and friends, watching fireworks and having a good time. I wondered what my family and friends were doing right then. They were probably out on the town, or maybe at home relaxing, having a barbecue, or watching the fireworks. Not me though. I was stumbling through the dark of night, scaling mountainsides, and trying not to get lost in the desert. I was jealous of everyone back home and it was distracting me from my duties.

Just then the voice of my commander came over the walkie-talkie. "Hello, everyone. We've decided that since it's New Year's Eve, we are going to do something nice for you. For the next ten minutes, until the clock strikes midnight, you are all going to offer up one song that you want us to play. You may vote for the song that you guys want."

This was a small joy! I considered my options and ultimately decided on *American Pie* by Don McClean, which I knew by heart from singing it on the bus when we took field trips at school when I was a kid in St. Louis. This was exactly what I needed, something familiar and communal, the perfect song that would remind me what it was like to be back home, comfortable and happy. I got on the walkie-talkie and tried to convince my teammates to vote for the same song.

When the clock read 11:59 p.m., I stopped at the top of a mountain. I had many more mountains to traverse before we would reach our final destination, but I wanted to take a short break to listen to the song at the top of the mountain. Despite sheer exhaustion, I was almost giddy with excitement, hoping they would play *American Pie* over the radio. I remember staring up into the stars; they were so beautiful, as were the mountains, and waiting blissfully for a moment of rest and normalcy that would remind me of home. I prayed that they would pick my song, literally prayed, hoping for just a little morale boost that would help me complete the mission. We still had so far to go before we were done. I just needed a little something to help me get through. It was, after all, a holiday.

And then, the opening synth notes of Miley Cyrus's *Wrecking Ball* started to play over the walkie-talkie. I was enraged beyond belief. I screamed and cursed into the night air and could hear my voice echo down into the valleys below. What was wrong with them? Not only was the song terrible, and not what I wanted to hear on that of all nights, but we hadn't even suggested it. No one had suggested it! Were they still playing mind games? I couldn't stop cursing, not for several long minutes, before I finally calmed down, picked up my walkie-talkie, and headed down the mountain and up the next one, and down that one, and up again, and again, and again… I felt completely broken inside and that was the worst New Year's ever, making me dread the coming year.

Going over maps in preparation for the navigations that night – the floor is flooded because there was a flash flood, we are under this small bridge trying to stay out of the rain

While navigations were not my strong point, I was excelling in most of my training. However, on one occasion, I was almost kicked out of my unit, though it had nothing to do with my performance and, as is so often the case for young men, everything to do with a girl. It was nearly a tragedy, one that I brought on myself that could have resulted in losing everything I had worked so hard for.

At the time, I was doing an intensive two-month training program in explosives engineering, which was the major specialization of my unit. The instructors held recruits to very high standards, which made sense given that we would be handling explosives and required us to get almost perfect scores on exams, just to pass the course. Though I was particularly worried about this course because of my poor Hebrew, I performed quite well.

A training exercise with special Israeli equipment

Toward the end of the explosives course, I learned that Talia would be visiting Israel. We had kept in touch by phone and sending regular texts and long-flowing emails back and forth to each other. In all that time, I had never told her my true feelings. This seemed like the perfect opportunity to do so in person. Unfortunately, she was visiting Bat Yam, which was six hours away, and I was on base every day taking my explosives course. I asked my commander, a man named Gal, for a day off so that I could see her while she was there. I knew he would never grant leave for a date, so I told him that my sister, whom I had not seen in a year, was visiting. In retrospect, if Gal found out I lied I could have gotten kicked out, right then and there, but I knew that would be my only chance to see her, so I took the risk.

Asking for time off was not a decision I made lightly. I understood how critical it was not to miss crucial training that would make me a better soldier and maybe someday save my life, but I was able to rationalize my desire since I was doing so well. One day wouldn't hurt, I told myself, and I could make it up when I got back and learn everything on my own.

It wasn't like I made a habit of missing training. Aside from the day I thought Batman had eaten my door, I had never requested a day off.

Gal never got back to me about the request, so I reminded him of it the day of, first thing in the morning. With a stern look, he informed me that my request was denied, and I could not leave base.

The right thing to do was shut my mouth, but that's not what I did. I had learned from the Israelis and argued with my commander. In fact, I even threatened to quit if I did not get the day off. The ultimatum came as a shock to even me. I regretted the words as soon as they had left my mouth. I couldn't believe I was willing to risk everything I had worked so hard for just to see a girl and, in retrospect, that was stupid. But the gambit had already been made.

Gal looked taken aback by the threat. He was the last person to issue such an ultimatum to, since he regularly reminded us that the door was always open and that we could leave anytime—we just shouldn't expect to be able to come back. The unit had no interest in soldiers that were going to quit, and if someone was going to quit, they wanted them to do it before going to war.

I fully expected Gal to kick me out of the unit right then and there, but, to my surprise, he did not. He considered my request and, a few hours later, he made me an offer. If I could pass that day's exam beforehand, I could take a twenty-four hour leave of absence.

The catch was that I only had two hours to take the exam and make my bus or I would never get to Bat Yam and back again within that time frame. It was a nearly impossible time crunch, but I wasn't about to let that stop me. I rushed to explain the situation to my teacher, who agreed to give me the exam early, though it would take fifteen minutes to set up. I used that time to get packed and then rushed back to hurry through the exam. Despite blowing through it at breakneck speed, I got a perfect score.

I then finished packing and was ready to go with fifteen minutes to spare to my teammates' utter amazement. Because of the lie they did not know why I was in such a rush to leave. On my way to the bus station, I called my good family friend, Udi, and asked to spend the night at his place in Rishon Letzion, which was next to the city of Bat Yam, where I was meeting up with Talia, and just like that everything was set. I had been issued leave of absence, set up accommodations, and made the bus on time.

Unfortunately, I had overlooked one not so small detail in my haste. I had forgotten to pack clean clothes. My bag was full of dirty clothes and army uniforms. There was no way I could meet Talia wearing either, so I jumped off the bus when we stopped over in Beer Sheva and rushed to the nearest mall to buy new clothes. In a mad dash, I grabbed a pair of jeans, a shirt, and a pair of shoes, all of which cost me $300, a considerable outlay on a simple soldier's salary, but I wanted to impress. I paid for the clothes and rushed back to the bus station to get on the bus before it departed for the next stop.

The entire trip took about six hours, from the base to Bat Yam. I was still in a rush when I got there, so I took a cab to Udi's place to take a shower, change into my new clothes, and drop off my bags. By the time that was all done, and I was ready to go, it was nine o'clock at night. I was hungry from not having eaten all day, but thankfully Talia was only ten minutes away. She arrived shortly thereafter.

We all chatted for a bit, and then Talia and I took off to the center of town, where we looked for a fun place to grab a drink. Bat Yam is not a big city, like Tel-Aviv, and there were not that many fun bars. We ultimately settled on an Irish pub because we could hear the music, laughter and the clack of billiard balls from outside. I was ravenous at that point, but Talia's stunning eyes took my mind off my hunger.

We grabbed a small table in the back so that we could talk over a few drinks. We toasted being reunited after so long. I told her about being in the army and my explosives course.

She talked about studying drama at her college. We talked and laughed so much that the time flew by, and, before we knew it, the bar was closing for the night.

I walked Talia home, building up my courage to make a move and tell, or show, her how I felt. When we were standing at the front door, I knew then was the time, so I leaned in for a kiss. She backed away and murmured a quiet, "No."

Through the sting of rejection, I apologized for misreading the situation, and we went our separate ways. She went inside, and I returned to Udi's place sad, hurt and alone.

She sent a text the next day, asking if we could meet for lunch. I politely reminded her that the previous night was the only night for which I could get leave and that I was already on my way back to base. With another five hours on the bus, I had plenty of time to stew in my heartbreak.

It was only later that I found out, through her social media accounts, that she had a new boyfriend at the time, whom she had been seeing for several months. She had made no mention of him at all, not that night, not in any of our texts or phone calls, and at no point before I had risked my entire military career, everything I had worked so hard for, just to have a chance to see her. She hadn't told me anything about him, and I never knew he existed until much later. This was probably for the best. I had already felt heartbroken. There was no reason to have felt foolish as well. Once I returned, my teammates noticed how distraught I was so I told them the real reasons I left. We decided not to tell Gal until we had finished training, and when we eventually did, he got a big laugh out of it and agreed that if I had told him the truth he never would have let me out, but regardless, he called me an idiot for trying to have such a romantic night under such difficult circumstances.

Soldiers in the IDF, and especially in Special Forces, must wear many hats. We are trained in many roles and jobs, or *pakalim,* as we call them in Hebrew. About a year into my training, most of us had at least two roles, either official or unofficial, sometimes more. My main job so far was as a Negevist, but I also handled explosives regularly, having done so well in the explosives course. We all had to be flexible and learn something about the different roles so that we could be adaptive and act on the fly.

We were now all going to learn a new official *pakal* on top of what we were already doing. They were going to divide our team into three groups that would each focus on one of three new roles necessary for reconnaissance missions, in which we would be doing many. The roles were "builders," who specialized in camouflage and building camouflage outposts; "lookouts," who specialized in reconnaissance technology and techniques and also called in airstrikes and kept track of the position of soldiers on the field; and "navigators," who were in charge of logistics and moving the group from destination to destination in an orderly manner.

We started off learning the basics of all three jobs because we had to know how the different roles functioned together, but then they assigned us each to a group to dive deep and train in our chosen role. We did not get to choose the role, though. Our commanders placed us where they thought best. Gal designated me as a navigator, which was a big surprise and disappointment, considering I was not very good. I wanted to be a builder because it didn't require me to communicate in Hebrew. I was terrible at navigation, something my commanders knew, as they had almost kicked me out of the unit for being so bad at it just the week before. Being a navigator meant that I would have to suffer through another two weeks of navigations training, which I would have done anything to avoid.

I took the matter up with Gal, but he was not very receptive to my concerns.

"Max, this is your chance to redeem yourself and improve!" Gal said with a laugh.

I doubted his reasoning. He was leaving the unit for

another position in a few weeks, his role to be taken over by Paz, who had just finished officer school and previously was the commander for the other team in our unit during basic training. So, I suspected Gal simply didn't care that much who was in what role. I begged for him to reassign me to a new job, but he refused. This meant, like it or not, I was about to suffer through another two weeks of navigation training. There was no avoiding it, so I sucked it up, got my map, compass, and walkie-talkie and joined the other navigators to learn my navigation routes for the next day.

Navigator training, as I had experienced, was fairly straightforward; you spend the day learning and memorizing your path and then head out at night to collect the hidden codes before heading to the endpoint. But, as I suspected everyone else who was made a navigator was good at navigating, which was why they were chosen, and the drills were designed to challenge them. We had to stop at many more waypoints along the way to search for even more difficult hidden codes and locations. Not being good at navigation, I really struggled to keep up. The first three days out in the field, I was only able to find two of six waypoints. I was getting a little better each day, but I could never imagine leading the entire unit to a designated position on a real mission.

The third night of this new phase of training, I was making my way to the endpoint when I ran into another soldier, Pal, or, as we called him, 'Pal Pal.' We waved and said hello. I asked how his navigation was going. He had found both points easily, whereas I found neither, though I was at least on track to reach the endpoint in time. We headed there together.

While we were walking, Pal looked over at me and asked, "Max, where is your walkie-talkie?"

I reached to the back of my vest, only to find empty air. In horror, I rummaged through my vest and pack. I checked my pockets. I checked every cranny of my person trying to find the damn thing, to no avail. Pal was laughing in disbelief, unable to understand how it was possible to lose such a critical piece of equipment.

The walkie-talkie had gone off an hour ago, so I couldn't have lost it very long ago. I retraced the night in my mind and then in actuality, going back up the mountain I had just climbed down looking where I had just been, to search for that damn walkie-talkie. After an hour, I still had not found it and it was getting close to the time I was supposed to meet at the endpoint. I decided to head there without the walkie-talkie. It was bad enough that I had failed to find the waypoints and lost my equipment. It would be even worse to show up at the endpoint late as well.

I went to the endpoint and, with my tail between my legs, told Paz, whom had now fully taken over for Gal, that I had lost my walkie-talkie. I was relieved that he wasn't as mad as I had expected. He said that we just needed to go search for it. I told him I already had, and it was a lost cause, but he wouldn't accept that as an answer. He assembled a team that consisted of me, Shmulik, Liron, and Pal to go find the walkie-talkie. They all laughed at me for having lost it in the first place, but we headed out together to find it. We again retraced my steps through a forest, up a mountain to the most likely place it might have fallen off and spent four hours looking without success. I used Shmulik's walkie-talkie to tell Paz that we couldn't find it.

Paz still wouldn't accept this as an answer. He had a personal stake in the matter. Both he and I could be thrown in military jail if we didn't find the walkie-talkie, which he reminded me sternly. Military jail is not real jail. One famous Israeli general once said that you weren't really a soldier if you hadn't been sent to jail. Army jail seemed more like getting a timeout then a regular Israeli jail. You get to keep your phone and can do basically whatever you want, but there are downsides. Jail time doesn't count toward your service time, which meant it would take longer to finish my three-year commitment. This didn't bother me, but what did bother me was that going to jail would likely result in being kicked out of my unit.

After five hours of searching, we took a break on the side of the path. Everyone was exhausted, and the whole search party was mad at me by this point. Shmulik was the most aggressive, calling me stupid for getting myself into the situation. He took his phone out of his bag, which was forbidden since they were only for emergency use and played *Turn Me On* by Nicki Minaj. I didn't know the song, but found it catchy, so I took out my phone and added it to my playlist. This was probably a ridiculous thing to care about given the circumstances, but I was hopeless and sitting in the middle of the forest with nothing to do while the other guys rested. It was going to be impossible to find the small black walkie-talkie especially in the middle of the night.

Paz called us on someone else's walkie-talkie to ask how the search was going. We gave him the bad news. Paz sighed and said that he and a few more guys would come and help search. By the time he arrived with a car, the sun was coming up and we all had a new burst of energy. We had more men to help search and we could actually see now.

Paz had brought more soldiers and two commanders with him. One of the commanders had a computer with my tracking information on it that he used to retrace my path. We all piled into the jeep and retraced my exact path. We came to a barbed wire fence that I had crossed on my way into the forest and to my relief and shock there was the damn walkie-talkie hanging from the fence. It must have caught on the barbed wire and slipped out of my holster while I was crawling under the fence. I had never been so happy to see my navigation equipment. It had taken six hours, but Paz and I both avoided unwanted jail time and a lot of explaining to our commanding officers. I was also pleased that we found the walkie-talkie hanging from the fence because, while I had lost the radio, at least I hadn't just left it somewhere.

After we hightailed it back to the end point everyone was already working on their navigation maps, planning for the next night. Before I could rejoin the group, Paz pulled me aside to ask how my week had been. I admitted that I was terrible at navigations and that the week had felt like torture. He asked what I would prefer, given a choice. I said that I would make a great builder, as I had explained to Gal before, because of my poor Hebrew I felt that was the best job for me. I also loved building things and thought camouflage was cool.

Paz listened carefully and took my words to heart. Unfortunately, the builders had already left for training and were on the other side of the country. It was too late for me to join them.

"How are you at word search?" Paz asked.

"I was really good as a kid," I said, though I hadn't done one in years.

Paz explained that doing lookout was very similar to doing a word search. Lookouts had to have a keen eye for details. Paz then informed me that I was going to stop my navigations training and instead join the reconnaissance team. I had never been so relieved in my life. I wouldn't have to do navigations training anymore, at least not after that week. I was stuck there until then.

"Should I get ready for tonight's navigation anyway?" I asked, which I did not want to do, but I was stuck.

A look of horror came over Paz's face. The last thing he wanted was to send me out to lose another walkie-talkie. "No," he said. "Tonight, you will stay with me and guard the equipment."

While I should have been embarrassed, as I was basically kicked off my Pakal, my excitement over not having to do any more navigation training overshadowed everything else.

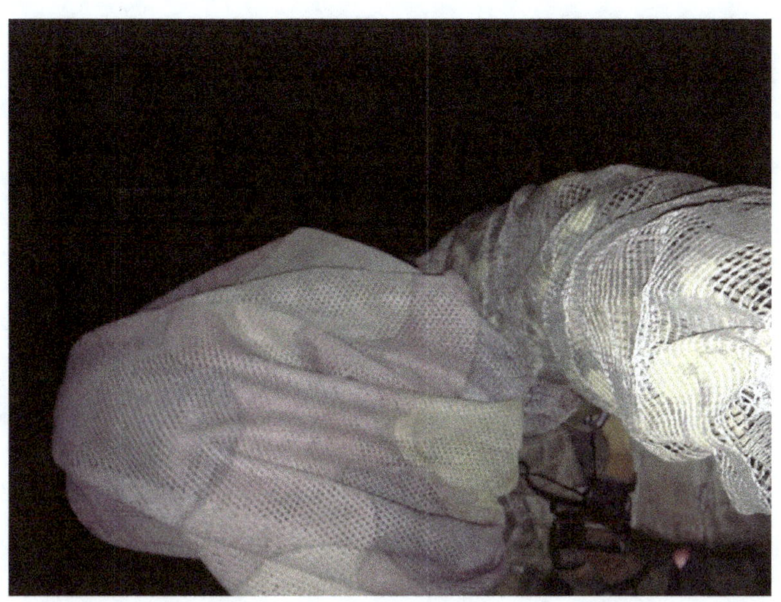

Myself camouflaged in a surveillance outpost in the West Bank after completing training

9

SURVIVAL

"We'll never survive!
Nonsense. You're only saying that because no one ever has."
~ William Goldman, *The Princess Bride*

As the name implies, survival week taught us how to survive in the wild and live off the land. We spent the first day in the northern part of Israel, in hilly and mountainous terrain, learning what plants were safe to eat and which were not. Unfortunately, this was not as informational as I had hoped. Survivalist techniques, in general and for a specific region, encompass a vast and complex set of topics that cannot really be covered in a single day. So, in short, I only remember one naturally grown flower that I was allowed to eat if I ever needed to survive in the north of Israel or south of Lebanon.

We spent the next three or four days in the desert, which was more helpful. We learned how to improve our navigation skills and find water, the most pressing concern when trapped in an arid environment. We were taught how to look at a terrain and see if there are any animal paths that have been made. We learned how to read the landscape from a high vantage point and identify the terrain, its challenges and its opportunities.

We learned to watch and track animals for clues about our surroundings. We tracked goats to find water, food and shelter. The IDF Bedouin trackers, who consist of an elite desert tracking unit, knew these areas well, and taught us how to track people and animals. Little details that most people miss are a key to understanding your surroundings. For example, examining feces would tell us how recently animals had been through an area.

We went out on many tracking drills in which two people would be sent out into the desert with a head start and it was our job to track them down. We learned to spot and follow footprints, even when people are trying to cover their tracks. We also practiced rope skills. In the wild, you have to tie everything down so that your shelter and supplies don't blow away in the wind.

By chance, my twenty-first birthday fell on survival week. This would have been funny if it weren't so depressing to spend my birthday in the middle of nowhere and away from family and friends. Thankfully, my team was supportive. They bought me a cake and we celebrated that night before bed. We even had poika, a traditional Jewish dish that's comprised of rice, meat, and anything else you can find around the house to cook slowly in a stew over an open fire. What I assumed would be the worst birthday of my life turned out to be one of the best.

The final few days of survival week were a comprehensive test of everything we had learned over the whole week. We were given a true test of surviving out in the wild. The scenario was this: we were trapped behind enemy lines, all alone in the desert, and had to make it back to Israel undetected. No one was going to be coming to save us. It was only us in the wild with the enemy in hot pursuit. We were on our own, no one but ourselves to rely upon.

We had only our wits and a few supplies: a little uncooked

food (though it wasn't enough to last), a lighter, rope, our gun, our backpacks and basic fighting equipment, and an Air Force map. This map only shows large details about the landscape, unlike the topographic maps we were used to that were much more detailed, adding an extra challenge to the navigation. This was all we carried. Everything else we needed to survive had to be acquired in the wild.

Because the scenario indicated that we were behind enemy lines and under pursuit, we had to avoid major paths and roads. Our instructors had patrols out looking for us the whole time, patrolling the obvious routes, playing the part of the enemy. If they found us, we failed the exercise. So again, we had to make our own paths everywhere, many of which were treacherous and took us far out of our way to avoid being detected.

This was a three-day exercise. I slept one night hidden beneath rocks on the side of a mountain, and the other night on a steep ledge of a canyon. There were patrols looking for us down below, so I made sure the terrain became so steep I could go no higher. I found a small crevice to sleep inside. To keep myself from awakening and rolling off the mountain, I tied a rope around my body and tied myself to a boulder. I tied my equipment to my leg. This way neither me nor my gear would fall down the cliff during the night. I saw a teammate's bag fall off a cliff at one point and he had to go down the canyon to retrieve it. As he was hiking down the canyon, I almost yelled, "That sucks man!" But I did not, out of fear of being detected. I certainly didn't want that happening to me.

My sleeping arrangement was clever, but it was all for naught. I was so stressed out that I couldn't sleep at all. I was on edge the whole night and woke the next morning feeling not at all rested. I might as well have just kept moving through the night.

Nonetheless, I survived and finished the exercise the next day and avoided detection.

Though I had left the extra navigation training to be a

lookout, we all still had to train many weeks in navigations because it was a cornerstone in our development. Mesacem Prat was our navigation final exam, a 100-kilometer navigation that takes three days. For our route, we were doing the famous trek known as Yam Le Yam that started on the Mediterranean Sea on the northwestern coast of Israel and ended at the Red Sea on the country's eastern border. We spent a weekend beforehand learning, charting and memorizing the entire route. Unlike before, when we were given our waypoints each morning, we were given all the points ahead of time and had three days to learn the entire three-day route before departing.

Unfortunately, I was not in good shape for that mission. I came down with a fever and had to see the doctor. My fever must have broken right before they took my temperature, because it read as normal, even though I still felt sick. The commanders didn't care how I reported feeling, though. I didn't have a fever, so they expected me to perform. They kept telling me to stop slouching and get back to work. I didn't want to slouch; I just felt terrible.

Two days into preparing the navigations, the medics took my temperature yet again, because I looked so sick, and once again the thermometer showed no fever. This time they got a new thermometer and took my temperature again. The third time around, on the new thermometer, I registered with a fever of 101 degrees Fahrenheit! The first thermometer must have been broken all along; no news to me, as I knew I was sick as a dog.

With this new information, I told Paz that I was legitimately sick and couldn't go on such a long and arduous navigation. He informed me that this was an important week. He told me that the unit would drop me if I did not go. This seemed unreasonable, but I understood the importance of that week. I could sit the test out, but then I would be off the unit. I tried my best to invoke my never-give-up attitude, and I set out on the navigation with everyone else.

While the commanders forced me to do the navigation sick, they did take a little pity on me. Paz was able to allow me to start one day later and go with the Palsar unit. In addition, we were supposed to carry fifty percent of our bodyweight in gear. They dropped my requirement down to thirty percent. They also had me radio in every hour or so to make sure I was alive and not somewhere sick and dying in a field. They also had the medic check my temperature at all of the end points for each night to make sure I wasn't getting sicker. These were not so much allowances on my part so much as exceptions made so that I could do the test. If I got sicker, they might have had to pull me out, though they would also have had to kick me out of the unit. I prayed not to get any sicker.

The test was very intense. I was alone for most of the time, trekking across Israel at night. During the day, we convened in three-man squads to build a camouflaged hideout in which to wait out the day and make plans for the next night. The commanders would radio us throughout the day to make sure we were planning and not sleeping for the next night. Once night fell, we would set out on the next leg of our journey. We traveled thirty kilometers each night, traversing difficult terrain much of the time. Our commanders had set the waypoints on mountaintops, forcing us to climb almost every mountain we saw on our way as we crossed the country. We barely slept for the three days; there was always something to do, whether it was traveling at night or building a camouflaged hideout during the day.

Even when we finished reaching the final endpoint, we were not done. The commanders liked to test our mental fortitude by giving us another task once we thought we were done. I had scaled seven mountains in three days. Now we were going to scale one more; Har Bell, a difficult mountain to summit on any day, but especially difficult after a three-day trek across Israel. Normally they made us do this last "surprise" or "haakptazah" (It was no longer a surprise anymore, as they did this every week.) while carrying a few guys on stretchers. They must have taken pity on us, or thought the mountain too steep to safely scale with a stretcher, so they let us leave the stretchers behind.

Har Bell still took three hours to climb, and we were not even done once we reached the summit. They administered a visual exam, asking us to name many of the surrounding areas we had just walked through. They wanted to ensure that, even after three days of exhausting navigation and travel with zero sleep, we still had a sense of our surroundings. This was a crucial part of the test that none of us knew was coming.

Once the exam was over, we were finally done. We loaded a bus to Bet-Lied and every last one of us passed out as soon as we were in our seats. We were awoken only two hours later, not in Bet-Lied as we had been told, but at Wing Gate, the athletic facility where I had done my first gibush, the Yom Sayarot exam, over a year ago. I now found myself there once again. The experiences were not so different. The commanders were yelling at us to get off the bus and line up in rows of three.

The *Mem-Pay*, or platoon officer, told us that we had done a good job finishing Mesacem Prat, but that we had one final challenge to complete to finish the week, a physical exam. We were now going to run three kilometers on the sand dunes along the beach outside of Wingate. Afterward, we would run through an obstacle course that included a six-meter rope climb, scaling a wall, crawling under and through barbed-wire fencing, and a few other obstacles, and at the end grab our rifles and shoot six shots at a target. The minimum we could miss was one. We had only twenty-five minutes to finish the exam, which would have been a reasonable amount of time had we not just hiked 100 kilometers in three days and scaled seven small mountains, plus another large one, while weighted down with heavy bags. We had gotten almost no sleep in three days. I was still sick. My body and brain felt like Jell-O. I felt like the walking dead. After all of that, they were giving us a pass-or-fail physical exam with a hard time limit that is usually meant for fresh soldiers who have relaxed all day and who have prepared to take this test. Failure would result in our dismissal from the unit. Fuck me.

Though exhausted to the point of ridiculousness, we complied. I had done the hundred kilometers in three days, the eight mountains, all while sick. I completed the obstacle course in twenty-one minutes, not twenty-five, and I hit all six shots. Once we were all done, we lined up and filed back to the buses and made the short-drive to Bet-Lied. Finally, finally, that terrible, long, grueling exam was over. I had succeeded, somehow, despite being sick and running a fever the whole time. I could finally get some sleep.

After successfully finishing Mesacem Prat we had another famous test coming up. Our Krav Maga exam. Generally, throughout our training weeks we would have a Hakpatzah or surprise where the Lochama (trainers) would pop out of nowhere and ambush us. We would be given 30 seconds to get our krav maga gear on and begin training. There were 2 different kinds of training exercises. The first was to actually learn Krav Maga and learn the basics on how to fight and defend ourselves against anything from being ambushed with someone trying to stab with a fake knife or how to use our gun as a weapon without bullets. We even learned how to takedown and disarm people. These were all practical and taught us the physical maneuvers of krav maga. The second kind of training was to train our minds, mentality, and overall toughness. Krav Maga is known for especially being very ruthless and we needed to learn that mindset. These kinds of training consisted of grabbing a fence while 3 people beat you, hitting a punching bag while people beat you, moving from one side of the room to the other while a gang of people tried to stop you, crawling over glass, nails, gravel. At times we were allowed a little padding which would protect us from leaving bruises and marks on our bodies but didn't do much for the force of a punch to the gut.

But even with these small pads Krav Maga did anything you could think of to toughen us up and make us get comfortable with pain.

Then one night as we were fast asleep, I heard the yelling Hakptazah Hakpatzah!! The Lochama are hear!! And as I heard that, in came 4 lochama, wearing their black shirts and army pants, with poles. They begin to beat us as we get dressed and run to the krav maga studio. From there we began to do sprints back and forth on the street outside the studio. We must have sprinted for over an hour because everyone was exhausted, dripping with sweat when we were done. Then before we could even get a sip of water, we were each pulled into the studio where we began the final training mission. I started off fighting 1-1 with one guy. After taking him down, he pulled out a fake knife and I had to take him down with a knife. Then once that was done, we formed a ring. The instructor in the middle called out a Max! and I came into the middle. I knew this drill; I knew what was going to happen. I was going to get ambushed by one of my teammates at any second, from any angle, I needed to be ready to fight him off. Then Tzeh! The Lochama yelled and Rotem came at me. After a minute of fighting he went back.

Tzeh! Demissi came from behind, kicking me in the back, and Mekonon in front of me. 2 v 1. After another minute of mostly getting beaten up by the Ethiopian duo, they returned to the circle.

Tzeh! Rappaport, Shahar, and Li popped out. This time I was more successful in keeping the trio in front of me. Taking the punches but still getting a few good ones in too. After another minute they returned to the outer circle.

Tzeh! In came Noah. He was the best of us at Krav Maga. He had practiced his entire life and was an absolute monster. This was going to be tough. At this point, after over a year of fighting with each other, I knew I couldn't win, I just had to try and survive, keep him at bay as long as possible. Lucky for me I had the longer reach and was able to keep him away from getting too many good head shots in. Another minute went by.

Tzeh! Finally, in came one of our commanders! Commander David! David was the one who was on top of the trash can yelling ahoo ahoo ahoo as we pushed it 500 meters. He certainly was crazy and this was going to be tough. But, to get a chance to beat on my commander, I couldn't let this pass up. I went all out, punching like a wild man at this point due to my near exhausted state. It comes out a draw and the minute ends. I then finish the 5-minute drill and return to the outer circle as another person enters.

Once the circle was over, we then started the gauntlet. Everyone formed two lines. One man was going to stand on the fence and get beaten by the lochama for 60 seconds, then rush out and push, shove, and beat a guy holding a pillow across the row of people. As he did this the row would be punching him all the way through. Once finally getting through, he then ran to a punching bag and beat on it for 3 minutes while 3 guys beat on him.

After a few guys went through this, and I in the gauntlet threw some pretty forceful punches to their guts, I heard... Max! you're next!

I then went to the wall and it began. After about 40 seconds in, the lochama's metal-tipped shoe came right into my rib. I saw stars for about 3 seconds while he continued to beat on me. Then everything went red. I could still see but couldn't feel anymore. Then Tzeh! He yelled and I ran to the gauntlet. I threw the person all the way back in a matter of seconds, rather than minutes, making my way to the punching bag. And from then on out, it was 3 minutes of bliss, hitting the bag while trying to avoid the other 3 guys. I not only survived but was the fastest to finish.

After this the last part of the night began, a trial began. This time focusing on skill rather than mentality. We would run around the base to go through different maneuvers we had learned to disarm, take down anyone who stood in our way.

We were no longer the ones getting beaten but were finally doing the beating ourselves.

And as the sun rose, the trial ended. I have finished my Krav Maga Trial, bloodied, bruised, drenched in sweat, but full of pride for finishing the challenging task.

The Gauntlet

Krav Maga training – Fighting Circle

Our training ultimately culminated into Mesacem Maslool, a two-week trial that would conclude our year and two months of training, the ultimate comprehensive test of everything we had learned so far in the army. They would test our knowledge, our skills, our grit and mental fortitude, all at once, forcing us to prove that we had what it took to perform on real missions. This was a major undertaking, and while it would be physically and mentally demanding, the Mesacem Maslool was also more exciting than our other drills and tests. We would be engaging in two weeks of nonstop war games that would allow us to practice our skills in realistic situations that mirrored real warfare.

We spent an entire week just preparing our equipment before finally heading out. We were supposed to start the week off with a joint mission with Shayetet 13, which is the Israeli version of the U.S. Navy Seals, by coordinating an amphibious assault on a beach. They would ride in by boat. We would parachute into the water, landing in the shallows with all our gear on, the water up to our chests. We would then convene on the beach and search for mines before continuing into the jungle as part of the next phase of our mission.

I was looking forward to doing this training mission; it sounded so exciting. Unfortunately, it never happened. Due to a conflict of scheduling and budget concerns, the mission was nixed. Shayetet 13 was busy. The paratroopers faced budget concerns and didn't want to use seventy parachutes that would be left at sea. Instead of parachuting into the sea and storming the beach, we took a bus to the north of Israel, hopped off at the beach, put on our heavy bags of equipment and began our march into the jungle. The night air was crisp, the equipment was all in place and we began our mission.

The hike into the jungle was another thirty-kilometer trek through hills and thick brush. Once we reached the area, we began our training mission. We were now doing war games. The scenario was this: a stronghold in Lebanon was firing rockets into Israel. We had to find and infiltrate the base, comb the area for enemies and booby traps, and deploy explosives to destroy all rockets and rocket launchers.

We closed in on the base and changed formation so that we could start combing the fields. Everything had to be done in silence, without saying a word, because "the enemy" was nearby. We maneuvered as quietly as possible through branches and vines, stepping lightly to avoid crunching leaves beneath our boots. We were on high alert, scanning the area for the enemy, played by none other than the lochema (the guys that used to beat us with sticks, to wake us up for krav maga training).

After twenty minutes of combing the terrain, Shahar Dover, our forward sharpshooter, located a blue missile launcher 100 meters to our north. Dover was our little blonde, Russian perfectionist. Coming in at 150 pounds and five foot five, although small he had a mighty roar. He did everything down to perfection and was an ideal soldier, making me feel I had a reliable member at the forefront of my team. He not only pushed those around him to be their best, but he did the same for himself. He led the team in stretches and sometimes gym exercises like runs. He took me under his wing at times and made sure I understood everything going on. When we were first doing navigation, I had a very tough time understanding the lingo. I never had to learn all those new concepts before, and maps weren't really my thing. Although Dover's English wasn't great, he pulled me aside and made sure I understood everything and was able to complete the navigation maps and be able to convey my navigation report on my own.

We convened nearby, and Dover, Schmidt, Paz, and Li, our *Chod* (or, forward operations chooliyot), fanned out to look for enemies. Whereas Dover was the perfectionist, Li, on the other hand, was the class clown. He was small and stubborn but incredibly strong. He was the arse of the group with a heart of gold. Many times, when others were feeling down, Li found ways to make everyone laugh and smile. Now, though, was not the time to fool around.

Dover found someone hanging out by the missile launcher. Schmidt signaled that he saw someone else on the other side of the launcher with his night vision goggles. Paz signaled for one of the squads to break off from the group and head west and up the hill to better surround the enemy.

Once we were all in position, Paz gave the signal to fire. This was not a live ammunition drill, so we didn't actually fire our guns, we simply pointed them at the enemy and yelled, "Fire! Fire! Fire!" or, in Hebrew, "Ash, Ash, Ash!" With the enemy now taken out, we advanced on the rocket launcher. Solomon, who I considered to be one of the smartest on our team, brought out the C4 and worked with his squad to assemble a bomb that would disable the weaponry. We didn't use actual explosives, of course. The C4 was really just blue Play-Doh.

Once the mission was over, the lochama, who had played the enemy, told us that two of our men had been injured in the firefight and we needed to carry them and their equipment off the battlefield to a safe-landing zone 500 meters away so that they could be helicoptered out. We couldn't use the stretcher in such thick woods, so I hoisted one of the injured men onto my back and carried him to the safe zone. This was the shortest part of the mission, but also the most painful. He was very heavy, and I was already loaded down with my own gear, gun, and ammo.

We regrouped at the "safe zone." The sun was now up, and we were about nine hours into our two weeks of war. They gave us five minutes to break, (AKA plop down on my giant bag like it was a bed) until our head commander called in on Paz's walkie-talkie. He said that we had another mission a few kilometers away.

Our next mission was to intercept an enemy supply truck and destroy the supplies. We were given the exact coordinates over the walkie-talkie. Li found the location on the map and planned out the best route. We were supposed to kill those in the truck and destroy the supplies with explosives. While we would still not be using live ammo, we would be using real explosives this time.

We marched to the location in double-time so that we could intercept the truck before it passed. We found the location and went into ambush formation. The squads fanned out around the location and got ready to attack. When the truck approached, we yelled "Ash! Ash! Ash!" from our hidden locations. The truck rolled to a stop, and we moved forward under the assumption that the enemy had all been killed.

This time, I was the one assigned to build and detonate the bomb. This was a live-fire explosives drill, with real C4, so everyone not directly involved in the explosives fell back to a safe distance. While we were using real explosives, we were not going to use it on the truck. We were going to blow up a rock instead; blowing up a truck would have been an expensive waste. It took me only a few minutes to finish the bomb. Rapoport then helped me set the electrical cord back a safe distance so we could set it off. We backed up from the position and Paz gave a countdown. Nine, seven, five, three, two, one—and, boom! The explosion erupted and shook the earth beneath us.

We continued doing missions such as those for four days, nonstop, with no sleep whatsoever. This may sound preposterous to civilians, but these are actual wartime conditions that we had to train for. It was only after four days that we were given any rest at all, a few minutes to restock on food and water, before the commanders were giving us our next mission.

Our next mission involved another thirty-kilometer hike through the jungle, this time to find a small urban city that had fallen into enemy hands. We were to locate the urban enclave, take out the bad guys, secure the position, and then defend the city from any retaliation or attack. For this mission, we would be using paintball guns, which we had never done before, so we were all excited, despite our exhaustion, to engage in a "real" firefight. Our team was going to first take the city from the lochama and then be the defenders of it from the other two teams.

We picked up our bags, threw them over our shoulders, and began the march over mountains and through thick jungle. The terrain was very difficult and the night was pitch black, without a star in the sky. At one point, while we were up on a mountain, Paz, who was leading the navigation, seemed lost. We spent four hours trying to find a way down the mountain. All the paths were blocked by walls of thick jungle. It would have taken hours to hack through all the vines, and we did not have the luxury of time. We had to get to our location in time to start the mission. We had to find a faster way to get off the mountain than trying to hack our way through the jungle. So, we continued to search as we circled around the top of the mountain trying to find a way down and back on to our path.

By this point, I had been up and doing missions for over ninety hours straight. I had never been so tired in my life, but the excitement of the mission ahead helped me stay alert, though my mind was starting to play tricks on me. At one point, I was walking in formation when Solomon suddenly stopped.

I went up to him to see what was going on. "Hey, man. Why'd you stop?"

He didn't respond.

I repeated myself. "Hey, Solomon, why'd you stop?"

Again, no answer. I reached out to pat him on the back, only it wasn't Solomon at all. My hand closed around leaves and branches. I had been talking to a bush the whole time. My mind was hazy and delusional from going without sleep for almost four full days. The experience was unsettling, and I wondered whether I could truly trust my own eyes under those conditions.

We spent the whole night circling the top of the same mountain and I had made plenty of new bush friends. Six hours had gone by and the sun was coming up again. This was not going as planned. Paz radioed the head commander for aerial support to find our location. They then radioed us our location and a path down the mountain. There was a small path, just 200 meters north of our location, that would take us down the mountain. Since the sun was rising, we found it almost immediately, which made the six hours of searching seem awful, but that is the nature of combat logistics.

Finally, off the mountain, we advanced toward the city again. We had lost so much time that we had to move double time to make it into position. We still had ten more kilometers to go, carrying our guns and packs the whole way, with the hot sun beating down on our heads.

As we came across the city it was clear that it was not really a city at all, but more of a town, consisting of twenty houses. Most of them were small buildings, but a few were larger two-story structures. The town was at the top of a hill with a single central road running down the middle. The land to the west of the hill was open terrain, but to the east side was a small wooded area, which we used as cover while we moved into position and made plans for attack.

We split into two groups. Group A's job was to come out of the forest, turn right, and then circle around and approach from the north. Group B, to which I was assigned, would do the opposite, bearing left and then coming up the path from the south. Each group would capture and secure its half of the town before meeting in the middle.

We advanced from our positions. As we entered the town from the south, my group split into two separate squads so that we could raid the first two houses simultaneously. Both buildings were empty, so we cleared them quickly. Across the road, in the upper level of a two-story building, we spotted a man through the window. The other squad fired on the window, pelting it with paintballs, while my squad advanced on the building undetected.

I entered the building along with Tamir. He and I had been working close together that week, since we were both in the same chooliyot. We stalked through the building quietly, clearing the bottom floor before advancing up the stairs. We could see the enemy fighter shooting out the window at the other squad. We popped up behind him and shot him in the back, taking him out of the fight with a splash of red paint.

We continued on and cleared the rest of the lower field. The other group had cleared the north side and we now had the entire town secured. There had only been five enemy combatants in the town, and we had dispatched them all. The town now cleared, we moved into defensive formations. The other two Special Forces teams from our plugot (platoon) were taking up positions and preparing to take the town from us. We did not know when or where they were going to come, but just like us, they had paintball guns at the ready, and would have a force of about forty men.

We regrouped in the center of town and split off into four squads of four men each. My squad was made up of Rotem, who was in charge, Noah, Yaniv, and me. Noah was my partner for that drill. He struggled with a stutter, but that didn't stop the fridge of a man, meaning that he was amazingly strong and well built. He was like a Jewish linebacker, only shorter. From the beginning, it was clear that he was the one person on the team not to be messed with when it came to fighting. That is mostly due to the fact he had been learning krav maga since he was little, but his size helped too. I was impressed how he didn't let his stutter keep him back and was a great speaker and communicator amongst the guys.

Rotem and Yaniv were also partnered. We were required to stay by our partners for the rest of the exercise and learn to work together as one. Our job was to hold the southeast side of town, which was most likely to come under attack because it was near the wooded area. If necessary, we would also leave the town and surround the enemy if they tried to enter through the woods.

We waited patiently in position to see how the enemy would advance. As I searched the fields with binoculars, I found it difficult to stay awake, having not slept for four full days at this point. The high-intensity situations were the only things keeping us awake at all. Just standing around for ten minutes was enough to make us doze off, but we couldn't doze off, not in battle, so I would dance around and shake my head to try to rattle myself back awake.

After twenty minutes of waiting, we moved into one of the two-story buildings and used the higher vantage points to better scan for the enemy with my binoculars. We didn't spot anyone but kept looking until Rotem got a call on his radio. The first team was entering the town from the northeast side. They had used the forest as cover to get close while being undetected.

Noah and I pulled out of our position and moved into the woods in an attempt to come up behind the enemy and surround them. We walked using stealth techniques and camouflage to move quietly through the woods. Unfortunately, we were too late. The enemy had already left the 'safety' of the woods. They were now in the town and had taken over the first two buildings. They were exchanging fire with Omer, who was pinned down under heavy fire on a rooftop. Omer was our magist (someone who carries the Mag machine gun), if you thought taking the negav was difficult, his gun was even larger and the weight he carried heavier. Omer started off as a pudgy little guy from India, but at this point, after taking the mag around for all of training, he was probably the strongest guy on the team. Although all that new acquired muscle did not save Omer from the unlucky mistake of being on that roof, as enemy paintballs pinned him down. In real life, people will search for snipers and sharpshooters on the roofs first, making the roof a terrible place to hide.

We crawled to the edge of the woods while the enemy fired on Omer, waiting for the right moment to make a move. He was drawing enemy fire and attention, which allowed us to get close. When David, who was the commander of one of the "enemy" teams, dashed from one building to the next, we were able to open fire and take him and his partner out without revealing our location.

We continued to shoot at those that crossed the street and picked off another four men when they exited the building, but they now knew our position and started to return fire. We fell back into the woods, trying to avoid the paintballs flying by us, where we ran into Rotem and Yaniv. We now had our four-man squad back, twice the firepower, so we turned around and headed back toward the town. We set up position in the trees, close to where we had been before.

David's team had now advanced and taken another building. We opened fire on them again, taking out another two men, as we shot through the buildings open windows. Now half of their team was down. However, they were more wary now, and harder to hit because they had taken up better defensive positions and knew where we were firing from. They returned fire into the woods, so once again we fell back to regroup.

We were going to find another position to shoot from, but before we could head back toward the town, we heard rustling and movement coming toward us. The enemy had sent a squad to flush us out of the woods. We decided to split up. Rotem and Yaniv headed to the south side of town to protect it from invasion. Noah and I found cover behind rocks and trees and waited in ambush formation for the squad they had sent after us.

We believed we could take a squad coming into the woods by ambushing them, but what we hadn't expected was for them to send two squads. We were now outnumbered four to one and there was no way we would win an all-out firefight. They were already upon us when we realized how outgunned we were, so we opened fire anyway, taking out one of their guys, before retreating backward. We headed south in order to meet up with the rest of our team on the south side of town.

We moved quickly, using the trees as cover. With David's squads hot on our heels, we took up defensive positions in one of the houses on the southern side of town. Unfortunately, the neighboring building had already been captured by the other enemy team, Team Razel. They spotted Noah in the window and opened fire on us. We backed up and hunkered down in the corners of the room.

At that point, we were surrounded and pinned down. Two squads from David's team were coming up on the back door of the house. Razel's team had us in their sights, covering the window as well as the front door that opened out onto the main street. There was no way out without walking right into enemy fire. The only option was to stay hunkered down in a defensive position and face David's squad head to head in an indoor firefight, a fight we would almost certainly lose being seven against two.

Then a paintball came through the window and hit Noah. He was out. Dutifully, he sprawled out on the floor and played dead, as was the rule of the game.

Now all on my own, I crouched down in the corner of the

room with my gun trained on the doorway waiting to shoot whoever emerged first. I could hear the enemy's footsteps, first outside, and then against the floors inside the building and moving through the house. The barrel of a gun poked through the door. It was Yakov, who was on the enemy team. I landed a shot in his chest before he could react. He returned fire, hitting me in the neck. His partner, Eitan, then came in behind. Together, they took the room, even though I had just shot Yakov.

"Hey!" I said. "He's dead. I shot him!"

"Fuck that," Eitan snarled. "We have to take this town. He's alive."

"That's cheating!" I said, exasperated. "Have you guys been cheating this whole time?"

Noah then awoke from the dead and started shouting at Eitan. "Yeah! What the hell? I shot you a while back. How are you even here?"

Eitan pointed his gun at my face, then my partner's face, moving his aim back and forth between both of us. "Do we have an issue here?"

Under threat of a paintball to the face, we stood down for a moment, but only a moment. Noah distracted Eitan while I escaped into the woods. Fuck them, fuck that, this means war!

But before I could get my revenge, the game ended shortly thereafter. Though we had lost much of the town, the commanders deemed the exercise a draw because of all the cheating. I felt a little outraged since they had started the cheating first and then threatened us for calling them out on it. In the end, it didn't matter. This was just an exercise, in real life we were on the same team, and we had all learned a lot. It was also the single most exciting exercise we had engaged in so far.

Picture taken after the drill

By the time the paintball exercise was over, we were going on a hundred hours without sleep. We were delirious, literally hallucinating, and not in our right minds. Our bodies desperately needed sleep, but we still had more to do. A caravan of supply trucks had arrived that needed to be unloaded. It was now Friday, and since religious Jews don't work on Friday night, we had to unload them immediately. With Shabbat only a few hours away, we unloaded the supply trucks, set up tents, and got sleeping bags. We hadn't packed sleeping bags because we hadn't expected to sleep. We also set up tables and food for Shabbat, a day of much needed rest. I had never been so excited about the prospect of cold schnitzel in my life, nor was I ever so happy for sleep, which we were finally permitted after setting up the tables and tents. Everyone passed out immediately, right there on the ground.

For Shabbat, they allowed us a day of rest and relaxation. We did nothing but stretch, eat food, and sleep as much as possible. We had been deprived of both sleep and a decent amount of food all week, and would be again after Shabbat, so we needed to stock up on both while we still could. For four straight days, we had slept not a wink and eaten little more than a can of tuna, two slices of bread, a bit of either beans, peanuts, or corn each day, all of it scarfed down in a few minutes between missions. This made the prospect of Shabbat, with a day to sleep and a little more food in our bellies, a heavenly experience. One of the guys on my team who was sent off to commander's course early, came back and brought popsicles for everyone in the unit. On the field we were in constant competition with the other two teams, always trying to be the best in the plugot, but we were also really friends and brothers just trying to make it through the grueling ordeal, so of course we shared the popsicles among the plugot.

Once Shabbat was over, we hiked another thirty kilometers up a mountain to a helicopter, which airlifted us to the south of Israel to start our second week. For me, training and drilling in the south was much better than the north because there was no jungle to contend with. The svach makes movement hard and laborious. We would no longer have to hack our way through vines just to get around.

The second week was similar to the first, though we engaged in more live-fire drills and in our final mission used actual explosives to blow up an old, abandoned structure. It also happened to be yom hashoah, so in the middle of one of the live fire drills, a siren sounded across the country. We all stopped what we were doing, stood up and remembered in silence the 6 million Jews who had fallen. In that moment I felt immense pride to be able to stand there, in the middle of the land of Israel, our homeland and train to be a soldier, ready to defend our country so such a tragedy will never happen again. Once the siren ended, we were given our final mission.

Our scenario was this: Hamas had established an army base at the top of a large mountain. Our mission was to climb the mountain undetected at night, sneak into the base, take out all the enemy combatants, and demolish everything.

We hiked up the mountain, completed the mission, and blew up the base with explosives. In previous drills, we would locate the target we were supposed to destroy with explosives, but then pause and move to a new location where we would blow up a rock or dummy target rather than a real truck or missile launcher. This time, however, we were given permission to demolish an old army structure that needed to be removed anyway.

As all things, even as we finished, we rushed onto the next task. I didn't even have a chance to see the explosion; but as it went off, the ground shook as I began my descent down the mountain. Those of the team who were "pulling the trigger" on the bomb quickly regrouped with us as we were making our descent.

There was a rumor going around that we were going to get an airlift off the mountain from a helicopter. Once the base went up in a ball of flame, we waited expectantly for the helicopter, but unfortunately it never came. Instead, we learned from our men calling in over the walkie-talkies, that the helicopter would be picking us up from another mountain thirty kilometers away. This was our last Haakptazah or as I like to translate it, "surprise fuckers, go climb a mountain while carrying your friends!" As we heard the news, the three teams were now in a race to reach the landing zone first.

We gathered our gear and raced back down the mountain we had just spent hours climbing. Going down is always harder than going up. Climbing up a mountain, you have to fight gravity. Going down the mountain, you have to beware the pull of gravity, aka falling off the mountain.

We made good time down the mountain, but we ran out of

water at the bottom. Paz radioed the head commander to send a water truck down. The commander refused. This was the last leg of our final week. Water or not, we had to complete the mission on time. We wouldn't stop for water if this were a real mission and not just a drill.

We carried on with the next leg of the mission without water. And as we got to the bottom of the mountain, we again ran into the lochama. They instructed us that each team had to open up our two stretchers and put a man on each. You might think of the two men in the stretcher as lucky, especially given the lack of water, but this was a role that no one wanted. Being on the stretcher felt like missing out on the mission. No one wanted to literally burden their own team with his own dead weight. I was thankful not to have to ride in the stretcher, but instead to be under the stretcher, contributing to the team.

The stretchers were difficult to carry but being under them rallied the body and focused the mind. Under the stretcher, everything else faded away. The aches and pains of carrying our own personal bags and gear disappeared. Our sore feet and bodies went almost numb. Tiredness, hunger and thirst seemed to dissipate. The only thing that mattered, once under the stretcher, was getting your friend and teammate home alive. This was just a training exercise, of course, but it all felt very real once you were under that stretcher.

We raced up and down several more mountains carrying the stretchers the whole way, right behind us was the Palsar team and team David. We were team Paz, each named after their commander. Each of us raced to be first and prove that we were the best. Up and down we went another twenty kilometers; for a brief moment toward the top of the hill, the Palsar team had gotten in front of us. This was unacceptable, we had to double tail it to beat them. Unfortunately, for them one of their soldiers developed heat stroke along the way. They had to stop and airlift him out of there. This allowed not only us but also team David to get in front of them and continue the race. Eventually, after ten more kilometers, I could see the finish! There was a small jeep with the mem pay (our platoon commander) waiting at a flat land right next to the tip top of the mountain. As we came in, we finished first, a kilometer ahead of team David and two kilometers ahead of team Palsar. Our prize Oren, our mem pay, said we had to finish what we started and climb to the very top of the mountain, which was that small hill a few hundred meters to the left. A little exhausted and disappointed, Paz rallied the troops and claimed it would be our final stand, and to give it all the rabak we had left. So as instructed, we put down the stretchers and raced up the last 300 meters to the very top of the mountain. There, Shy, a tall, lanky, Sephardy boy from my team, who was infamous for snoring like a wild bear at night, had secretly been carrying with him a bottle of champagne in his bag the whole time. He opened it up and we celebrated finally having finished training. Once the other teams arrived, we returned down the mountain in anticipation for the helicopters to take us the hell out of that desert.

When the Blackhawks finally arrived, we loaded up and got an airlift to the Air Force base in Tel-Hashomer. There we would be loaded onto Hercules planes so that we could parachute back into the desert and complete one last march to the ceremonial spot for the Gadsar Tzanhanim, which would mark the completion of our training. We fell asleep in the Blackhawks and we fell asleep again once we were on the planes. The planes where previously I was so nervous, I would feel the butterflies in my stomach exploding, now continuously dozed off, barely able to keep my eyes open. We had been awake for a hundred hours prior to Shabbat and another seventy-two hours after that single day of rest. There aren't words for how tired I was. My brain could barely stay conscious. I kept getting woken every time the bell sounded for the next group of jumpers to exit the plane and then fall asleep again, until finally it was my turn to jump.

When my turn came, I kind of just stumbled toward the door and fell out of the plane. It wasn't until the force of gravity and the air resistance hit me hard that the adrenaline kicked back in and I woke up. By that time, the cord of my parachute was pulled, and I was falling through the air at a brisk thirty miles an hour or so. Just with enough time to look up and enjoy the beautiful view, I prepared myself to land and *blump,* smacked the sand dunes soft ground and performed my paratroopers' roll. (I had gotten better from my first time)

I then quickly grabbed my gear and met at the meeting point a kilometer away. We were supposed to then march another thirty kilometers to the ceremony, where we would be declared warriors, but due to the heat and two soldiers getting heat stroke on our previous hakpatzah, only a few hours earlier, the higher ups stated that the heat conditions were too strong for us to complete the march. This rule is called "Omas Chom," which means that if the temperature and general heat conditions reach a certain point, it is illegal for soldiers to train outside. Finally, some luck was turning our way, I thought. After all, it was over 100 degrees outside. Therefore, rather than hike the thirty kilometers, the head commander of training sent an egged bus to take us to the ceremony.

At the ceremony, the head commander of the training gave a speech of our accomplishments in training and how he could now feel confident sending us off to the unit as combat ready Paratrooper Special Forces soldiers or Gadsar Lochamim. There would be another ceremony in the following weeks, in which our parents would be invited, but in his eyes we had already finished our training and were now true *lochamim*, or warriors, of the unit. Our commander said that since we didn't do the march, we finished early and the buses were scheduled to get there at night. They called ahead and the bus company said they would try to get there earlier but for now we just needed to sit and wait. So, all of us, finally sat down on the grass and fell asleep. But just as that was happening, a few cars pulled into the lot. Out from the cars came a gang of Jewish mothers! At second glance, I realized it was some of the mothers of the guys in our team. My mouth dropped in shock. I could not believe that our secret military ceremony was crashed by a gang of Jewish mothers. I had no idea how they found us, but somehow, they did and as they arrived, so did the cartons of food they had in their cars. Together we helped them set up a table with a spread fit for a king. With hummus, barekas, pita's, cakes, and many other middle eastern delicacies, we drooled in delight. But before we could eat, every Jewish mother wanted a nice group picture to solidify the moment; it was the least we could do.

The second it ended, we sprinted over and began to devour the food. Like monsters we ate until everything was gone. I can honestly say I have never had food so good as that day in the grass where I went from starving, sleep deprived, and utterly exhausted, to having a mountain of food shoved in my face by over twenty Jewish mothers. And once we were full, we slept in the grassy shade, relaxed, noshed, laughed and enjoyed life until the buses finally arrived, six hours later to take us back to base. Little did I know that soon a countdown would be ticking down and I would have twenty-four hours until going to war with Hamas.

The picture we took for our Jewish mothers (we were staring at the food on the grass in front of us)

Popping the champagne bottle at the top of the mountain when we finished training (before the jump)

Helicoptering to the next phase of training

Udi with me at the end of training ceremony, 2014

Udi with me when I visited him in the army, 2002

Getting new equipment as we join the unit. New vest, knee pads, and boots, the best a young soldier could dream of

Induction to the Unit Ceremony (at base) with the Team

10

ש

"Don't watch the clock; do what it does. Keep going."
~ Sam Levenson

July 2014

Shin + 24

The countdown was on. We had exactly twenty-four hours until we would be going to war with Hamas. Our clocks ticked down each hour, or *shin*, as we prepared. We were recently stationed on the border of Gaza after the three kidnapped Israeli, yeshiva boys were found. We were out in the desert preparing for war while Israel began to get pelted with rockets coming in from across the border.

Israel had conducted major wars in Gaza before, but this time felt different. Unlike in 2012, when there had been no ground invasion, IDF soldiers were now going to move into Gaza in mass numbers. I would be one of them. I couldn't shake the feeling that, in twenty-four hours, I could be walking into my own grave. I barely even understood our mission, a last-minute operation that the higher-up commanders had handed down to us.

Once we were four hours into the countdown, we would not be allowed to use phones for any reason. We would be cut off from the outside world. "Call your parents. Call your family. Call your loved ones," Commander Paz instructed. "Say goodbye now."

Shin + 6

I climbed to the roof of a two-story building that stood in the middle of a training field to make my goodbye phone calls. I could have stayed in my tent, but the romantic in me wanted a majestic view if this would be my last time speaking with my loved ones. From my vantage at the top of the building, which was at the top of a sandy hill, I could see the desert spread out, fading into the horizon. Our tents were lined up just down below, where I saw my friends–teammates, brothers–getting ready. In a few short hours, we would be heading off together into the unknown.

Camp

From the rooftop, I called my loved ones, family and friends, everyone who meant anything to me. I was only twenty-one years old, but there I was on the phone saying what could be my last goodbyes. We were forbidden to speak about the operation because of security concerns. I couldn't even tell anyone what we were doing or where we were headed. I had to lie. Rather than voice my concerns and fears, which were real despite my resolve, I had to say that everything was fine. I had to sound busy and carefree as normal, possibly concerned because everyone knew there might be war soon, but I could not show in any way that I was in the middle of it all.

I told them that I was not currently involved in ongoing operations and that I would be performing field drills in the northern end of Israel. None of this was true, but I steadied my voice as I told these lies. I did not want them to hear the fear. These were my problems, my burden to bear alone. I did not want my family and friends worrying about me.

Afterwards, I hung up the phone, thinking how fucked up the situation was, sending our sons to battle and them saying goodbye without their family knowing that is what they were doing. I contemplated all the things I would be missing out in life if I were to die there in Gaza: Girlfriends, my dogs, having a job, traveling the world, going to college, marriage and having kids, all those things might never happen.

I went back to my tent and checked over my equipment again to make sure everything was prepared. The smallest piece of tape had to be wrapped properly. Every buckle had to be fastened. All of my necessary supplies needed to be packed, plus just a little extra in case of emergencies, but not so much as to weigh me down. We debated whether one foot of string was good enough to bring versus two feet. This was the kind of meticulous detail we covered when we decided what went into our bags. Some of the other soldiers had family who had fought in the second Lebanon war. They had told stories about packing double, even triple, the gear required and feeling foolish when they could barely lift their bags—until the extra gear saved their lives. These stories scared us. It was better to be over prepared than underprepared in war, or so we thought, so we over-packed. My bag was heavy by the time I was done, heavier than any other bag I would ever pack again in my military career, but at the time it gave me a much-needed peace of mind.

The second Lebanon war was not the only war we talked about in preparation for our entry into Gaza. There was Israel's withdrawal of all military personnel and Israeli civilians in August of 2005 from within the Gaza strip. It only took five months later in January 2006 that Hamas won an election in the strip, making itself the governing force in the area. With their win, they celebrated by killing their opposition as they had a military takeover against their opposition Fatah, which ended in June 2007. Once they had finished defeating their enemy within their borders, they moved on to targeting the enemy outside, Israel. Israel at this time in 2006 was fighting one of its worst wars with Hezbollah in Lebanon, known as the second Lebanon war. Between 2007 and 2008, Hamas, now having full control of the Gaza strip, fired thousands of rockets into Israel. Israel's response was in December of 2008 to begin the first of many Gaza, Israel wars or major military operations, with "Operation Cast Lead." Like all these operations, they began with heavy Israeli Air Force and artillery bombardment to attempt to destroy the Hamas rockets and militants. Then on January 3rd, 2009, a fifteen-day ground operation commenced and ended when Israel believed they had sufficiently destroyed Hamas' military supplies. Three years later in 2012, the rockets from Gaza came firing down on Israel's cities again and "Operation Pillar of Defense" was on. However, unlike Operation Cast Lead, this time the soldiers did not go in. We were told from friends of friends that were in the operation, they would be literally sitting on the border waiting for their shin to hit zero, but it never did. The ground forces never entered into Gaza. Now in 2014, my friends and I were preparing ourselves to go into Gaza and neutralize the threat.

Despite all of this preparation, we still felt unprepared.

Our team had just finished training, and everyone was still being moved in and out of positions. There were currently thirty of us on the team, but that would drop to eighteen as a dozen of us would be selected to become trainers and commanders. Almost daily, our roles and positions evolved and changed. This helped us learn the different positions, but also interjected a bit of chaos and uncertainty as we prepared to go to war. Who would carry the stretcher this day? Who had a specialized weapon and which one? The answers to questions such as these could change suddenly without everyone being able to keep track. We would ultimately be shifting around almost down to the wire. This was not typical, but a result of finishing training right as we were headed into a major operation. Those who would not stay to go to war, had other assignments, such as becoming commanders for the new recruits or drill instructors. Even though there was a war and there were men ready to fight, training and drafting new recruits does not stop.

After double and triple checking my equipment, I went for a walk to clear my mind and calm my nerves. When I returned to the tents, the whole unit had big grins that stretched from ear to ear. This was a big surprise, not what I expected from men that were headed to war in a few hours. They told me that the operation had been delayed for a day. We had another twenty-four hours.

I was suddenly relieved. Another twenty-four hours to live! Though I should have been grateful, I was not. It was now clear how unprepared I was for war. I felt good about my training and my physical shape, but my mind was not in the right place. I needed to steel myself against what was coming by detaching from my life and the rest of the world. I had to wall myself off. There was no other way I would be able to do this and get my head into the right state for war.

Fortunately, I had time. The delays kept coming. They were of different lengths, sometimes another twenty-four hours added to the clock, sometimes it was two or three days.

However, we were not idle during this time. We trained every day, doing drills and exercises in the desert, and sometimes a few of us would be sent off for a few days of training to learn more specialized equipment. One time, two other teammates and I were sent back to our old training base, Bach Tzanhanim, to specialize in a few more weapons. I guess they figured if there was time, might as well have some of us learn some more weapons. I watched the incoming soldiers struggle with basic training, and while I was aware of the hell they were going through, I had my own problems and struggles. The training on these guns was supposed to last two weeks, but we had to ascertain all the knowledge in four days so that we could get back to the border in case our team was deployed into Gaza. We had a lot to learn in those four days. We spent all three nights sleeping outside, next to the firing range, even though there were open beds in the base. Soldiers from outside of the base aren't technically supposed to take beds on base without an approval from the head of the logistics on base, of which there was no time to get. However, usually the commanders who were sent to train the new soldiers in our unit, the Gasdar, would look the other way so that we could get a good night's rest. However, the logistics commander or 'Rasap' was a coward and afraid he would get caught by the logistics base commander and made us sleep outside on the firing range.

After four days, we returned to the border and rejoined our team. We kept waiting and waiting. The days turned into weeks. Eventually, a whole month had passed, and I was still in the desert waiting. I had no idea when it would end. Practically daily, I made the climb to the top of the building on the hill to once again say my goodbyes. A month solid of daily goodbyes; it felt like a sick joke. I had to keep coming up with new lies to explain to my parents of where I was and what I was doing, for I could never tell anybody the truth.

Then the hakpatzah occurred and I was going out to protect my family and friends for the first time, as described in the prologue. Hamas terrorists had infiltrated through a tunnel into Israel and were suspected of going off to Kibbutz Nir Yitzhak or Nir Am to try and kill as many people as possible. Finally, our team was put on a real mission to protect people from this possible attack. Unlike in years past, in 2014, the threat from rockets was all but neutralized due to Israel's military "shield" over its lands called the "Iron Dome," which was a device that intercepted the rockets coming from Gaza in mid-flight and blew them up. However, now there was a new threat; Hamas had been digging underground and was able to go under Israel's border and infiltrate the country. Our mission was to destroy these tunnels so we wouldn't have men with AK-47's coming out from the ground trying to kill everyone.

Our main mission was to infiltrate the south of Gaza and locate and capture four homes that surrounded two of the known tunnels. Our intel indicated that these were attack tunnels leading into Israel. Our mission was to go in the cover of night, capture the surrounding homes around the tunnels and then blow up the attack tunnels. This mission was estimated to take forty-eight hours to complete.

We met each day to talk about our assignment. The operation was so top secret that we had to put our phones into a box and lock them up in a metal container whenever we had meetings to discuss the mission. We were afraid that Hamas would hack someone's phone and eavesdrop on our conversations. Once the room was secure, we would go over plans and gathered intelligence.

After reviewing our plans so that I could recite them in my sleep, we all knew our jobs by heart. We even knew each other's job by heart. We replayed everything backwards and forwards so that, when the time came, we would be ready. But, as the days ticked off, and we had now been waiting on the border for almost a full month, we began to get bored. We knew our mission better than the backs of our own hands. We were so bored that we spent our off hours thinking about anything else, playing chess or checkers, or just working out, anything to keep our minds elsewhere.

Every day, I watched the clock get reset. Shin+24 never ever became Shin + 0. They just kept postponing the mission and restarting the countdown the next day. Until, that is, when they did not.

On July 16, 2014, the clock kept counting down.

Shin + 10

With only ten hours before we were going to infiltrate Gaza, we again went over all the details. We talked about the plan. We checked over our rifles, vests and bags. I made sure all my tape and knots were fresh.

Shin + 8

The buses arrived on our makeshift base in the desert. Paz commanded us to load our equipment onto the buses. This was normally when the countdown would restart, and we would be given another day to prepare. Not this time. Today, the clock just kept ticking down. Tick tock, tick tock, we could almost hear it in our heads as we loaded up the buses. We now started to believe that this time was real.

Shin + 6

The buses were loaded. Our equipment was ready for transport, and so were we. We went over the mission with the head of our unit one last time while we waited.

Shin + 5

By now, the clock was still counting down. We really started to believe that tonight would be the night. To pass the time, I watched some motivational videos on my phone. I started talking with my team about the mission to pump each other up.

At some point, I remembered my family and friends back at home. I had called back home every day diligently. There was no way I could have forgotten on that day, when it mattered most, when we would actually move into enemy territory and put our lives on the line. I once again made the climb up the sandhill and to the top of the two-story building in the middle of our makeshift camp. From the roof, I had dialed my parents. When they picked up the phone, I told them I just wanted to say hello before heading out on a training mission in the north of Israel. This was, of course, a lie.

"Are you connected to Gaza at all?" my mom asked, having heard about the fighting. "We heard about the rockets and are so worried about you."

"No, Mom," I lied. "I am safe and sound. I am in the north of Israel training, but I won't have my phone for the next few weeks. I will call you when I finish."

"Ok, Max. Stay safe."

I told my parents I loved them both and hung up.

Shin + 4

When they started confiscating our phones, we knew the mission was a reality. We left them in a small box. We boarded the buses. The box did not. We sat waiting to ship off. It was finally happening, and we were all a little scared imagining the war movies we had seen as kids. Even though I was considered a young man, I suddenly felt like a kid once again. No matter the training I had received, which was a shit ton, going to war for real is scary. There was a heavy weight on my shoulders. But to stay pumped up, I thought of war movies and of glory and honor, and with the fear came a little excitement too. I applied Camouflage paint.

Ready for war

Shin + 3.5

We were on our way to Gaza. Those who did not finish with the camouflage paint continued to apply it while we rode. It wouldn't be long until we crossed over the border.

Along the way, we pulled over on the side of the road to pee and stretch. While we were stopped, some of us were still peeing at the time, a truck full of Haredi men blasting music pulled up alongside us. This was the kind of thing you would see in Jerusalem, not in the middle of the desert. They got out and came to greet us as the music blasted from their truck. They wanted to talk to the soldiers, which was a very Israeli thing to do. They started dancing and singing, forming a circle as the boombox on top of their van played the hoorah, right there on the side of the road, everyone dancing to *Am Yisrael Chai* (The People of Israel Live). As we loaded up onto our bus, they handed each of us an XL energy drink.

The only thing I could think was, how the fuck did these Haredi men, driving the Jewish version of a clown car, find us in the middle of the desert, with camouflage on our faces, right before we left for war? I guess that's a mystery for the books.

As I got back on, people were recording last words and jotting down final messages to their families, in case they didn't make it back from the mission alive. Some men were praying. These kinds of moments, with the prospect of death breathing down your neck, can make you feel spiritual. Under my uniform, I wore a shirt with *tzitzit*, which are biblical fringes that religious Jews wear under their shirts. This was not something I had done before, but I hoped it would protect me. I wanted to come back home in one piece. I also prayed silently to myself, which reminded me why I was on the bus and doing what I was doing. I thought of my friends and family, everyone on my kibbutz, and everyone behind me whose lives were also in danger.

Shin + 3

By the time we arrived at our first meeting point, I had achieved a feeling of almost peace. My predominant feeling stepping off the bus was that of pride. By that time, the sun had just set, and dusk was turning to dark.

I unloaded my bag, barely able to lift it even with both hands, and put on both of my vests, one a bulletproof vest and another for carrying ammo on my body. It took all my strength to get my pack up and on my back. I lost my balance and almost fell over just trying to get it into place. Instantly, with that gear, I had almost doubled in weight, going from a 170-pound soldier to over a 300-pound soldier.

The team formed two lines and started marching through a grassy field, moving up and down the hills. In the distance, I heard the sound of artillery firing. We eventually passed through some tall trees and came up to several large artillery tanks. Each time they fired, the ground shook and I would almost lose my balance.

We marched on past the tanks until we reached lower flat ground. The terrain there was green with tall brown grass like large weeds but because it was desert, it was also very sandy. Overhead, artillery and mortar fire lit up the sky. Shells were flying back and forth. We were, literally, in a warzone. There were mortars falling all around.

Paz commanded us to spread out and dig foxholes. I found a good spot and took off my bag. With a shovel in hand, I dug out a hole for cover. I had never felt so scared before and that my life was so in my own hands as it was then. I dug as fast as I could, so fast that my commanders in the Gibushim (try-outs) would have been proud. This was not training though. This was the real thing, and my body moved almost automatically out of desperation to survive.

We were three men to a hole. I dug for all three of us while Shy and Omer were making last-minute adjustments to the large machine gun, the "mag." I put shovel to earth for fifteen minutes straight before starting to become exhausted. I checked on my teammates. The mag was almost ready, too. I was excited to get help with digging, but there was no time to wait. I went back to digging while they finished with the gun. This was a matter of life and death, I reminded myself, as I leaned into that shovel.

Sweat was pouring off my face, which had to be red from exertion. Shy and Omer must have taken note because they came over to ask if I was okay. We could barely hear each other over the steady repartee of the tanks firing and the sound of mortars overhead. I told them I was fine, just hot.

They looked at me quizzingly. "Are you wearing something under your uniform?"I told them I was wearing the dry-fit shirt with *tzitzit*. They looked at me dumbfounded, and said, "Take it off, you idiot. You're going to get heatstroke."

They were obviously right. My extra shirt, meant to protect me, was slowly killing me. I handed over the shovel and stripped off my vest, body armor, uniform, and finally my shirt with the tzitzit. Even though my godly shirt was killing me, I felt it would have been disrespectful to just throw it on the ground, even in a warzone, so I rolled it up and put it in my bag. I then went back to digging. With all three of us taking turns, we finished the foxhole for three people, in thirty minutes, the fastest I had ever dug one, and a time that would have, again, made my gibush instructors proud.

Just as we finished, Li, our navigator and Paz's partner, came by on his rounds. Li was a great guy, a bit of a clown, but now, possibly for the first time ever, he was serious. He instructed us to take cover in the foxholes and wait for further instruction. The three of us went down into the hole we had just dug. We pushed our bags to the side of the hole and lay down next to them, looking up at the sky. The sound of heavy artillery was still blasting all around us. The ground continued to shake, almost as much as Shakira. The sky lit up periodically from rockets and mortar fire, but between flashes of light we could see the stars twinkling in the sky.

The stars reminded me of how, as a boy, I would visit the Lake of the Ozarks in Missouri. My dad would take us out on our boat where we would spend the whole day at the lake. At night I would sit in the backseat and stare up at the stars. I had never seen so many stars in my life, certainly not in Saint Louis. Those were simpler times, nicer times.

My daydreaming was cut short by the report from more mortars landing nearby. The earth shook around me in my little hole. When the dust settled, I looked back up into the sky to see not just stars, but helicopters, fighter jets, and rockets. The rockets exploding, the stream of exhaust from the jets, it almost looked like a Fourth of July celebration back home in the States.

It was then that I leaned over to Shy and started talking about how surreal our lives had become. It was so surreal that there were shells and rockets going off all around us. We could be killed at any moment, and all we had were ourselves and each other. That was a relief, actually, as these were my brothers now. We had gone through so much together in training, preparing for this, and here we were now seeing each other through.

With that in mind, we tried to do the most unimaginable thing possible: We tried to sleep. We knew that Li would be coming by eventually to gather everyone, but we did not know when. This was a relatively safe place in the sense that no bad guys would wander up to us in such a fortified area, and while we could be blown up by a mortar at any moment, being asleep was probably the better option in such a situation. So, we put our heads down and tried to get some shut-eye. Amazingly, even with the explosions going off overhead, we managed to doze off for a little rest until Li came by and thumped our helmets with his hand to wake us up.

Shin +2

It was time to move. We emerged from our foxholes and, with a Jewish moan that would make Larry David proud, we put our heavy bags back on. We formed into two rows again and moved out. My stomach was churning. We moved so silently that we could almost hear the sand crunch between the soles of our boots and the firm ground. The darkness and the noise from the rockets were enough to mask most of our movements and sound. We were like a silent serpent moving slowly across the land, an apt metaphor given that the symbol for the paratroopers in Israel is a snake with wings. We literally snaked across the terrain, undulating left and right moving in military formation, as we made our way toward Gaza.

We moved from checkpoint to checkpoint, stopping at different buildings along the way; and to be honest I do not know why we stopped at all, but that is what we were instructed to do. Each time we stopped, we would crouch down for a moment and point our guns into the shadows and look over any hidden area that seemed suspicious ,constantly searching for the enemy.

Along the way, around the third stop, I started to get sick to my stomach. It felt like my abdomen was hotter than the rest of my body by as much as twenty degrees. My stomach was overheating beneath the body armor. That XL energy drink hadn't helped either, and neither did my fear. I ended up having to go off to the side to vomit. My partner, Ishay, came over to make sure everything was all right. I reassured him that I was fine, just a bit sick, and that it would be okay. I wiped my mouth and stepped back in formation with the other guys.

Shin + 1

We continued on. By this time, we had been marching for an hour. By my rough calculations, we were a little over halfway to the gate. Since I wasn't navigating, I was with the men bringing up the back of the line. We generally had no idea where we were in relation to the target, but we did have watches. Since we moved on time, always and without fail, we could use the time to judge how much further we still had to go.

My stomach felt much better after having puked. I was starting to feel confident again and ready to take on whatever task lay ahead. As a breeze hit, I looked up into the sky. There were still helicopters overhead, flares flying every which way, and the flash of rockets and mortars. These were still alarming, but less scary than they had been even just an hour ago. I was already starting to acclimate to wartime conditions. I was still scared, but I felt able and ready.

We marched on, moving swiftly, until we neared our destination and stopped a hundred meters back from a large fence. We were at the edge of Israel. Beyond the fence lay Gaza. We had to kneel and wait for the guys in the front of our unit to run over to the fence and blow it up.

A half-hour passed before the call came over the radio to tell us that they had blown open the gate. I gathered myself and got into formation. From that point on, I knew that there would be no turning back. The countdown was almost complete. No one would be resetting the clock, and there would be no more extra days to prepare. This was it. The mission was about to start for real.

Nearing the fence, we passed three Israeli tanks. The tank crew greeted us as we moved by, but as much as I wanted to stop and gawk in awe at the really cool tanks, I could not, I had to keep moving.

Shin + 0

We stepped past the gate, now blasted open, and entered Gaza to begin our mission.

11

SHOTS FIRED

"Do not pray for an easy life. Pray for the strength to endure a difficult one." ~ *Bruce Lee*

Stepping past the gate and entering Gaza was like entering a strange land. Of course, the actual ground was no different, the same sandy but firm terrain, spotted with bushes and weeds that kept the earth from blowing away and forming dunes, as on the other side of the border, but everything felt different after crossing over. We had left the safety of our homeland and entered what was now hostile territory.

We marched through farmlands, as we had done hundreds of times in training, but we now moved with a sense of purpose. Drilling had been about running us through the ringer to test our mettle, so the commanders had piled on handicaps and ridiculous tasks. Now, out in the field, we were to move as quickly and efficiently as possible, to avoid detection and an unwanted fight. When we came to farm fences while in training, we avoided damaging them. Now we simply destroyed the fencing as fast as possible and continued forward. This was not Israel, but Hamas territory, and the people here wanted us all dead. We did not have to concern ourselves with property damage.

We marched all night, surrounded by Israeli tanks, as we moved further into Gaza. We were fearful, but also determined. The need to stay alert and focused superseded my own fear. I was too scared of being ambushed or picked off with a potshot to indulge that fear on a visceral level.

Our march then came to a standstill. I was in the back and couldn't tell what the guys up front were waiting on. The unit was held up for two whole hours. Whenever the line stopped moving like that, men would at first go down into crouching position and, if time felt like it was going on forever, our tired eyes would shut, and we would fall asleep while waiting. However, here in Gaza you would think we would not shut our eyes, we would stay awake and be focused for all 2 hours. You thought wrong even in Gaza the lack of sleep started to get to us and already some of us were falling asleep, though I did not blame anyone for being exhausted given that we hadn't slept well in days due to training missions. Some of us took turns resting while the others kept guard. Those on guard weren't allowed to sit, because they needed to be ready for a sudden encounter. We had to crouch down on our heels in what is known as kneeling position, or matzav kreyah in Hebrew. However, crouching on our heels for hours was painful and led to cramping, so most of us ended up sitting at some point anyway.

We were supposed to arrive at our objectives before sunrise so that we could operate under the cover of night, but this did not go as planned. Unforeseen complications held up the operation, and my unit wasn't closing in on the first house until the sun was already rising. The target was a small house with a cinderblock wall running around the perimeter. We took cover among palm trees a few meters from the house. To the untrained eye, the house was unassuming, with little scraps of trash everywhere, but we knew that these piles of trash could be used to hide booby traps. We had to move carefully as not to trip any hidden wires. There were little pieces of string among the trees, and I was worried these might be wired to explosives, but upon closer inspection they turned out to be nothing. I made it a point not to step on the strings anyway out of paranoid caution. No one wanted to be the guy that stepped on a mine and got blown to pieces, so a little extra caution seemed warranted.

Each team had a different role in the mission. My team and Team 20 worked together to surround the house while Team 10 prepared to move around the wall and infiltrate the building. With the sun now beating down on our backs, Team 20 swooped around the wall and entered the building while our heavy machine gunners gave cover fire to ease their entrance. Everything went according to plan, and they took the house without any resistance. There was no one inside. Israel had warned Gazans with leaflets and phone calls to leave the area and that anyone who remained would be considered armed enemies, not civilians, and dealt with immediately. If Hamas had been there, they had cautiously abandoned the position.

We left Team 10 behind to hold the position while the rest of us moved to the next objective. We continued down a hill and moved into another sandy backyard filled with more trash. There was a four-story building that looked like a hotel on my left and a small box-like cinder block building to my right. Our path forward ran through the two buildings. The tall building, which would make for good sniper positions, worried me the most. The hotel was riddled with bullet holes and bombshells; some of the walls had fallen to rubble, perhaps the air force or artillery had already taken shots at the building, which made me even more wary.

An order came in for our team to run ahead and clear the sandy path from booby traps between the two buildings. My partner and I had been carrying a piece of heavy equipment meant for this exact moment. We sprinted to Paz, who, behind the cover of a wall, gave us our instructions. We were to move forward onto the path, along with two forward companions who would cover us as we set up the device. The rest of Team 20 would hang back and provide more cover.

Providing cover in Gaza

The four of us moved forward onto the path where we noticed a partially buried wire running across the path. This was clearly a trap. We stopped and got to work. My partner and I set our guns aside and concentrated on setting up the equipment, fully trusting our teammates to protect us while we worked. We had the device set up in a minute flat and then we all fell back. After a short countdown, the anti-mine and booby trap device detonated and blew up everything in the path. If there had been a trap, the device would have taken it out.

Clearing one of the many paths

Before the dust cleared, Team 20 moved forward with weapons drawn and took over the little cinder block hut on the right. The commander peered inside and found three men with their hands on a detonator for the booby trap we just disarmed outside. Their plans foiled, they surrendered and came out of the hut without a fight. The sight gave me a shock. These men, clearly Hamas fighters, were the first non-Israeli's we had seen since entering Gaza. They were in civilian clothes, totally unassuming, and with nothing to identify them as a threat. The only thing that made them a threat, other than the tripwire and explosive device we had been lucky enough to spot and disarm, was their presence after the evacuation order had been given. By failing to vacate the area, they were automatically a threat, as far as we were concerned.

Team 20 dealt with apprehending and arresting the three men while my team continued to move forward. We crossed the path and several of our men peeled off to clear the next house, which we planned to use as our operating base because it gave a clear vision of the two tunnels that we intended to destroy. As they cleared the house, we hung back to secure the position, provide cover and prepare to take the next house ourselves.

My sergeant asked me to take his bag for him since he was entering the next house first and needed to be light on his feet. I agreed to take the bag on one condition: that I would be the one who got to shoot the rocket launcher that was in his bag. He shrugged and agreed, and I clapped with joy. Despite the chaos and danger, as ridiculous as it sounds, we were having fun. We had spent over a year in training pretending to play war games and we were now playing the real game of war.

The next target was a complex compound consisting of a three-story house, a small shack and other structures, as well as a farm out back. There were live animals on the farm, as many of the people who lived there were forced to leave livestock behind when the evacuation order was declared. The inhabitants might not have been necessarily sympathetic with Hamas. Some might have simply been civilians who were unlucky enough to reside so close to the tunnels.

We came upon a path that led to the targeted house banked on both sides by a row of palm trees. We used the trees as cover and moved in closer to the target. Halfway to the target, I was ordered to stop and use the bazooka from my commander's bag to take out the shack in front of the house, thereby dispatching any booby-traps or enemy waiting in ambush. I set up the bazooka and took aim. I slowed my breathing and let out all the air from my lungs before perfecting my aim. Click, pulled the trigger. BOOM! The rocket fired off and hit the middle of the shack, blowing the rooftop off.

I steadied myself and watched the dust cloud rise and settle over the shack. It was a perfect hit and any threat at the location was now neutralized. With a smile and a rush of adrenaline from getting to shoot a real bazooka, I tossed the bazooka behind me, whispering "*Hasta la vista, baby*" to myself, and moved forward toward the house to join the rest of my team and start clearing rooms to take control of the complex.

"Hasta la vista, baby"

The team divided into four-man squads, or *chooliyot*, and we stormed the different rooms in small groups. Most of the team, including my sergeant, moved up the small exterior staircase to the first floor of the home and then split up to secure two floors at once. Elazar and I moved downward and began to clear the basement. Heading down the steps into the basement, I noted a propane tank to my right and stopped and yelled above to report its presence before continuing.

After getting the okay, Elazar and I continued forward, coming to a stop in front of a big black door. I checked for booby-traps and found nothing suspicious, though the door was locked. Our sergeant commanded us to kick the door down and go inside. With a large oomph! Elazar kicked in the door, causing it to swing wide open, and we entered at once. Weapons drawn, we scanned both ends of the room. "Naki!" we each yelled, which translates to *clean*, meaning that the room is clear. No one was inside.

When we finished clearing the whole building, we regrouped and reported the big things we found in every room. On the first floor, they found an AK-47 assault rifle, a pistol, high-capacity magazines, and a few grenades in the family room. The house clear, we set up guard stations to defend the area. Now that we had taken the complex, we had to defend it from attack. While many soldiers were put on guard, I and a few others began a more thorough search of the house. The weapons stash from earlier had just been sitting out, but there might have been hidden stockpiles as well.

Elazar and I returned to the basement to conduct a more thorough search. The big locked door was suspicious. We found several large knives, as well as several Hamas pamphlets and books that laid out detailed instructions on sniping and bomb-making. We went back upstairs and found flags and uniforms in the kid's room.

The longer we rifled through the house, the more we came to know its occupants as real people. The beds were hard, practically like sitting on the floor, and the family room had magnificent chairs and luxurious sofas crowded around one small television. My English allowed me to read several books and documents that my teammates couldn't. There was a book of Hamas propaganda in the kid's room that denounced Israel as the devil and even composed Jews as having horns. I flipped through documents and came across personal records of the inhabitants, including medical records from when the son had broken his leg and had to go to Egypt for treatment two years before. I gained a vision of the enemy that became more eerie as it became more real and human. They were ordinary people doing ordinary things, but they were also aligned with terrorist fighters that sought the destruction of Israel, my friends and my family.

After a few hours, we had finished searching through everything in the house. I took a turn helping to guard the front door so another man could rest. The day was now over, and night was once again falling. We had successfully entered Gaza, and the war, for me, had begun.

That night an ambulance drove by. As Omer was on guard duty, he looked out at them. They looked back and drove away. As he told our commanders this story, we all realized that we had to leave immediately. Now the enemy knew our location.

The next day I heard over the radio that Hamas operatives had taken over an ambulance in our area and were using it as cover while they shot at Israeli soldiers. I knew that this was the same ambulance Omer saw a day ago. My first thought was wondering what happened to the paramedics inside the ambulance. I assumed they must have been killed by Hamas. I imagined a carjacking scene, where those poor men and women were trying to help some injured person, and right from under their noses they were murdered, and their ambulance hijacked by those they were trying to help.

Under the laws of war, it is taboo to shoot at or destroy an ambulance or those working for it. However, when that ambulance is now shooting at you and your friends, you must defend yourself. A few hours went by and I again heard over the radio that the Israeli Air Force had neutralized the enemy. "Good, now we don't have to attack an ambulance. That would have been uncomfortable," I said to Tamir.

We spent the next few days in the area, switching houses almost every night so that the enemy could never be sure of our location. On the third day, we had to change to a house that was past our "red line." Even though we were in the heart of the city and very deep into Gaza, we would always create barriers for ourselves on where not to go, so in case we saw someone there, we would not confuse them for allies. Those rules helped us know where our allies were and where they were not, then when some stranger popped up in the distance we did not need to hesitate before shooting them down. However, tonight in order to maintain our safety from mortar attack, we were going to cross our "red line."

As we quickly prepared our stuff, I looked over the small window in the kitchen that gave us the only view to our new home across the street. It was a two-story house with a wall surrounding the entire property. It looked like the kind of villa I always heard of college kids renting in Mexico during spring break. The path we took to our new villa was a straight one out in the open. There was no cover, so we knew that the only thing between us and a possible bullet to the head from a sniper somewhere off in the distance was speed, and the cover of darkness. Then as our sergeant, Tamir, gave the command, we each sprinted across in pairs to the wall. Once at the wall, we had one man crouch down in a squatting position. Then Tamir and Shy jumped on his legs and quickly climbed over the wall. As they gave the all clear for the initial 'landing in' we continued to jump over in the same fashion. As it came to my turn, my adrenaline helped me overcome the heavy bag on my shoulders and I boosted myself up onto the wall. Yet, with all my grace, I was unable to prevent myself from flopping down onto the grass like a flounder as gravity overtook my newfound weight, and I came crashing down on the other side.

I quickly recovered to my feet and once I jumped over, I noticed that Tamir and Ofek were about to blow open the door and enter the building. We all made our distance around the corner quickly as not to be too close to the front door. Then, 7,4,2, boom. And the front door along with half of the living room and the kitchen went kaboom. As Tamir entered, I took

Omer with me to search the garden, car, and one of the two newly formed guest houses inside this villa. As we entered the guest home, we saw a small office with a closet. As my heart raced, we quickly opened the closest to find no one hiding inside. We then came outside and turned the corner in a speedy fashion, but just as quickly in the room across from me was a man with his gun pointed at me and mine at his. And then, right before I pulled the trigger, I looked up and noticed the face. It was not an enemy but Mendelson, the second in charge of our unit.

We both took a deep breath, shocked that we almost killed one another. Then in Israeli fashion we walked past each other with Mendelson sputtering, "You idiot. What were you doing?"

"You idiot," I responded, "you're not supposed to even be here. We're the ones clearing this area."

Then just like nothing happened, we quickly returned to the building where Tamir was waiting for our report that the outside areas were all clear.

After the area was given the all clear from enemy personnel, we again searched through the two smaller buildings in this large villa for supplies. We found several guns and a big stack of cash, as well as military uniforms with badges that indicated that the owners had climbed high up the ranks of Hamas. In the outside areas, we found papers that indicated that one of the men also worked for the Al-Jazeera news company. I wouldn't have guessed that major international news companies would hire actual literal terrorists, but I also wasn't surprised.

As we were clearing the house, a call on the walkie came over. It was Paz, my officer. He was with the other half of the team working on clearing the tunnels. He told us all to stop what we were doing and slowly raise our hands. As the radio call went off, everyone started to do so. Then I heard again over the radio, "Oh thank god it's you." I realized that there must have been some miscommunication to which house we were moving to. Paz had then told Tamir that if we hadn't responded in that manner, he was about to have his half of the team gun us down.

In the IDF, our greatest fear isn't the enemy. Our greatest fear is shooting our friends. Friendly fire due to miscommunication is very common in war and we, above everything else, did not want that to happen to us.

Once the house was cleared, the snipers in our unit set up on the second floor. The wall surrounding the perimeter of the property made it difficult to see much from the first floor, so we relied on our snipers as lookouts and cover. For our part, we watched the yard itself so that we would be ready to intercept anyone that actually ran into the villa.

Snipers all set up

Eventually, we got bored watching the egg-shell colored paint dry, so Tamir told us to clean up the mess we made from the explosives. We found a broom and swept up the splintered wood and crumbled drywall and piled the debris in a corner of the kitchen we had just blown up. *This is crazy,* I thought, *sweeping up a warzone*.

We were two hours deep into cleaning when we heard laughter outside. We stopped in our tracks. There were people outside speaking in Arabic. We couldn't see them, so they must have been just outside the fence. We raised our weapons quietly, preparing to ambush whoever stepped into the yard, when *crunch*, Elazar stepped on a plastic bottle. The sound tipped off the men, who had now stopped talking, and outside the large walls, we heard the pitter patter of their feet as they turned and ran.

Tamir shouted to the snipers upstairs. "Hey! we have at least two scouts here running north!"

Several seconds passed in silence. Then came the loud bang of a sniper rifle firing from upstairs. Another long moment of silence, and then three more shots from the rifle shook the whole house.

"We got them," someone shouted from upstairs.

Everyone downstairs cheered. Several of us climbed the stairs to ask the snipers what happened. Solomon greeted us and explained that Rapoport, the sniper from my team, was the one who took the shots. They saw the three young men fleeing down the street. Rapoport dropped the first one with his first shot. The other two scattered, one dodging for safety while the other grabbed a woman off the street as a human shield. She was screaming while he held a gun to her head. Rapoport waited patiently with his rifle trained on the man, until the woman bucked the guy off her, and popped him in the head. While she scrambled away for safety, Rapoport shot the man dead. As the target fell, the third man leapt from his hiding place to try to pull the injured man to safety. Rapoport shot him dead as well.

"Where is Rapoport?" I asked.

Solomon motioned to one of the other rooms. "He's upset."

The men were barely men at all, two of them looked about sixteen, barely old enough to drive in the States. We all hung our heads, feeling bad about what had just happened and the three bodies in the street, but we also knew these young boys, if they had escaped, would have reported us to their commanders. Then it might be us lying in a pool of blood. As I heard this story, I took a moment to think about the situation we were in and compared it to the only other thing I knew that showed what war was, the movies. *Saving Private Ryan, Lebanon, Full Metal Jacket*, this was nothing like those movies. Except I believed that one message tried to come through. The fact that none of us wanted to be there. No one wants to be at war. None of us wanted to hurt anyone, but I was fighting for those who needed protection, making me determined to complete the mission and destroy all Hamas terrorists' tunnels.

Soon we all gathered again and talked about what to do. We couldn't stay in the same location, not after blasting it half to pieces, and certainly not after the encounter we had just had. As the sun came down, we moved onto the next house.

Days rolled by and we realized the small "two-day" mission we were given, to come into Gaza to destroy two tunnels and leave, was not going to happen. The mission turned into a much larger operation named Operation Protective Edge and would be known as the next big Gaza Israeli war. This left another obstacle on our path. Since we thought the mission was going to be two days, we brought with us just enough water and food for two days. By day three, we started to run low on supplies and because we were so far into Gaza it was impossible for supplies to reach us. Thoughts of exhaustion, hunger and major dehydration began to enter our minds but with the threat of snipers, mortars and enemy ambushes, those worries were put aside.

Working on demolishing the tunnels

Tunnel

Entering the tunnel

On our fifth day in Gaza, around two o'clock in the afternoon, I was on guard duty in a new house that we had captured the night before when I saw the shadow of someone in a window 150 meters to the north of our position. The man was standing in the center of a closed window screen, on the second floor of a strange building with three large vertical orange and red stripes. It was the most bizarre paint job I had ever seen.

I had been searching for enemy snipers with my binoculars, with the curtains drawn shut. In the corner I peeked through the sliver of curtain and was then able to search the area without being seen. I went from window to window, searching every building. Of course, it would have been easier to open the curtains and stand in the middle of the room, where it was possible to see in all directions, but this would have opened me up to sniper fire.

Operating under the stress of deadly conditions, for days on end, can play with your mind. The previous night, while doing the same thing with night-vision goggles, I thought I saw lights go on and off in a nearby building. I grabbed another teammate, Shy, to come investigate the building with me, but we turned up nothing. I was just being paranoid due to sleep deprivation and anxiety. I had probably hallucinated the light. It was very possible I was hallucinating the shadow of the man in the window, too.

Also possible was that I had spotted my first sniper.

I wanted a second opinion, but we couldn't leave our guard spots unattended while everyone else was out searching more homes. I switched spots with Omer, another teammate, so that I could watch the front door for him while he took my spot. I pointed out the window to him and asked if he saw a man.

From my post, he called back, "Max, you got one! There is a man in that window! You're not crazy this time!"

Thermal imagery of Hamas terrorists in Gaza

We switched back into our places. He reported the find on his walkie-talkie and asked for permission to open fire. Before we got a response, Mendelson, the second in charge of my unit, marched through the door with his chooliyot, (a group of four soldiers). I reported the sniper that we had spotted. He immediately crouched down and took my place by the window, pulled open the curtain, took out his sharpshooting scoped rifle, and began to take aim. However, he had to wait for permission to shoot to come over the radio, since the enemy was in an area where there were allies.

"Get command to give us permission already!" Mendelson shouted at me, as if I could do anything to hasten the process. Command is very strict about not firing without confirmation and permission. With so many close calls, everyone was afraid of friendly fire. But we knew that no one from our unit or the surrounding units were supposed to be in that specific building.

A tense minute went by while we waited.

"Fuck it. Let's shoot," someone yelled.

But, before he could pull the trigger, the radio went off telling us to hold our fire. The Palsar Tzanhanim, another

Special Forces paratrooper unit, had just moved forward and was taking control of the building and had soldiers on the first floor. However, the man on the second floor was not one of our guys. We radioed the Palsar to let them know that an enemy soldier was on the second floor of the building. They decided to handle the situation on their own so we wouldn't risk friendly fire.

From there, I closed the curtain in frustration and went back to searching for more enemy snipers.

It had now been three days without food and water. All I thought about after the man in the pinstriped building was getting some water. Every fifteen minutes I would go to Tamir and ask when the supplies were going to come. Even though we rationed, everyone was out of supplies and it was impossible for any vehicles to get to us. So, because of us getting the wrong info in the beginning, Tamir had to deal around the clock with someone asking when water was going to arrive. Some guys even contemplated drinking their own pee. But Tamir reassured us that the supplies should come soon. Finally, by that evening, a vehicle was able to reach us and from the small hole in the top popped out Amitai with a big smile, but even more important, with some damn water and tuna. Amitai was the Rasap for our unit, which meant he was in charge of supplies. So, finally after three days of nagging Tamir, we were able to fill our bellies and quench our relentless thirst, and all this right before we changed our guard rotation to nighttime rotations. This meant that instead of doing two-hour shifts, everyone would do fifteen minutes, and then get thirty minutes to sleep. That way no one could fall asleep while on duty.

Eventually, food made its way through and we feasted like kings, all of Israel was supporting us–sending packages filled with coke, mango juice, bamba, and many other treats that made it to us so deeply into Gaza

Day 5

I had just gotten off guard duty and several of us were asking around about what the next mission is going to be, until suddenly, the head of our unit, Neria, rushed into the building in total panic. Neria was about 5'10, Ashkenazi and started his military career with the paratrooper infantry brigade 202. After rising through the ranks, he had such a knack for authority and leadership that he eventually became our unit commander. Neria had the kind of stern face that when you looked at him, you knew he was in charge. As he rushed in the door, he told our commander that he needed our team's emergency rescue squad, which consisted of five people, including myself. One of the teams from Palsar Tzanhanim had been ambushed by the enemy. At least one man had been seriously wounded, he said.

We sprang up, grabbed a stretcher, and in the middle of the day left behind the protection of our building. As I stepped outside, the sun was blinding, we were so used to working at night it was strange to be out, in the open, during the middle of the day.

We headed to the area where the incident had occurred, carefully retracing the same path that we had taken the night before so as not to wander into any booby-traps. One man carried the empty stretcher while the rest of us moved with guns drawn, pointing them at windows and up towards rooftops, ready for someone to pop out at any moment. We were on edge, and not just from possible traps, but because we were now exposed. The enemy had been in the area and some might still be lingering in the shadows.

I could feel the adrenaline rushing through my veins and hear the blood pumping in my ears as we ran to the site with the stretcher in tow. I no longer noticed the pounding sun or weight of my armor and equipment.

We made our way past buildings and up and down sand dunes until we reached the scene where our unit commander ordered us to make a perimeter of the area. My heart was pounding. We were surrounded by buildings and someone could pop out of a window or alley and start shooting at us at any moment from any direction. Someone had just been shot in this exact way and, of course, it could easily happen again. The rescue mission was opening us up to ambush. Just as Rapoport had killed one of the enemies while he was trying to pull one of his own to safety, we were now the one's risking it all to save our brothers.

We stood guard, unflinchingly, until Tamir, my sergeant, came by to explain what had happened. The man inside had been shot in the head, though Tamir assured us he would be okay. He wanted us to stand guard until the doctors (Israel has real doctors that go into combat with soldiers.) inside signaled for us to bring the stretcher. We would then evacuate the wounded soldier quickly and get him to safety.

We listened to all of this intently but dared not turn to face

Tamir. Our eyes stayed trained on the surrounding buildings so that we could hold the position safely. Not turning your head when spoken to, especially by a commanding officer, goes against the body's natural reflexes, but we had been trained never to turn away from our duties or potential dangers.

We waited for what felt like hours, but may have only been minutes, until the order was given. We sprang into action, rushing into the room with the stretcher and loading the man onto it. It would take four men to carry it. We hoisted him up and began our march towards the M.A.S.H. station, the medical facilities, for further care.

We had to carry him over a few kilometers. I was, of course, all too familiar with being under a stretcher. During training, I had carried stretchers across sand dunes and mountains countless times. I had carried empty stretchers, stretchers with men on them, and stretchers loaded down with sandbags. But this was my first time carrying a wounded soldier on a stretcher. I was running on autopilot, doing the task I had trained for a thousand times before, and fueled by a sense of real urgency. This man, my brother in arms, might actually be dying.

And so we carried him as fast as we could. Eventually, Tamir ordered us to stop and take cover. We needed to cross over a small sand dune, worn into the terrain by passing tanks kicking dust to the side of the path, but there was a team of men exchanging fire with the enemy up ahead. We ducked down into the sand dune with the stretcher still on our shoulders, waiting for the firefight to end. The sound of guns firing slowed down but did not stop. Time was running out.

I looked down at the man on the stretcher. The bandages wrapped around his head were soaked through with blood. The sand caked to his face was red. His wound was worse than it had looked. The bandages were not only staunching the flow of blood but also holding his brains inside of his skull as well.

Given his condition, we didn't have time to wait. We had to sprint up and over the dune. We hoisted him back up and made a break for it, running up and down the dune. Thanks to our speed, and a good deal of luck, we made it across without getting hit by enemy fire.

We carried the stretcher another kilometer or so until we came to a large sand dune with several Palestinian flags flying at the top. We raced up the dune, where we were met by a medical team of six Israeli soldiers. They took the stretcher and thanked us for our work. We paid little attention to them. There was no time for even sincere expressions of gratitude, no time for contemplation, as this was a warzone. We raced back down the hill and got into formation, weapons drawn in case the enemy approached, and waited for our next orders.

Tamir returned from speaking with the medics and we moved out again. There had been another incident with the Palsar. We were now going to respond to that as well. We retraced our steps back to the same general area where we had picked up the other wounded soldier, but this time stopped at a different house a few blocks down. When we arrived, there were eight soldiers writhing on the ground, screaming in pain. These were not random men but familiar faces. I had gone through training with these men. I hadn't known the other soldier we carried to safety, but these were my friends. I was horrified to see them in such pain, their bodies riddled with bullets, and I could see literal holes in their chests and stomachs as they lay in a pool of blood on that cold concrete floor. I was aghast at the screaming and yelling and not being able to directly help them. Since the room was packed with medics and doctors, we had to stand by and help guard the house while they prepped them for extraction.

Within a few minutes, two more rescue teams joined us, and we had three teams to defend the house, which had become an impromptu hospital for the wounded. We stood by anxiously while the men were given acute care to try and save their lives. When the doctors gave the word to Tamir, we again sprang into action—it was time to get the wounded out. We loaded the men onto stretchers and as we had always been trained, "1,2,3" I yelled, and we lifted them up and started carrying them out.

However, unlike last time, those men needed to go into tanks for they were going to go quickly across the border and from there airlifted to hospitals.

As I saw Natan's face wincing in pain, I tried to console him as we carried him. "*Iheyah besader achi, yesh lanoo Otcha Achsheli*," I said, which meant, "You'll be okay, bro. We have you now."

He smiled and said, "Oh man, I'm in the Palchan now. How cool. Let's go blow stuff up." I chuckled. I guess the morphine the doctor gave him was in full affect now.

We again had to cross the sandpit among a hail of gunfire. With no other option, we took the risk and sprinted across again. We took a slightly different route this time in order to deliver the man to the tank waiting for us. We loaded up my friend onto the tank, while it was getting shot at from all around. Within a few seconds he was safe inside the tank and we were heading back to the house for the next person.

We took an indirect path back in order to avoid the gunfire and grabbed another man. By the time we dropped the second man off and returned for a third, we were all exhausted. We were overheated and sweating, every muscle hurt, and our legs felt like jelly. But there was no time for our kvetching (Yiddish for complaining). Our friends were still lying in the room, horribly wounded and needing help. We had to get them out. However, a medic, Rom, who was a member of their team took note of our condition and sent us to drink water so that we wouldn't pass out. I could only imagine how he must have been feeling while his own teammates were lying on the ground in agony.

We chugged down the water and then grabbed the next man and hoisted him up on the stretcher. The water helped to make us feel less exhausted, but the third man was heavier than the first two, which made the trip even harder. The medics had told us that he felt embarrassed about being wounded and advised us not to engage him much. I tried not to make eye contact or talk to him, but at one point he looked at me and grinned. He had a morphine lollipop hanging out of his mouth while he told a joke. I knew then that he would be okay. I smiled back at him in relief.

We neared the tank. There was more shooting than before. The area was unsafe. We took cover behind some bushes and fencing and looked for an opening. Unfortunately, we didn't have much time. Our friends were bleeding out. We decided to take a risk and again load the man into the tank under fire. Luckily, everything went well and no one else was hit.

Once again, we dashed back to the house, but by the time we got back, there were only two injured men left and they could both walk on their own. Done transporting people, we took up a defensive position around the house.

Finally, with a moment for reflection, I was able to take in what the commanders had told us about what had happened. They explained that they were ambushed inside the house. But that didn't make any sense. How could the enemy sneak up on the building without being seen?

It was then that I remembered the tunnels in the area. Was it possible that there was a tunnel opening in the area that we didn't know about? I started inspecting the area to look for anything suspicious. There was a small hut a few feet away. Upon closer inspection, there was nothing out of the ordinary with it. Tamir saw me walk closer to the hut and yelled, "Max, don't go inside. We cannot lose eye contact with one another, one second we see you the next you could get kidnapped."

Eventually, after a few minutes, Tamir announced that it was time to go. We were going to exit the area and escort the last of the wounded soldiers to the tanks. Since they could walk, we didn't have to use the stretcher and we could all keep our rifles up and ready. We scanned for the enemy as we moved. We were deep inside Gaza. There were tunnels everywhere. The enemy could pop up anytime, anywhere, and start firing on us.

I found this last trip the most worrisome because we had to move slowly to accommodate the two injured men. They were in severe pain and had limited mobility. It would have been faster to carry them on the stretcher, but they had turned down the offer out of pride. They wanted to walk for themselves rather than burden the team, and while this was counterproductive, I understood where they were coming from. I, too, would have wanted to walk on my own two feet.

We made our way slowly to the tanks and loaded the last two men up. They were safe and sound, and we were finished. All the injured were off the battlefield, and we were ready to leave the area and move to the next target.

But, within seconds of loading the last two men, we heard the blast of rifles as we came under sniper fire. We dropped down to the ground. I crawled behind a small bush for cover. We couldn't tell from which building the fire was coming, but we knew it was aimed at us because every few seconds the sand would jump into the air as another bullet landed. We stayed low; our rifles trained in the direction of the path we had followed there. This was where the shooting had been earlier, so it made sense that the enemy had followed us.

Earlier, the shooting had been indiscriminately aimed at anyone in the area in an Israeli uniform, but we were now pinned down under the fire of a particular sniper. There was something strange and intimate about the exchange of gunfire. This was the first time I felt that someone was actually trying to kill me, personally.

The shots kept coming and we couldn't pin down the source. We had our weapons drawn, but we could not shoot blindly into the area we just came from, other Israeli soldiers were still in the area, and god forbid we hit them. Rather than return fire, we stayed pinned down while the head of our unit called in another tank. The tank rolled in and let out a smoke-screen. As I crawled behind the tank, I could hear *pop pop* as the sniper's bullets bounced off it. With the tank and smoke-screen for cover, we dashed away able to escape from the sniper, unharmed.

12

MY LAST DAY IN THE WAR

"Life is 10% what happens to you and 90% how you react to it." ~ *Charles Swindoll*

Another night went by, and we were now on our sixth day in Gaza. We got very little sleep the night before, which is the norm when at war. We rotated fifteen-minute guard shifts, once an hour with our chooliyot. That night, my chooliyot was in charge of guarding the front gate. This meant fifteen minutes guarding, and hopefully forty-five minutes to sleep, which is difficult even on a good night. This had not been a good night. The sound of enemy mortars landing nearby, and our tanks returning fire, shook the house and kept us up all night long.

I was charged with guarding the front gate of the house. The light from the explosions was visible through the peep-hole in the door. A moment after each flash the whole house would shiver.

The firing didn't slow down until the sun started to come up. I was relieved to have survived the night without incident. I had been afraid that this would be my final night, that a mortar would hit the house, or enemy combatants would pop out from around a corner or from an unknown tunnel. None of those things happened and I began another day in Gaza with my team.

Later that day, over the radio, Neria, finally declared that the mission was a success and we were ready to move onto a new location. We had gotten into a routine, going further west (further into Gaza) taking a new house each day and hunkering down. However, this new location was a few kilometers north which was unchartered territory and intelligence believed it to be even more dangerous.

Studying the map for the new location in Gaza

Nonetheless, it was time to move. We prepared during the day, packing our bags and resting when possible. We went over the mission at least three times to make sure everyone was on the same page. My Hebrew was still not great, so I was a little unclear on the details, but I was accustomed to being a little out of the loop and had learned to trust that I would perform in the moment.

When night fell, we left the house in formation and retraced our steps so that we could restock supplies along the way. I was supposed to get a new piece of equipment for clearing booby-traps, mines, and IEDs, like the one I had used on our first day. As we began our journey back, we stopped in the alleyway next to the first house we had taken on our first night in Gaza. Our sergeant and a few teammates peeled off to go set explosives in order to demolish our last house and cover our tracks. We waited in the alleyway while they worked. After a while, the countdown came in over the radio, 7,4,2, BOOM! and then the house exploded in a ball of flames as the explosives sparked a gas line. From our vantage point, we watched in awe as flames swallowed the house. Like boys setting off fireworks, we hollered and cheered at the sight.

Tamir returned and we regrouped back into formation. We marched on, sticking to the same path we came in through to avoid any mines or IEDs. I glanced periodically at the ground as we marched, scanning for traps, and in doing so, I noticed the change to the ground. The tanks and other military vehicles had torn up the landscape. The ground was covered in debris and rubble. What was once hard ground beneath my feet was now soft dust, except the dust was so thick it felt like trudging through a foot of murky, brown snow. It was not lost on me the damage we had wrought blowing through this strange land. Mostly, I kept my head up, though, always searching for the enemy.

As was typical, we got lost on the way back and what was supposed to be a short march turned into an all-night affair. We went in circles trying to find the destination where we were supposed to pick up the new equipment. Despite all the unplanned detours, we made it to the restocking point in time, though we were annoyed and tired once we reached it. And as we reached it my favorite moment came. I got to sit down in the middle of bushes for cover, lie back on my human-sized backpack and drink some cold water.

Not much later, I was up again helping Tamir and Paz collect camelbacks from the team to refill with water and then went to pick up the explosive equipment. I stood by the equipment vehicle, a large armored vehicle, waiting for my large green explosive box used for clearing the path, but a fresh one never materialized. I went over to Amitai asking where my stuff was, but he had no idea. Paz then gave me a large sandbag with a claymore inside. Though not exactly light, the device was much lighter than what I was supposed to be carrying, so I was as happy as could be.

I went back and helped distribute everyone's water and then repacked my bag with the claymore. Everyone now ready, we regrouped into formation and set out. We were going to have to be more careful now since we didn't have the right device for handling ground-based booby traps. We moved a little more carefully, a little more slowly, though we felt relatively safe because the path we were on had been flattened and widened by tanks rolling through. The path was well traveled, and any booby traps would have probably been set off by the weight of the tanks.

An hour into our march, the line came to a stop. We were near our target, but had arrived early, so they let us sit down and rest. So once again I plopped down on the ground, leaned back on my bag, and this time passed out. I was awakened to what seemed like a few minutes later, though in actuality was a few hours, by the sound of an armored vehicle known as a D-9, which was effectively a bulldozer on steroids, rolling down the path. The D-9 was twenty meters away, approaching fast, and showed no signs of stopping. Everyone jumped up and bolted out of the way, except for Elazar, who in disbelief that he might get run over, took his sweet time getting up and jumping out of the way at the last second before being pancaked. We hollered angrily at the vehicle as it passed. The driver, who seemed confused by our presence, continued plowing forward. A line of three Merkava Israeli tanks followed up behind him. We watched them pass, annoyed that the driver was paying so little attention. "The few, the proud, the glue-eating mentally-challenged D-9 drivers," I murmured.

A D-9

There was no time to be shocked about almost being flattened by our own men. Our commander was already ushering us into formation and continuing the march. A group of six of us, including me, were cut off from the rest of the unit by the long, deep divot left behind by the tanks and we had to sprint to catch up with the others.

On the way to the next meeting point, the shoulder strap on my bag snapped, forcing me to hold my 100 pound bag with my left arm and my gun with the right. With the string and tape I had packed, I made a fruitless effort to fix the bag while marching, which distracted me from my surroundings. In enemy territory, situational awareness is a matter of life and death, which made the bag malfunction not only a nuisance, but also a real danger. And the only thing I could think of was, *why god fucking damnit did this strap break now! How am I supposed to fix it, while watching for the enemy, and keeping up with the rest of the group*? However, while thinking that, I decided to continue carrying the bag with one hand and keep going until I found a moment to try and fix it.

As we continued forward, we soon came to a large dirt hill and began scaling its steep banks. Like clockwork everyman got to the top of the hill then lost their footing in the loose sand, and one by one, each man went tumbling down, like Jack and Jill, to the bottom of the hill. As I fell, I saw Rapoport and Solomon, our snipers, sitting at the bottom, waiting for the rest of the unit. They looked relaxed and calm, chilling and talking. I took a seat next to them, realizing this was the meeting point. With a few moments until the others arrived, I knew I should use the time to mend my bag, but as I sat down, my sheer exhaustion gathered all at once and I fell asleep there on the ground.

I awakened to the rising sun. As daylight started to break over the horizon, Li came by and bopped me on the helmet. "Time to go," he said. We jumped up and into formation, the tanks starting to roll out, and we were headed on our way to the next mission. With disappointment, I was no more prepared than I had been earlier with a broken pack and both of my hands full while we marched. There was nothing to do about it though than deal, so I held the bag in one hand and my gun in the other and continued to curse my luck quietly as we walked forward.

As we moved into a new area, we stayed on high alert. This was new and dangerous territory where anything could happen. I kept my gun ready as best as I could with one hand on my bag, as we made our way through a big crop field with a few houses spotted around the perimeter. While moving through the field, an explosion sounded, though we paid it little attention because the sound of tank cannons firing and mortars falling had become an erratic beat in the background, almost white noise. There were four tanks at each corner of the field, and we assumed the blast had come from one of them. We saw nothing alarming or out of the ordinary, at least not at first, until we moved further and came across a fifth tank in the middle of the field that had fallen into a crater and flipped over. We realized that the explosion, or one of the explosions, had created the crater.

Thankfully, all of the tankers were safe. They had helped each other out and no one reported any serious injuries. Given that everyone escaped unscathed, I thought it was kind of funny to see a big mighty tank flipped over on its head. The tankers were understandably angry and shouting, cursing up a storm. In retaliation, the other tanks started firing rounds in the windows of the nearby houses. As the explosion blasted through the rooms, I thought, *well, I guess there is no need pointing my gun over there*.

My unit continued forward further and then, inexplicably, stopped in the middle of the field where we had no cover. We dropped low and pointed our guns towards the houses in case we came under fire. Hunkering down in an open field where the enemy could take up higher ground and cover in the adjacent houses was a dangerous situation. We still had three operational tanks in the area, along with other special forces units everywhere, which meant there was plenty of backup available, but it also drew unwanted attention to the area while we were exposed in the middle of the field. *All of the backup in the world wouldn't mean much after already taking a bullet from a sniper*, I thought.

From the back of the line, I had no idea why we had stopped, especially while so exposed. We started moving soon, but then stopped again every few minutes. Something was holding up the line. It wasn't until we got further down the field that I could see what was happening. We had stopped the first time while the first team cleared a house and we were now waiting for another team that was crossing the road in front of our path.

When it came my turn to cross, I gathered up my courage, looked directly at the spot I needed to go to and sprinted forward. Unbeknownst to me, just as I went, a large wooden utility pole started to come down on my path. Ishay tried to warn me, but his shouts were out of earshot. The large power line whipped my helmet and across the back of my neck, but thankfully did not deliver a shock. I brushed the line off and continued.

As I finished my sprint, I joined the rest of the line, where they were waiting to take the next house. I noticed to my left that Team 20 was already clearing the house, so the wait wouldn't be long. As I looked in front of me, it was then that I recognized our location. This was the same sandy road I saw on a map earlier, where I was previously going to use my explosive device to clear the way. We needed to be very cautious.

"Walk on each other's footprints!" Paz shouted, instructing us to minimize danger by stepping in the same place so that we wouldn't trip any booby traps.

The path was short, and it took less than a minute to wind our way through. Safe on the other side, we stood before three green houses and a large building behind them, that was my team's target. We cut a hole through the clear tarps and made our way through the green houses, moving through the tall weeds that went up past our knees. Inside the houses, rope was strung from the ceiling and hung down to head level, blocking our view and hindering our passage. The hanging black rope, along with an early morning fog that went up to our knees gave the whole area a very eerie feeling. However, all I could think about was how I was still encumbered by my broken pack and hoped desperately for a quiet moment inside one of the houses so I could mend it. Once we got to the last house, we could clearly see the target building. It stood three stories tall and was made from black bricks. There were several windows on the upper stories that would give snipers an excellent position.

My Kita, or class in English, which represents another way of organizing half the team—in this instance, nine of us went with Sergeant Tamir, and the other half with Officer Paz. Stopped within the last small green house, we all dropped to one knee. The grass there was literally up to our stomachs and some even went past our heads when we knelt. Still fiddling with my bag, I knew I should be more focused on the here and now, but it had caused me nothing but trouble. I finally gave up with it and trained my gun on the target, ready to blast anyone who popped out. We were fifty meters from the target now. Even though there were large holes cut to move in and out of the green houses, the rest of the tarp had blurred my vision of the house.

I watched as Paz and his group made their way to the side of the building. 7-4-2 'pop' went the explosive. They tried to blast through the wall to no avail. Paz then radioed the situation to the unit commander who gave us permission to then try and go through the front door. Paz's chooliyot then set up an explosive device and carried it to the front door, but just as they got close to the door…

…BOOM!

A giant explosion caused the whole building to erupt in flames.

I saw the flash as it happened and a split second later, heard the swooshing sounds as things flew past me. Then suddenly, BANG!

It felt like a baseball bat struck me on the side of my head. My hand reflexively went to my head and found nothing. At first, in shock, I thought nothing of the fact, but then blood started pouring down my face and into my eyes. I checked my head again, in the spot where it hurt, only to find a lot of blood this time. It covered my hand.

Before even looking up, I instinctively started to yell, "I got hit! I got hit!"

Then I began to hear the sounds of screaming coming from the blaze in front of me. I traded worried glances with Ishay and Omer, realizing that this was a horrific situation. I immediately shut up, no longer calling attention to my wound, realizing now that there were others in worse condition. I had been hurt, but the wound was not a grievous one. I could continue. I had to do so, for the others, but first I had to bandage my wound. I took a deep breath, realized blood was gushing from the right side of my head, and so I laid down on my left side and asked my partner, Omer, to come help. He rushed over and told me to calm down, though his own face was so shocked and ashen that I started to laugh from the absurdity of him telling me to calm down.

With shaky hands, I reached for bandages in my bag and began wrapping my head. A few deep breaths were all it took to get me in the right headspace, and my hands stopped shaking. Unable to finish the bandage myself, I asked Omer to tie off the last bit. In his haste, he did a poor job and the bandages immediately slipped down over my eye. He looked upset with himself; more upset than me.

"It's okay," I reassured him. "Just do it again. I have to be able to see."

He pulled the bandage back and then rewrapped it, tighter this time so that it would stay in place.

As this was going on people started to run forward, to the house, to the other teammates, all over. The situation was in chaos, no one knew what to do. Then I heard "ZAMBIAH!!!" Tamir shouted. Silencing the crowd and drawing everyone's attention to him. Tamir, started barking commands to a team of around twenty people who had come with stretchers. We had help.

My helmet felt heavy, so I pulled it off to keep it from interfering with the bandages. By this point, I felt mostly functional and fine, as far as I could tell. My head hurt, but I could move, and the blood had stopped pouring. I figured whatever hit me probably just scraped the side of my head. So, I tried to jump to my feet to help the injured, but Omer grabbed me by the shoulder.

"You are not going to move," he said. "You're hurt."

"Fuck off!" I yelled.

Tamir looked at me and ordered Omer to make sure I didn't move.

Grudgingly, I yelled back to Omer, "Fine! I won't move, but then you go get them!"

Tamir noticed the red bandages and the blood. He told Omer to stay by my side and not to let me move. I didn't try to argue. I was injured, others were injured, and this was not the time or place to start disobeying commands. I sat there, upset, unable to do anything but curse quietly to myself. Not only could I not help, I was a burden to the team. However, I needed to find a way to do something!

Thankfully, there were others to whom I could provide assistance. Soldiers from other teams poured in to help. As the soldiers came by I would help direct them to where the more wounded soldiers were. I continuously yelled, "Go forward! Go get my brothers! They're the ones who need help!"

More and more of them came by to help me, and every time I shooed them away. I did my best to provide intel on what had happened and who was where, but the more time that passed, the less I knew about what was happening on the ground. All I knew was that others needed help more than me. I could hear their screams.

Within a few minutes, everyone who needed assistance was getting it. Everyone looked shocked and horrified. There was blood everywhere. People were screaming, moaning and shouting. I was not so shocked by the sight of blood and suffering. After all, I had been an EMT in Mada. This was not new to me, but I understood the horror and did my best to put on a brave face. Every time someone looked at me, I smiled and asked them how they were doing. I insisted that I was fine, that we were all fine, and everything was going to be alright. There was nothing else I could do, aside from lay there, assure those around me that we would be okay, and point my gun at the corners of the building, hoping there would not be a second attack. But if there was, I would be ready.

With everyone now having received immediate care, the order was given to get the injured evacuated. I gave my bag to Omer, who was uninjured. He would stay at the front while I would walk back. I felt ashamed to be walking back. I wanted to stay and help, but orders were orders and we had to leave. At the very least, I thought, I will help someone who cannot walk get back, that way there will be more able-bodied guys in the front. I was able to assist someone who had taken shrapnel to their shin and needed help walking. Most of the other injured were being carried out on stretchers, which I also tried to carry but was shooed away by those already under them. We headed back to the tanks that were waiting for us by the road. I saw Noah, from my team, on a stretcher with a morphine lollipop hanging out of his mouth and a blanket covering his legs. I was aghast, but he shot me a wink and a huge smile as he sucked on his morphine lollipop, which gave me hope.

There were two armored vehicles by the tanks, waiting to receive the wounded and ferry them to safety in Israel. Having sustained a head wound, I was classified as being in critical condition and was to be evacuated immediately. But I refused to accept the diagnosis and stayed until the last of the wounded were loaded up. I did not want to go and hoped they would run out of space, which is what happened. The seriously injured were taken first. The rest of us, who were not in critical condition, were ordered to return to the house that Team 20 had just taken over. There were five of us sent back, one still on a stretcher.

We went back as told. I sat next to Shmuel from my unit. He was not from my team but had taken shrapnel under his eye and in his leg. He must have been over 150 meters away from the house. Hagay, from my team, was also there because he, too, had been hit in the head with shrapnel, though he, too, was walking around fine. My friends from team 20 were also there keeping the house secured, and they looked upon us with anguish and horror. One of the officers already had tears in his eyes when he saw me. One look at the blood-soaked bandages wrapped around my head and he lost his cool. He went into the other room, slamming the door behind him. I could hear him sobbing in anguish.

Everyone handles tragedy differently, and I didn't blame him for breaking down, but I was determined to keep my cool. I maintained a smile at all costs in order to keep things light. Positive attitude, whether it was warranted or not, was what we needed. Another friend, also injured, sat down next to me. His face and his leg were swollen and there was a piece of shrapnel lodged halfway in his cheek, right under his eye. But he was also smiling; a kindred spirit. We started cracking jokes about what had just happened.

Our charade didn't last for long. Several men brought in a stretcher with a blanket pulled overtop to cover up a body. Fearing the worst, I asked Hagay who was on the stretcher. He did not answer, but the look on his face said everything. Someone had died.

Right then, we received orders to vacate the building. The tanks had arrived and were ready to take us away. I rose to my feet, helped Shmuel do the same, and together we walked out to meet the tanks. There was now a sea of people outside. The other paratrooper Special Forces units sent groups to help evacuate, and it was now impossible to find my own teammates. I followed the other injured to the street where the tanks were supposed to meet us.

Along the way, I ran into Ben, one of my good friends from the Garin. I was surprised to see him in Gaza. He was still in training. Apparently the IDF was allowing any of the Special Forces trainees with at least a year of training under their belt to fight in the war, even if their training wasn't complete. They needed more boots on the ground now that we were locked in an actual ground war. We gave each other a big hug, both relieved to know that the other was alive, if not well. We rarely heard news of how others were doing, unless their names showed up on a list of casualties, but I had received no such word since entering Gaza. We were always worrying about our friends, especially while we were in Gaza and cut off from the outside world. So, seeing a friend with my own eyes, knowing he was alive, was a deep relief.

My blood-soaked bandages must have alarmed Ben, because he kept glancing at my head. I smiled and tried to assure him that I was okay. There was no time to catch up, swap stories, or indulge in long goodbyes. We parted, happy to have seen each other, and carried on with our orders.

I met the tanks at the pickup spot and left along with the last of the wounded. I was there with three other injured soldiers. We crammed into the last tank, along with the four men operating the tank, and tried to get comfortable. Someone outside asked the commander of the tank if there was room for a *goofah* in the tank. This came as a shock to me, as there was barely room in the tank for the eight of us, and certainly not for one more. I had never even heard of a goofah and had no idea what that word meant. I asked Shmuel, "What's a goofah?"

With a deep sad response, he said, "It's a dead body, Max."

I then understood why silence had descended over the tank. We ended up leaving without the dead body, which they decided to transport in some other way, but it was as if the body were there with us regardless. My mind wouldn't let it go. I knew someone had been gravely wounded, but not who, and now that we had confirmation that there were casualties, it was eating at me not knowing who had been lost. Based on what I had seen so far, I assumed that two of my friends had been killed in the blast.

The tank ferried us out of Gaza. The ride was uncomfortable, but with the latches closed, I felt safe within its cramped, armored spaces. When we stopped and exited the vehicle, the brightness of the sun was blinding, as if I were leaving a cave.

"Where are we?" I asked the commander.

"Out of Gaza," he said.

When my eyes finally adjusted to the light, I could see that we were at the border where we had crossed the gate. Due to all of the tanks and armored vehicles crossing the whole area now looked like a vast wasteland.

They had us lie down on stretchers. I hated being on a stretcher, so I cracked jokes with the medics to lighten the mood and distract myself. They lifted me onto a truck, along with four other people, two of whom were friends that had been injured with me. One of them began to freak out about the tourniquet that had been around his leg for what he thought was hours. He was afraid he was going to lose his leg. I reassured him that everything was going to be fine and that we would be back on our feet, both of us, in no time. It took a while, but eventually he calmed down.

The truck drove us somewhere for about five minutes, all I could see was more barren desert. This was where the helicopters would pick us up and airlift us to the hospital. As they got close the helicopters kicked dust and debris into the air as they landed. There was little we could do to shield ourselves from flying sticks and rocks while on stretchers. The helicopters had limited space and took the most seriously injured first, which was fine by me, though it did mean that I would get pelted by flying debris several more times as the helicopters took off and landed.

I waited patiently on the stretcher, talking to the other soldiers, until the next chopper arrived. They loaded me into the helicopter and administered a quick medical checkup once I was onboard. It turned out that the medic was on the same elite team as my Chilean friend, Martin, who I knew from my Garin, at my home in Kibbutz Nir Oz. We took a selfie together on the helicopter and sent it to Martin.

While the helicopter zipped through the air, the soldiers performed another checkup. The medic cut off the kneepads that my father had just bought me before the war and was about to cut off my shoes until I yelled for him to stop. These were not standard army boots. They were only issued to Special Forces soldiers upon completion of training and only Special Forces were allowed to wear them.

"If you think you're going to cut off my shoes you have

another thing coming," I said. "You of all people know how hard it was to earn these shoes!"

The medic was in 669, an Elite Special Forces team and had the same pair of boots. I threatened to rip his off and take them if he cut mine off. He finally acceded and allowed me to take the shoes off normally before continuing the examination. There were no hidden injuries. Shortly thereafter, we arrived at the hospital landing station.

Once the helicopter touched down, the medics carried us by stretcher to an ambulance, the famed Magen David Adom ambulances of Israel's emergency response system, which I knew intimately. It was surreal to be a patient in the kind of ambulance that I used to work in. They gave me my own private ambulance for the quick five-minute ride from the landing station to the hospital. While the driver and medic performed another assessment, I told them how I had been a medic for Magen David Adom just two years ago. We all got a good laugh out of the irony of the situation.

Though faring well up until that point, all things considered, I started to get overwhelmed when we arrived at the hospital. Reporters surrounded us as they unloaded me from the ambulance and wheeled me into the hospital. There were cameras everywhere. People were trying to shove microphones into my face. Everyone wanted to know what had happened. Their clamoring made my head spin as if the ground was lurching. The medics rolled me straight through the crowd and past the double doors into the emergency room. The harsh hospital lights were just as blinding, if not more blinding, than the summer sun, especially after days of operating by night, observing the world through the faint green light of my night-vision goggles.

Once inside the ER, I tried to convince the Israeli doctors into letting me stand up and move into a hospital bed on my own. I employed what we called "Israeli negotiating," which is a euphemism for yelling at people.

The medics and doctors left me alone in my room for a

while. Eventually, a nurse came by and questioned me about my background and medical history, jotting down notes about my name, place of residence and other basic information. I answered her questions impatiently and kept asking what had happened to the other people on my team. I wanted to know that my friends were going to be okay. She had little information to share. After answering her questions, I asked for a phone to call my parents. I had been dreading this call since the moment I was inside the tank. I did not want to scare them, but how was it possible to tell my own parents that I was in the hospital with a head injury and that others had lost their lives? There was no easy way to break the news.

The nurse was kind enough to lend me her phone. I took a deep breath before dialing the familiar number to my parents' house. The phone rang several times before my mom picked up and said hello in a confused voice.

"Hi, Mom. It's me."

"Max!" she exclaimed. "Oh, my god, how are you? Where are you? Is everything alright?"

"Yes, Mom, everything is alright," I promised, and then explained what had happened. I told her I was at the hospital after being hit in the head with shrapnel. "They don't think I will need surgery."

My mother was in shock. She barely said anything.

"Look, Mom," I continued. "I need you to call Udi, Eli, and Joey to let them know that I'm in Bellinson Hospital." Eli was the head of my Garin and was a guardian and father figure to us all, always helping me navigate and understand the many nuances in Israeli society. Udi and the Nebel family were some of our closest friends in Israel, who time and time again helped and supported me. I remember when I first was getting settled in the army, I got stuck in Beer Sheva and Udi drove two hours each way to pick me up and take me back to spend the night at his home. Otherwise, I would have had to sleep on a park bench because the buses had stopped running for Shabbat. I don't know what I would have done without him. Joey and the Price family were my cousins in Jerusalem who time and time again welcomed me into their home and really into the entire American Jewish community in Talpiot Jerusalem, giving me a place to call home in the Holy City. There were many more people I wanted her to call but I knew that once these three were informed everyone else would soon follow.

My mother promised to do as I asked. The doctor came in then and I had to get off the phone. I promised to call her back after talking to the doctor.

The doctor took me to have x-rays done. I asked him about the status of my teammates and if it would be possible to see them. There was still no word and he said that he wanted us to focus on me at the moment. The x-rays came back showing a piece of shrapnel in my head. What had seemed like a scratch was actually a ball of metal, about the size of a fishing weight, lodged in my head. I waited while the medical team came up with a plan of action. They determined that I would need surgery after all.

For the first time since the injury, I was scared about my situation, though most of this fear was because I knew that I would have to call my mom back and let her know I was going to have surgery. I called her back, as I had promised, and told her that I would need a very minor surgery. "You don't need to worry," I said.

"Do I need to come over?" she asked, sounding frantic now.

"No, no, please, don't. Everything is fine."

There was a long pause on the line.

"Call me when it's over," she said.

"Of course," I said. "Love you"

"Love you, too."

The hospital staff took me to a room to be prepped for surgery. This was when I finally got to see a few of my teammates who were also there to be operated on. What a grim gathering! It was one big surgery party. We were glad to see each other and get confirmation that we were all okay, but we were also sad to be there and frustrated that we did not know what was going on back in Gaza. We wanted to know what had happened. None of us knew the full story of the explosion, who was safe and who was not, though it was clearly a booby trap. The hardest part was not knowing.

Shortly thereafter, I was taken in for surgery. The doctor gave me local anesthetic only, rather than putting me under, so I was awake for the entire procedure. I listened to the Red Hot Chili Peppers, my favorite band playing in the background while they dug into my head with a scalpel. I was able to talk during the procedure and learned that the surgeon had been in the same unit as me when he had served in the IDF. I couldn't believe the coincidence and it made me feel like I was in good hands. I remember little else about what we talked about, though we chatted throughout the surgery, which seems preposterous now, given that they were removing shrapnel out of my head, which had almost killed me.

When the surgery was done, they wrapped my head in fresh bandages and sent me on my way. I couldn't feel half of my body due to the anesthesia but was otherwise fine.

A nurse came to take me back to a room to rest. Floor 7, room 724, my new temporary home. I again asked the nurse what was going on with my team in Gaza and my friends at the hospital. She said they were not allowed to tell us anything until we saw a psychologist. "Fucking hell!" I yelled. Now it was another person I had to deal with. I demanded that they immediately send in the psychologist. She promised to work on it.

Shortly after she left, people started to trickle in. There was Eli, Udi's family, my cousin Joey, and Dana, who was another soldier from my Garin, and my adopted family from my kibbutz, Aviv, Liat, and their kids. And many more.

Family portrait of my kibbutz adopted family

The whole day, old friends and family came in and out. People I barely knew showed up. There were even people I didn't know at all. I didn't know how they had all found out that I was in the hospital. I could only guess that word of mouth spread quickly. Strangers were coming to thank me for my service. They brought cakes, presents and flowers. I was utterly humbled. Eli even went out and bought me a McDonalds' burger, at my request, so that I could finally have some 'real food.' A Big Mac was the first thing I ate after coming home from war and within thirty minutes, I was running to the bathroom to throw it up.

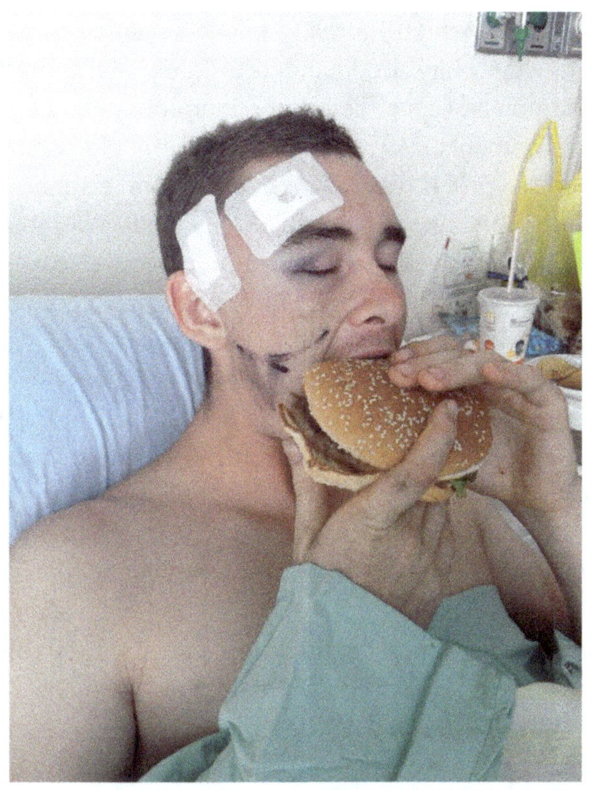

Max eating a McDonald's burger at Bellinson Hospital

The biggest mistake, though, was not the burger, but a picture that Udi took of me eating it at my mom's request. My mom took one look at the picture and said that she was booking the next available flight to Israel. She called me on the phone just to yell at me for telling her not to come. I hadn't wanted to bother her, though, in truth, it would be nice to see her. My father couldn't come, unfortunately. He had to stay home and hold down the fort.

I kept pestering the nurses and doctors to tell me about my team and what was happening in Gaza. They mostly ignored me or simply said they were working on it. I was sure they were lying to me. The psychologist finally came near the end of the day. He asked me a few questions and then assured me that I was okay, which I already knew. I wanted to know that the others were okay. I demanded to know about my friends, but he had no answers either. After examining me, he just left.

A few moments later, Nikolai, one of my old commanders, came in to see me. It was a shock to see him. I almost jumped out of bed and saluted, but half of my body was still numb. Now that Nikolai was in the room, everyone else left, and it became clear we were going to have a serious talk about what had happened. The sorrowful look on his face was all I needed to know that the news was going to be very bad.

"There was a booby trap in the house," he said, solemnly. "Paz, Li, and Dover were killed on the spot. Eighteen others were wounded."

I sat in silence trying to absorb this information. Paz, Li and Dover, three of my brothers were now dead, just like that, gone.

I took a deep breath, struggling to be strong and hide my emotion in front of my former commander. "Okay," I said. "How about everyone else? They're okay?"

Nikolai gave me a status report of everyone who had been injured. Noah and Shahar Shalev were both in critical condition and still undergoing surgeries. I was surprised, having assumed that Noah was okay given that he had smiled at me as he left, but it just goes to show how you cannot tell. Hidden injuries are hard to spot, especially when lots of shrapnel is involved. Nikolai explained that Noah had been very close to the blast but would hopefully be okay after surgery.

"How is the rest of the team doing inside Gaza?" I asked.

He told me that they were regrouping and would be continuing the mission without us. This gave me a sense of pride. I was down, for now, but my team would never give up.

The status report done, and my questions answered, we hugged one another and then he headed out to tell the others what he had told me. I thanked him for bearing the news, even though much of it was bad.

After Nikolai left, my family and friends rushed back in.

Dana leapt on the bed and gave me a big hug. I could do little but sit there passively and breathe, struggling to take in all that I had learned. It had been a long day and I needed to sleep. Dana stayed at the hospital with me that night, for which I was grateful, unable to believe my luck to have such an amazing group of friends, all thanks to Israel, all thanks to my Garin.

The next morning, another volley of strangers came with more gifts and well wishes. I was thankful, but also overwhelmed. My room was overflowing with cookies, cakes and candies; too much for any one man, so I donated it all to the kids downstairs.

My mind was stuck on a loop: *I have to get out of this hospital. I have to get back to my team. I need to get back to Gaza.*

The doctor came by that afternoon to say that the surgery went well, and I should be able to leave the hospital within a week or two.

"That's too long," I said. "I am feeling fine. I need to get back to Gaza now!"

My friends and family, still keeping me company in the hospital room, looked at me in shock, but I would not relent. Eli laughed, but he too had been to war and I knew he understood. I threatened to walk out and grab the next taxi to Gaza, if the doctor would not release me. We argued back and forth for a while. The doctor promised to revisit the discussion the next day, after I had finished one more day of the antibiotic. In the end, I gave in and promised to wait one more day. Having made the decision, I resolved to go with the flow and do as they said. It was, after all, only one more day. I stopped fighting. I put on a smile. I dutifully performed for the hundreds of people stopping by my room. But, on the inside, my heart was back with my brothers fighting in Gaza.

The following morning, the doctor returned, this time with the head of the hospital, who coincidentally also happened to have been in my unit in his younger days. They said that, while I could leave, they highly recommended that I did not. Without a second thought, I got up and started to leave. I did not get far. As I started to walk outside my room, I ran into my mom who had just arrived from the States. She looked me up and down and then dropped to her knees and cried. I helped her back to her feet and gave her a big hug.

"I'm fine. I'm fine," I said.

We walked back to my room and sat down. It was clear I would not be leaving the hospital that day after all. We barely had time to talk before Brigadier General Rami Zur came into my room. He was a stocky, bald man of average height and dressed in his army work uniform, or in Israel known as Madey Bet. This was my first time seeing such a high-ranking military official in person. I leapt out of bed and gave him a salute. He laughed and told me to sit down, asking, how did I, an American boy, end up there?

It seemed like a lifetime ago, but I thought back to that time on Udi's base over 12 years ago.

Before and after the explosion, thanks to Google Maps

13

HEALING

"Why do we fall? So, we can learn to pick ourselves up." ~ *Batman*

After finally explaining to Rami about myself, he then asked me to explain my situation and the incident in Gaza for his report. I recounted every horrifying detail, trying to be as specific as possible. Afterward, he took my mom outside and explained everything to her. Rami then came back into the room, and I asked him when I would be able to go back to Gaza. I wanted to return at once. He would have none of it and started yelling at me to think of my poor mother. We argued back and forth, but in the end, he won, of course. I agreed to stay another two days in the hospital while I finished my course of antibiotics.

Before leaving, Rami asked if I had any relatives in Israel. I told him that my cousin Joey and his family were in Jerusalem, and my friends, the Nebels, felt like family, and I knew I was always welcomed at the Vered's in Bat Yam, whom also felt like family, but in reality I spent most of my time at my kibbutz with my friends and adopted family. Rami said that I needed a family in Israel and that I should consider him like a father. He told me that his family would be my family, too. I laughed and thanked him for his generosity but did not really believe him. However, he came back several times that week and invited my family over for Shabbat. (He would have me over for Shabbat many times, months after the war, and it was only then that I understood that he had been serious about his offer.) From that moment on, whether I knew it or not, I not only had a family at my kibbutz, my close family friends in Bat Yam and Rishon Letzion, and real family in Jerusalem, but I also now had a family in Reut – Modiin, too.

Shabbat with Rami and his family

General Rami Zur and I playing ping pong

General Rami Zur

My mom spoke with General Zur for a while before he left. She then called my dad and told him that he had to get off his butt and come to Israel, too. He arrived by plane the next day. He was the first to fill me in on everything that had been going on in America since I was hospitalized. I was still without my phone and out of touch with the news. He told me that Fox News had interviewed my sister, Karen, and that multiple newspapers had run small stories about me. This media attention came as an utter shock; I did not realize anyone outside of Israel had cared. However, inside Israel there were thousands of people constantly coming into the hospital to say thank you to all the wounded soldiers.

I spent most of my time in the hospital meeting with those well-wishers, most of them strangers, and while it was overwhelming, it was also incredibly gratifying to know that the country cared and was behind me. These visits meant a lot to me, and I wanted to return the favor. As soon as I could, I started visiting the rest of my teammates in the hospital, as well as my friends from the Palsar that had been injured. Some of them were people I had carried to safety on a stretcher the day before I myself was carried out.

The five days in the hospital passed quickly. My parents stayed with me in Israel, as well as many other friends and family, many of whom I had not seen in months. I was the first of the injured from my team to be released from the hospital and, as such, it was my responsibility to visit the families of my fallen teammates and commander.

The day after I was released, Eli, the head of our Garin, my mom, and I drove and paid Shiva calls to the families of Paz, Li, and Shachar. I was the first person that was actually on the battlefield when the tragedy struck that talked to the families of the dead. Whenever I met with the families, Eli and my mother hung back at first. It was just me and the grieving families alone in a room together. I offered to answer any of their questions. Some wanted to hear about the battle while others just wanted to hear stories about their lost son in the army. This was the first time I had really spoken one on one with any of my team mate's parents. Each conversation was difficult, just as hard for me as calling my own mother a few days earlier. The trip was draining. At the end of the day, I returned to our hotel room and crashed, trying desperately to dream the nightmare away.

Two weeks later, I returned to my team. By then, the war

had ended, and we were going to begin a new operation in the West Bank. Our old commander, Gal, returned to the team for a brief time, taking over for Paz, who had fallen. The head of our unit, Neria, thought a familiar face would help us get back on our feet. It didn't really matter to me, the tragedy was still a tragedy, but it was nice to see Gal again.

Gal had only stayed with us for a month or so until we received our new commander, Shuki, who we spent the majority of our time with in the West Bank. Shuki was a tall, slender, strong Sephardi guy. He very much reminded me of Paz in many aspects. He also wanted what was best for us and made sure the team cared for one another and stuck together during the hard times.

Shuki had hurt his finger while in commanders' course and his index finger now looked like a little hook, so even though he was our commander, we always would yell Shuki and put a little hook up whenever he walked by.

Making fun of Officer Shuki

On a Saturday night, forty days after the incident, I was at home, on my kibbutz preparing to head to base when I got a text message informing me that Shahar Shalev had succumbed to his injuries. He was the last of us to fall. After Shachar Dover, Shachar Shalev had been the next closest to the blast. He had struggled for forty long and painful days in the hospital but, ultimately, did not survive. The entire team attended his funeral. I stood among the crowd, side by side with my brothers, watching as they lowered one of our own into the grave. As soldiers in uniform, we felt it necessary to appear strong and not cry. As I stood there, watching him lowered into the ground, I felt as if I were saying goodbye to all of the fallen. None of us had been able to attend the other funerals, all of us either in the hospital or still fighting in Gaza. As the funeral ended, we said our goodbyes and made sure to give the biggest of hugs to his family and to the families of all our fallen brethren.

After the funeral, we all boarded a bus together, no one daring to break the morbid silence, and headed to the West Bank where more conflicts and missions would ensue.

Final goodbye to all those that we lost–at Shahar Shalev's funeral

14

RETURNING TO THE UNIT

"There is nothing like returning to a place that remains unchanged to find the ways in which you yourself have altered." – Nelson Mandela

Getting back into the swing of military life had not been easy. After five days in a hospital and a week outside recovering, being with my parents, I was finally healthy enough to fully return to my unit and team. The war ended when I left the hospital and my team was given a week off to relax after what we had gone through. This meant that I was returning just in time to start preparing for our new operation, which would be in the West Bank.

This was a strange time for those of us who had gone straight from training to war. The war had felt like a climax that had come too soon, and now we were returning to regular duty—except that we had never done regular duty. We didn't even know what our regular duties looked like. We would spend the next month learning about our duties in times of peace, but we were shocked, feeling like war veterans yet still learning the basics of a soldier's life. Being a solider isn't entirely, or even mostly, about being at war, but we wouldn't have known that based on our brief experience.

We started this new journey by returning to our base, Bet-

Leid, where we would spend the next four to six weeks learning about our peacetime service duties. These were often combat operations, just not in a wartime setting. The nature of the terrorism that Israel faces means that the IDF must defend Israel from groups like Hamas, Hezbollah, or other isolated events of terrorism in the West Bank, even when we are not officially at war. For two weeks, we practiced various types of operations. We learned how to sneak into the West Bank unnoticed. We learned how to enter a terrorist's home and capture them at night. We learned how to operate quickly, quietly, and efficiently in order to capture the enemy without creating an incident or scene. We spent two weeks learning how to conduct those kinds of stealth operations.

In our third week, we learned how to control riots. We went out into the fields and trained with the border control units on how to use rubber ammunition, tear gas, and other non-lethal tools used for riot control. We played a riot control game in a fake urban environment constructed just for those training exercises. This was effectively an elaborate game of capture the flag. Some of us would play rioters and the others a crowd control team. The "rioters" threw tennis balls at the control team in order to simulate rocks. The control team fired tear gas back, though, of course, we used *real* tear gas because, fuck it, why not? The rioters tried to get around the control team and capture their flag. The control team was supposed to prevent the flag from being captured while also apprehending the rioters. The control team only had to touch the rioters to capture them. This all very much reminded me of playing capture the flag back in St. Louis at Solomon Schechter Day School when I was a little kid, except for the obvious stink of tear gas in the air.

The following week, we learned how to run checkpoints. We were taught important phrases in Arabic, such as "May I see your I.D.?" and "Please turn the ignition off and take the keys out." And, of course, "Open the door. This is the IDF." We learned how to perform a checkpoint, primarily by watching a video called *What Not to Do at a Checkpoint*. The video was made up of various scenarios, many of them so absurd that we all busted out laughing. My favorite scene involved two IDF soldiers stopping a man who was driving a watermelon truck. They asked the man to unload all the watermelons, one by one, so that they could inspect the truck thoroughly. The soldiers then instructed him to load the watermelons back onto the truck and scolded him for causing a traffic jam to back up at the checkpoint. We all laughed. This seemed like an obnoxious and ridiculous task, something we would never ask someone to do, but the instructors assured us that IDF soldiers had done things like that before. Almost all our rules and videos instructing us on how to act and not act were created from real life incidents that occurred in the past.

Viewed in that way, the video was somewhat profound. The lesson of the video, which was not to be a jerk, was deceptively simple. The truth was that, as IDF soldiers, we would have immense power over civilians. There is a lot of responsibility for someone who is only twenty years old, maybe not even. So, as funny as the video was, it was also important. We couldn't be jerks. We spent all week learning how not to be jerks, something my mom had taught me as a kid, but the lesson was worth repeating. Later, while doing checkpoints, I would think back to those videos to remind myself not to abuse my power or make a bad impression.

For our last week, we were mostly allowed to relax before heading to the West Bank, but first we had to attend group therapy with a psychologist. Though not officially forced to participate, we were ordered to attend the group meeting. Many of the other guys on my team already knew the psychologist, having gone to a previously forced therapy session right after the war, but this was my first time seeing him. As the session began the whole team sat in a circle about 10 minutes of awkward silence began. Eventually, Ariel, a small guy from the team who had been in commanders' course during the war and just finished and returned to the team spoke up about how he was feeling, how the war had affected him, how things were at home. I never really thought about the guys from our team that were not with us in Gaza. I can only imagine the only thing worse than being there and getting hurt, feeling like a burden, was not being there at all. But the fact that he spoke about how things were at home stuck with me. It was strange for anyone to ask about how things were at home, home life is easy, it was the army that was difficult. However, while in the army things had been generally good, we always had each other. Although there were hard times, everyone there understood how difficult things were, everyone was carrying the same pain on their shoulders, similar to carrying a heavy weight like how I would carry a person 1-1 up a mountain in training. It was almost impossible. But then when you have 2 people carry that same weight, that are going through that same pain, it becomes much lighter. When it is 4 people, under a stretcher, carrying that weight, going up and down the mountain feels easy, like you can go up several mountains now. When it's 20, the whole team, the pain seems as light as a feather at times, it feels like you can go on forever. But then you go home and all of a sudden you went from 20 people carrying that heaviness, to carrying it all on your own again. I'm not one to focus on my feelings so the next thought in my head was.. when is this going to be over and I can go back to our beach volleyball game? Our base had a gym, a boxed-in sanded volleyball court, soccer and basketball courts, and a rec room with televisions, Xbox, and a pool table. I was super excited to make use of the facilities and spend the week chilling with all the guys.

However, there isn't really such a thing as relaxation time in the army. We spent a lot of the last week working out and learning our *cav*, which was what we called the area we would be guarding, which, in our case, was Schem, a major city in the West Bank. We studied the geography, including the nearby villages and borders in the region, the city itself, as well as prior incidents that had occurred in the area. The idea was to be as prepared as possible.

At the end of the week, we were officially done with our practical training, and they shipped us out to a base by Schem, to join the rest of our unit. Upon arrival, we soon learned that the majority of our time there would be spent doing patrols. We took alternating shifts, typically doing eight hours on patrol and then eight hours off. Guarding the borders of Israel was an honor, but after being in a real war, it was also boring by comparison.

We had been in the West Bank for a week when Neria, The head commander of my unit, Palchan Tzanhanim, sat everyone down and explained his goals and expectations for our presence in the area.

"Look, I understand we have just finished a very intense trial in our lives," he said. "Many of you are still very much on edge from the war. But I want to make this one thing very clear to you all: our mission here is to keep peace and order. If you get into a situation where you need to harm someone, you have then failed your mission." This was a 180 degree turn from Gaza. We just came from hunting down terrorists and blowing up tunnels and terrorist strongholds, to what seemed like glorified policemen. The transition was strange. But now the importance of our actions changed. The head of our unit made our objective very clear: we needed to help, not hurt anyone. There always seemed to be a misconception that we were defending the Jews from the Arabs living in the area, but the real fact is that we were keeping the peace. If a Jew wanted to pick a fight with an Arab and an Arab with a Jew, they both had one thing in common, they would have to go through us first. To those of you who have never been in the West Bank, this task may seem a lot easier than it is in reality. In the West Bank everyone hates everyone. The Jewish settlers want the Arab population to leave and vice versa. There is always conflict and there seems to always be this underlying hatred, almost like a sense of racism between the two cultures.

Learning the political rules and geography in the West Bank was extremely complicated, and, although, we had to understand all the subtle differences of what and who is allowed in the A, B, and C areas along with what that even means, the overall "golden rule" that applied was what we learned in the videos, "don't be a jerk," and, hopefully, then people will be peaceful and get along.

Our Unit commander's speech served as the guide and at times a trial for my time in the West Bank.

15

RIOT

"Chaos was the law of nature; order was the dream of man." ~ *Henry Adams*

The IDF is known for its capabilities, but not every mission is a success. My unit learned this the hard way in Gaza, but we would receive gentler reminders in the West Bank. Some missions went spectacularly wrong, while others just ended up being fruitless busts.

One morning we were assigned a mission to destroy enemy tunnels in Nablus. We were to sneak into the city that night and infiltrate several target homes to search and destroy any tunnels and weapons. This was a joint mission to be carried out in conjunction with another Special Forces unit, Oketz, the elite commando dog unit. Their unit commander and several soldiers would be joining us on the mission.

We spent the day going over the basics of tunnel fighting and demolishing tunnels. We practiced interactive models beforehand, as we did with all missions, but this was our first time searching for tunnels in the West Bank. There would be a certain amount of learning on the job. We spent the whole day preparing until everyone understood their jobs and everyone else's roles, but, ultimately, there is no substitute for real world experience.

At 2:00 a.m., we loaded into several small armored vehicles and headed out. Once we got a few kilometers from the house, we hopped out and began our silent march to the target houses so that we could sneak up on them.

We exited the vehicles and began to descend the side of a mountain toward our targets. There were stairs down the mountain, since it was an urban area, though it still took us some time to descend all the way down in our gear. We regrouped at the bottom in a dark alleyway, trying to remain unseen.

We were divided into teams. Team B from my unit moved forward first, clearing the path and setting up defense positions around the house. Their job was to protect my team while we went in and worked on the tunnels. When Team B gave the word that they were in position, the commander and the breaching group went to work on the door with tools that quietly unlatch the hinges. The hinges gave a small pop and the door swung open.

They rushed in first, followed by me and three other guys. By the time my team got through the door, we saw that the breaching team had already subdued an old man who was watching television inside. They told him to stay in his chair while they questioned him about who else was in the house. They told him to talk quietly so not to alert anyone else of our presence. I searched the house while they questioned him. We immediately noticed brass panels on the floor that looked like they were covering something. I pointed the panels out to my commander. Together, we lifted the panels up to see what was underneath only to find water pipes.

We continued our search. Part of the team went outside and tried the backside of the home, but we still had no luck. In an effort to find the tunnels, we spent the next hour turning the house upside down, though we were careful not to make a mess or break anything and to always put everything back where we found it. Although the people living in this house were suspected of being terrorists and committing illegal activities, we were searching for proof, and without it there was no reason to act nasty to anyone. Not finding anything, we moved onto the other house that our intel suggested might also have a tunnel.

By this point, we felt discouraged and didn't think we would find anything. Once again, we quietly removed the door and went inside. There was no one up this time, so we started searching through the house quietly, trying not to wake up the occupants. We found no sign of tunnels and eventually abandoned the mission. It was now four o'clock in the morning, and we were supposed to be done and out of the city by five o'clock when people would start waking up for their morning prayers.

Disappointed, we headed back up the mountain to our vehicles. Everyone remained alert, as we were still very much in danger just being in the city. As we climbed the giant staircase that led up the mountain, I began to count how many damn steps there were; 420 steps in all. 420 steps that I kvetched over as I hauled my gear all the way back up, reminiscing of my time at Mikvey.

Riots were common in the West Bank. During my first riot, I was on top of a mountain, watching it transpire below. My squads' mission was to sneak up close to the town from a high vantage point and watch to make sure none of the rioters whipped out a gun or Molotov cocktail.

As the morning began, Ishay, Rapoport and I made our way down the hill where we were posted to get a closer view. Rapoport was our sharpshooter, I had the binoculars, and Ishay had the walkie talkie. As we got closer to the village, we needed to start to crawl forward so as to not be seen by anyone. Once we made it close enough to be within Rapoport's range, we hid under some small rocks and began our observation mission. However, the Arabs down in the village also did their own observation mission. We noticed that many of them would walk around, kick over trash cans and look in bushes at the outskirts of the village. I understood that they were also looking for any IDF soldiers that would be hiding and waiting for the illegal protest to commence. Then one of the men started to make his way up our hill. He walked about halfway to us when, ring ring ring my phone rang! I immediately grabbed it and turned it off, but it was too late. The Arab man had heard and was now walking in our direction. Rapoport, Ishay and I all ducked our heads under the rocks, hoping he wouldn't see us; if he did our reconnaissance mission would be for nothing. As he got fifteen feet away from us, Ishay and I prayed he would not notice us behind the rocks. At that moment, his friend down the hill called his name and he ran back down. As he left, I looked at my phone to see who could have called me at that crucial moment. It was my beloved mother, wanting to wish me a good Shabbat. Little did she know that because of her mistimed call, my life was put in jeopardy. After that close call, the illegal protest turned into a riot, as it always did. After the first 20 minutes went by, I got bored and decided to be the sportscaster for the exciting games down below.

"Two points goes to the Israelis for that amazing tear gas throw, right in the middle of the crowd. It looks as if the Arabs have cornered commander David. Will he be able to outwit them and escape? In came David's three squad members ready to bail him out. One point to the Arabs for having him call in reinforcements."

The Riot from afar

The riot from afar

After a long 6-8 hours, this mess finally concluded,

everyone got tired and began to go home, we were finally able to head back and relax for Shabbat.

My second riot was a more intimate affair. I was right in the thick of the chaos. In a way, my role was much smaller, but also more hands-on.

The riots unfolded like a game of chess, each side setting up their pieces, making the first move, and waiting to see what the opponent did next. They came out of the woodwork and set fires to tires and gathered rocks for throwing. We deployed our control units in strategic locations to take advantage of chokepoints and other exits around the village. No matter what, we could not let the riot spill over into the other nearby villages. This wasn't so hard since the village had only one major exit and entrance.

Looking for people carrying Molotov cocktails, guns, or other immediate threats to our friends' lives

My group was assigned to control the left side of the village and even enter deep into the heart of the village, if necessary. We had the low ground, which had more buildings, alleyways, urban street corners, and other hiding places that required us to be extra vigilant. Anyone could pop out and hurl rocks, or worse, at any time. Molotov cocktails were known to be a favorite of the rioters, but if this deadly bomb was used, the sharpshooters on top of the hill were supposed to take them out. Generally, to combat the sea of rocks and slingshots, we countered with tear gas and rubber bullets. However, if we ever saw a gun being aimed at us, or a Molotov cocktail about to be thrown, live fire was obviously allowed.

My group crept up to the edge of the village unseen and got down low to wait for our orders. Using a loudspeaker, the commanders on the main street ordered the rioters to stand down, but they never listened in the past, nor did they this time. They started hurling rocks at our commanders and the other soldiers on the main street. One of the rioters spotted our group to the south and yelled for his friends to retreat. They knew that if they got too close, we would swoop in, grab and arrest them. One might think, why not just go to their homes and arrest them after everything went down? The reason is that they all wore kufiyahs (religious face coverings for Muslims). We could not arrest a person without indefinite proof. So, the only way we knew to stop them was to catch them in the act. Therefore, the whole act turned into a dangerous game of cat and mouse where we did not want to get injured by rocks and they did not want to get caught and thrown in jail.

Before they could fall back, our sleeper cell team, who had camouflaged themselves inside the village, jumped into action and went after one of the individuals that appeared to be in charge of the riot. They successfully tackled him to the ground and were able to make the arrest. However, they were then surrounded by about three-dozen angry men that were hurling rocks at them.

As they were starting to get pelted by rocks and bricks, the squad I was on, including Tamir and Taye, jumped up and ran to intervene, carrying a shield in one hand and a tear gas grenade in the other. I tried to protect my friends with the shield, but quickly realized that this was futile. There were too many of them and they were attacking from all sides. The order came down to fire tear gas to break their line and give us an opening to retreat through. As the tear gas went off, the crowd started to choke and disperse, and we were able to successfully fall back to the low ground.

We regrouped and then advanced forward again. We moved into the town to push back the rioters. Along the way, we pushed up against small groups of Palestinian men, two dozen or so in a cluster, all of them chucking rocks at us. I tried to stay at the front of my chooliyot, using my shield to protect our bodies from the flying rocks as they zipped by, but my Sergeant, Tamir, pushed passed me to the front of the line.

We showed no fear, because we could not afford to look weak, but behind our tough faces we actually did fear for our safety. We were the ones with riot gear and military equipment, but it was not a battlefield and the goal was to deescalate the situation, not escalate it. Meanwhile, we were outnumbered ten to one, and if things started to go bad, they could go very bad. We weren't allowed to use firearms without prior authorization, not even to defend ourselves, because it would be deemed excessive force and we could go to jail. It was better to get beaten up than sent to prison.

We ignored those fears while holding the line and pushing forward. Though we were outnumbered, they slunk back in fear, and we quickly approached our "red line," which was the last position we intended to hold, it was a driveway with a beaten-up white sedan. Like in the war, once we reached our "red line," we did not want to continue further. However, unlike the war the reason then was because we did not want to cause duress to the innocent people living further inside the village. Again, our goal was to contain the riot. However, before I could reach the red line, a large rock struck my right shoulder. I barely felt the blow due to all the adrenaline pumping through my body. I was more concerned about my sergeant, who had pushed forward despite not having a shield. I pushed forward to shield both of us. Unfortunately, the shield wasn't big enough for two people and multiple rocks struck me. As the rocks began pelting us hard, I reached for my rifle and took aim into the crowd. By law, I was not allowed to fire on people throwing rocks at me, even if it was with a sling that could make the rock a lethal weapon. However, as I pointed my rifle at the rioters, just the sight of the rifle was enough to disperse the group.

With a moment to catch our breath, we paused to regroup. I took cover behind the truck and scanned for people throwing rocks. There was a tan house to my right with a small gate in the front and barred windows. There was a young boy in the window, no older than three, just sitting on the sill and watching us. It struck me how scary the situation must have been for him, to have armed soldiers outside of his home, fighting with the people from his village.

I took off my black mask and waved a friendly hello, and the boy gave me a look of confusion. Then I waved again and made a funny face, hoping to show him that we were friendly and meant no harm. That time the boy's face lit up with a smile that stretched from ear to ear. He waved back enthusiastically. I made another funny face, and he started to laugh, clearly enjoying the attention.

My sergeant, noticing me interacting with the boy, told me to stop. "In ten years, he'll just be another rock thrower," he said.

My sergeant was right, of course, but I didn't stop waving at the kid. Maybe, just maybe, interactions like that would keep him from growing up thinking we were bad guys.

The young men that had dispersed returned and started

throwing rocks again. We raised our weapons once again, trying to scare them away. It worked, but they just came back again. We played this game of cat and mouse for a half hour or more, them coming back to throw more rocks, us chasing them off, and then the same boys and men returning again. Our main force, which was closer to the center of town, continued to fire tear gas, which helped disperse the crowd further.

Throughout all of this, we continued to hold our ground by the house. But I never forgot the boy in the window only a few meters ahead and to the left of me. Between the volleys of rocks that came in and our reaction of lifting our rifles, which was just to scare them away, I would look over at the boy and smile and wave.

Once more, rioters joined and formed an even larger group at the center of town. We then decided to use a special armored vehicle to get closer to the protest and spray people down with water that smells like feces. The whole town center smelled literally of feces, which helped break up the crowd. The male teenagers were still throwing rocks, and we needed to keep the crowd dispersed if we were going to keep the situation under control.

I thought for a second about protests and riots and came to an understanding, the "protest" they claimed to start was never meant to be a protest at all but instead a deadly riot, as evidenced by the rock throwers, slings, and tires burning right from the beginning. And it continued…

The rock throwers kept throwing rocks. We fired more tear gas in response. At one point, a teenage boy picked up a tear gas canister and tried to hurl it back at us. This was super common, and it was never hard to pick up a tear gas canister. This happened all the time, making it almost a useless tool. His aim was poor, though, and the canister went straight through the window of the tan house in front of us. I was shocked and outraged. I had been hoping to preserve the innocence of the young boy inside. I didn't want that event to scare him and I didn't want him to hate us.

I started to rush toward the house to save the boy. I was going to break the door down and grab the canister, but Tamir stopped me. *Look up!* he exclaimed. The boy's mother had already carried him to the roof to escape the tear gas, so he was already safe. There was no point in breaking down their door and making the situation worse. As I looked back at the rioters, they seemed to laugh at me; laughing that I had cared for one of their own and was willing to put myself in harm's way in order to help them. As I looked at them, disappointed and ashamed, I tried to calm myself down and forget what a fucked-up world we lived in.

Surprisingly, the water with a scent of feces and tear gas had worked to break up the protest. I think that the addition of that 'stinky water' was enough to make most of them want to stand down and go home, but the main group was still under attack by boys throwing rocks. We rushed to their aid and pushed everyone back. At that point, the protest was mostly broken up and it was time to clear out. We fired one more round of tear gas to get everyone to back up so that we could leave without them hurling stones at our backs. The tear gas worked, causing the crowd to once again disperse long enough for us to get back to our armored vehicles. The Palestinian teenagers that had been throwing rocks had all lost interest, exhausted, stinking of tear gas and feces, they all went home.

In the end, we had succeeded in keeping the riot from getting out of control and spreading to other villages, but it was hard not to feel deflated. This was no long-term solution. There would be more protests and more riots and more rock throwers. And my sergeant was right, that boy would one day be one of them, perhaps remembering the day our tear gas canister came hurling into his home, no matter the fact that it was thrown by his own neighbor. We had stopped the riot, and successfully completed our mission, but did little to curb the ongoing problems or offer any real solution.

I felt that the most impactful act I had committed that day, to hopefully finding a real solution between the conflict of those two peoples, was when I made funny faces at the young Palestinian boy in the window. But as I thought about this, I also remembered Tamir's words, that "he would become another rock thrower one day," and I realized that he was tired. Tired of all the conflict, tired of the wars, tired of having to bury his friends from explosions, gun fires, stabbings and so on. And as I thought more about this, I realized that those on the other side must be tired, too; at least I hope they are. Tired of the conflict, the wars, tear gas, burying their dead from gun fire, explosions, and so on. But then I thought why not just come to a truce? Then as I remembered the Camp David accords in 2000 and the constant times Israel had tried to make peace, I also remembered the fact the world gives millions upon millions to these people in aid. I came to the conclusion that the issue was not those people who were throwing rocks. It was their 'elected' corrupt government that was scapegoating the State of Israel for its problems. They were taking bribes and enriching themselves instead of using the money to help the people. So, in the end, I realized that the only way any real change could happen would be a revolution, if the Palestinian people rose up against Abbas and their corrupt government in the West Bank, left the past behind them and created a reasonable peace treaty with their neighbor, then there may be peace in the Middle East. As I thought of this, I recalled the Arab Spring a few years earlier. How the Egyptian people realized that their leaders were not acting upon the people's best interests and were in fact corrupt dictators who only thought to free themselves instead of their people. The Arab Spring gave me some hope that they would then elect a government that would try to help their people and that, hopefully, those revolutions would come to Gaza and the West Bank. But they never came. Quite frankly, the grip that Abbas, the leader of the Palestinian Authority and the head of the government of the Palestinians in the West Bank, was too strong. And as strong a grip as he had, Hamas' in the Gaza Strip was that much stronger since Israel had left in 2006. So, the scapegoating and brainwashing of its citizens to blame their poverty and problems not upon those that led them but outside bodies like America and Israel continued. So, your average citizen in Gaza and The West Bank, instead of trying to find a way to change the government so they could have the freedom to succeed economically, politically and otherwise, would instead continue to burn flags, throw rocks, stab Jews, and create bombs, hoping that those actions would end their economic poverty and lack of social freedoms. And I was still there, still on the ground, trying to make sure no Arab or Jew was trying to purposely kill the other.

16

THE GOOD AND THE BAD

"We don't learn much when everything goes right. We learn the most when things go wrong."
~ Simon Sinek

On my first seyoor, or patrol, a man arrived at one of the gates we were guarding, which separated the border between the West Bank and Israel. Even though everyone knew the gate was closed and only open between 6 a.m. to 10 p.m., this man came rolling up in his car, asking for us to let him through at 11 p.m. No one was allowed to cross the gate after ten o'clock. He knew the rules but begged us to let him cross. He was with his grandmother who was having a medical emergency. Her oxygen tank was going to run out soon. She needed to get across the gate.

I explained that the gate was closed, and we weren't allowed to open it back up without permission coming down from high up the chain of command. We offered to report the situation, but we couldn't make any promises. So, we radioed in for permission to let them pass.

While waiting for permission, we went to the car to find that it wasn't just him and his grandmother, but his whole family in the car. We started to question the man about why he was over here in the first place, if his home was on the other side, the Israeli side. He continued to beg us to let him through.

One of the other soldiers who had been guarding the area for a long time knew the man because he passed through the gate every morning. The other soldier who was regarded as the vatick, or simply the one with the most experience, said that we should let them pass, though he didn't actually have the authority to open the gate at that hour and we could get in trouble for doing so. There were hospitals on both sides of the gate so the grandmother wasn't in a dire situation and would have been fine even if the oxygen ran out. They had options and would make it work, either way.

Nonetheless, after a thorough search of the car and none of the passengers turning up anything suspicious, and since we had a fellow IDF soldier who had been working in the area for over a year and a half vouching for the man, we opened the gate and waved him through. This was totally illegal. We would have been in major trouble if someone found out, but it felt like the right thing to do. We would have felt awful, of course, if something had happened because we broke the rules. The rules were there for a reason. But we also wanted to show kindness and felt that their reasons and pleas were sincere.

After the car had crossed over, I felt proud. I had just helped this Palestinian family in crisis. More importantly, we set a precedent that I have learned is shared by the whole of the IDF. To keep the peace, we needed to be an example of morality. Yet, we also must be incredibly cautious and avoid being naïve. Naïveté will get people killed. So, after checking the person's story, having a soldier vouch for the man, and checking the vehicle of all weapons, we could then consciously break our rule and let the man pass through our gate and rush his grandmother to the hospital. This action not only made me feel personally proud but to also be working in a place where this was the code of conduct, made me proud to be an Israeli.

Not every mission worked out so well, as I learned when we engaged in a joint operation to sneak into an Arab village known for housing Hamas operatives. This was a complex operation with different teams carrying out different objectives all within a few blocks from each other. My team's mission was to capture a man named Anas. He was a terrorist who was known for being involved in the deaths of over a hundred Israelis and was a bomb maker. He always carried a gun on him, and we were told that he slept with one under his pillow. However, the guys on my team said that his name, Anas, in Hebrew, meant rape. "We are going to rape the rapist," the guys on my team kept saying and laughing.

We trained all day for the mission, running over different scenarios so that we would be ready for whatever came, and headed out a little after midnight. We met at a rendezvous point a little outside of the village where the different teams split up to go their different ways. It was past two o'clock in the morning when we started to move forward.

Ready to go out on a mission in the West Bank

My team and the Palsar team were together since our missions were two blocks away from one another. On our way to the village, we had to cross a small farm with a bright exterior light. We were about a hundred meters from the farm, on the side of a hill, when a dog started barking. A farmer came outside to investigate. The dog was barking in our direction, trying to alert its owner who trudged up the hill toward us. He spotlighted two of the guys from the Palsar unit that were in front of the group. Realizing that he was looking at a military operation, he spun around and turned to run.

The soldiers up front ordered him to stop, but he kept running. "Stop or I'll shoot you," one of the soldiers said. This was a bluff, but it worked, and the man stopped. We swooped in and detained him but didn't know what to do with him. He didn't seem like an enemy combatant, but if we let him go, he might alert the people in the village and ruin the mission. This reminded me of the movie *Lone Survivor*, but this was real life. Since our mission was only going to take one night, we decided to handcuff and blindfold the farmer and bring him with us on the mission.

We pressed forward and came to a road that led to the heart of the village. This was where we were supposed to peel off from the Palsar and conduct our mission. My commander and I met with the commanders from the Palsar to confirm that we were ready to split up. It was at this time that the Palsar decided to unload the prisoner on our team, which was baggage and a liability that no one wanted while on a mission. We didn't argue though and had to take the prisoner with us. The commander of the raid was the unit commander of the Palsar, and he was calling the shots.

The commander of the Palsar pointed to the house that we needed to capture. "See those lights up there?" he asked. "That's your guy's home."

This was not the house that we had mapped out, but the one next door. Our new commander, Eyal, assumed that we had just gotten the location wrong. Shuki was finally getting surgery for his hooked finger. and Eyal, our new commander was taking his place while he recovered. He had just started the job and did not know us very well yet.

Our team pushed forward, Eyal and I leading the way. We made a hasty advance on the house which turned out to be a mistake because Tamir in the back, who was tasked with watching the captured farmer, was not able to keep up, and his chooliyot in the back of the line fell behind and got lost. Unaware that we were missing a full third of our twelve-man team, the rest of us pushed forward quickly, closing in on the house, which was now 200 meters away. Rushing to keep up with the commander, none of us noticed the four men were gone.

We opened the unlocked front gate, rushed into the courtyard and closed in on the house. My group of four men took up a position in front of the house, and we waited for the other two groups to get into position so that once we infiltrated the building, they would have every escape route covered. We now had two groups in place, but the third group was nowhere to be found. It was only then that we realized that we had left them behind.

Everything started to go wrong and, to make things worse, the commander of the Paratrooper Special Forces was behind us, watching the whole calamity unfold. We were missing Tamir's entire chooliyot. On top of that, my commander's walkie-talkie had started malfunctioning and was unable to hear our sergeant, Tamir, yelling at him over the radio. We had to stay there in front of the house, dangerously exposed in enemy territory, waiting for the third chooliya to arrive. Twenty minutes went by and Tamir made his way to us absolutely livid, having gone to the wrong home next door because no one had told him that the Palsar commander had changed the target house at the last minute.

The next problem we figured, right before we barged in, was the other house was not the wrong house. *We* were at the wrong house. The Palsar commander had given us the wrong location after all, which we only discovered when we radioed in for permission to bust in the doors and capture the guy inside (Intelligence had drones overhead watching us). Being at the wrong location, we had to wait another five minutes to confirm that we were at the wrong house from the intelligence teams. The whole thing felt like a sitcom, some great dumb tragedy of errors.

We regrouped and headed to the house next door. The house was fenced in, so we picked the easiest looking gate to break through. Another bad call. The team tasked with breaking open the gate spent five minutes trying to do so unsuccessfully. They eventually called me to just try and pry it open with a crowbar, making a ton of noise in the process. Then suddenly, a middle-aged man in pajamas came out to politely open the gate that we were supposed to have quietly broken down on our own.

We rushed in past him, but it was too late. We hadn't taken

up proper positions around the house. If the target had been there, he very well could have escaped by now.

While the other two chooliya's took up positions around the house, others questioned the man that had answered the door. They searched him for weapons, finding nothing, and then the *Shabak*, or the Israeli version of the FBI, questioned him in Arabic. Not knowing Arabic, I had no idea what they were asking him, but was later revealed that the target terrorist no longer lived there.

In the end, the whole mission was a waste of time and an utter embarrassment. We had fumbled almost every aspect of the mission and all our best-laid plans had gone straight into the garbage. Worst of all, the whole thing had transpired right before the eyes of the new head of the paratrooper Special Forces, or otherwise known as our *magad*, which added further insult to injury.

17

OPERATION DEAD LEG

"The best defense is a good offense." ~ ***Jack Dempsey***

The mission was a two-part operation. First, we would sneak into Cfar Kadoom, an Arab village, and camouflage ourselves to remain undetected in the environment. The name sounds like it should be out of an Indiana Jones movie; however, this village is that stinky little place with all the riots, I spoke of earlier. Second, we would lure those who were known for causing unrest and antagonizing riots within the village outside and capture them in the act of attempting to start another riot.

We performed a dry run of the first half of the operation, sneaking into the village, a week before the actual mission. We slipped into the village at three o'clock in the morning, while everyone was fast asleep, and held our locations for an hour to make sure they were solid and undetectable. Before entering the village for the first time, a cold chill went down my spine, the same cold chill I got before every mission. While not pleasant, this feeling kept me alert, sharp, and on my toes.

We had to take a long path around the village to avoid a dog. Any barking would likely have awakened the people, so we walked to another side of the village and entered through an olive tree forest. We took soft steps to avoid crumpling leaves or breaking sticks. Any noise could have been too much noise. The most difficult part about sneaking into the village was passing through a field of cut grass that offered little cover or camouflage. In order to remain undetected, we moved forward in waves. Two men went first, traversed fifty yards or so, and then assumed a prone position in the field, aka, they lied down. Then two more would head to that position while the original two moved to the next spot. In this way, we avoided too much simultaneous movement that might have resulted in detection. As there were eighteen of us, this maneuver looked very much like a snake constantly weaving through the short cut grass

Moving quickly but quietly, we made our way to the center of the village without alerting anyone to our presence. However, we would then have to turn inward and enter the lights of the village, where it would be almost impossible to hide. As we approached the lights, a dog in the middle of the village started to bark. I jumped back quickly, trying to hide, understanding that this could ruin the entire mission. We waited for several long seconds for the dog to quiet down and to be sure that no one was coming outside to investigate. When, after several minutes, no one in the village stirred, we believed we were safe to come out and continue.

We had to move in faster now, ducking into corners and shadows rather than lying flat as we had in the field. This allowed us to take advantage of the terrain and move faster, quickly reaching the target location, a garden-like area where we could take and hold a position undetected. We hunkered down and waited for the other groups to radio us that they too had reached their own positions. Several minutes passed and, just as we were starting to get comfortable, we received the radio call to leave. Everyone had reached their locations and we could now go. We exited the village just as quickly and quietly as we had come. The trial run was a success. Aside from a single dog spotting us, we had entered the village and left without anyone knowing we were there.

A week later, we performed the same operation once more, only this time it was for real. We prepared our equipment, went over a first aid drill in case anyone was injured during the mission, and then ran more drills involving the takedown and apprehension of the enemy so that we would be ready when the time came. Those 'simulations' were similar to my high school football drills in that we would close off all means of escape and corner the target, grab him by force and not let go until the target was down on the ground. We practiced tackling in pairs, which is how we would perform the operation, ganging up on the targets so that we could overpower and incapacitate them quickly. The drills went smoothly, and we felt fully prepared for the task at hand.

That night, we put on our gear and parked outside the village a good distance away to avoid detection of the vehicles. The big difference was that instead of waiting until 3 a.m., we began the operation at midnight because we needed to find that perfect time where everyone was in their homes but not asleep. We would attempt to bait the enemy outside of the home by having an army vehicle drive in and honk a few times. This would trigger the target from leaving his house, and he would go outside and attempt to start a violent riot with the goal of killing those inside the vehicle while those of us waiting in the bushes would be able to catch him in the act.

We were divided into two groups with distinct roles and gear. Some of us would be fully armed and equipped to offer cover and protection. The rest, including myself, were going in with no guns and almost no gear, nothing except for a helmet and bulletproof vest. We were tasked with running in first and taking down the target, while our friends with weapons and equipment would cover us from any outside threats.

Exiting the vehicles and entering hostile territory without even a gun made me feel naked. However, confident in my teammates' abilities, I was not worried. Once again, we snuck into the village, around the dog, past the olive trees, and through the field. We moved confidently, having done this before, but carefully. When we came upon the second dog in the village center, we were then aware of his presence and quickly maneuvered around her without causing her to bark.

We were getting ready to make our move when we heard a car heading our way. My group ducked behind the corner of a house. We had only a second to find cover, ducking behind whatever we could find—a potted plant, a stairwell, a telephone pole, anything that provided even a bit of cover before the car passed by. I leapt behind a trash can, stood still, my heart pounding, as the car rolled by. Thankfully, the driver did not notice any of us.

When the car passed us, we immediately got back into position. We then had to wait for phase two of the mission, which consisted of nabbing the target. The second in charge of our unit, Boaz, was supposed to drive a big armored vehicle directly into the middle of the village and honk a few times in order to draw out the enemy.

My chooliyot was hiding in a garden under one of the villager's homes. A ten-foot wall and several buildings surrounded the garden, giving us plenty of cover. We could hear voices in the nearby houses, the sounds of casual conversation. It gave me an eerie feeling to be hiding so close to people that, if they knew we were there, would emerge and try to kill us.

We waited until we saw the lights in the distance of our Israeli vehicle. As he rolled into town, Boaz honked the horn three times. We watched as lights flicked on in the various houses. We could then hear more men talking only a few feet away, so close that we could have participated in the conversation, if only we spoke more Arabic. Peeking over the wall, we saw a few people starting to gather, but we did not act. We held back, waiting for the crowd to grow. We wanted to be sure that our target, one of the leaders, was in the group.

Eventually, the crowd moved forward and advanced on the vehicle. Although we could not see them from within our position, we could hear them starting to throw bottles and rocks at the car. We then had legal grounds to arrest them. I looked over at Tamir who was waiting like an angry bulldog ready to be let off the chain. He told me that there was a man in a red sweatshirt; he was our target.

Over the radio, I waited on the toes of my feet, ready to sprint, and then I heard, "Cod cod 3,2,1, Tzeh!" and sprung from my hiding place in the garden and sprinted toward the crowd. Another team was coming up from behind and we trapped the leader between us. I spotted the man in the red sweatshirt who, realizing that we were coming for him, tried to make a break for it. I darted toward him and he tried to dodge, but my commander stuck out a foot and tripped him. The man went flying onto the ground. I leapt and tackled him, pinning him to the ground. Within moments, five of my teammates had swooped in to hold him down. We each had one of his limbs. My weight was on his back. He tried to struggle but was outnumbered. There was no resisting. I zip-tied his arms and legs and we carried him to the armored vehicle.

Within seconds, everyone was inside the vehicle too, with the terrorist bound and blindfolded. The driver raced away from the village. Several rocks struck the armored car, but no one cared. We had succeeded and were jumping for joy inside the armored vehicle.

Afterward, one of the commanders said that no one had thought the mission would be a success. There were too many things that could have gone wrong. Fortunately, everyone did their job well, the stars aligned, and we got our guy.

Finishing the dry-run for Operation Dead Leg

Eating schnitzel at 2 a.m. after a successful mission in the West Bank

18

ALL I WANT IS TO GO HOME AND ENJOY SHABBAT

"Honesty is a very expensive gift, don't expect it from cheap people." ~ *Warren Buffet*

We arrived at a scheduled protest to find no activity. It was rainy and cold, and we were standing in mud an inch thick. There was a Palestinian man with a microphone who told us we could go home because there would not be a riot that day. Normally, we wouldn't take such claims at face value, but everything seemed peaceful. My commander and I talked to the guy in charge, and he assured us that nothing was going on, there was nothing scheduled, even though they did have the microphone already out. If their claims were true, and there wasn't any violence, then we had no reason to be there. This was a compelling point. I asked Boaz, the second in command of my unit, what we were even doing there when there was no riot, no violence, and no objective.

Boaz told me not to listen to them. "Our best defense is a good offense," he said. "We should wait at the entrance to the town until the actual illegal protest begins at 12:30."

The shitty muddy scene

None of us really wanted to stay. Rain was pouring down and we all just wanted to go back to base and relax on Shabbat, but we had to stay and stand guard. As the time grew near, we saw a few men starting to put down roadblocks, which is technically illegal, and taunted us to respond. They knew how to get under our skin. The Palestinian son of a bitch in charge, or we assumed he was in charge because of his microphone, told us to watch out for the border police who were behind us because they might just shoot us in the back. He was referring to a friendly fire incident that had happened two days before in which the border police accidentally shot and killed one of their own during training. If they were trying to make a provocation, it worked. Then Boaz took out a tear gas gun and unloaded the entire clip, all six rounds, at them, which was in his right given that they were putting up illegal roadblocks. This was all the justification we needed to respond. Although I knew we had legal justification to do this, this felt like an overreaction. For us to respond to their taunts this time felt beneath us. However, trying not to be a jerk when the people on the other side are literally provoking you is very difficult.

After that exchange, things went quiet again. They stood in one area and we stood across from them at the edge of the village, just staring at each other. Occasionally, someone threw a rock our way, but they were infrequent and small enough that we just ignored them. Nothing like the sea of rocks coming through the air at the first two riots I encountered. We stood at the edge of the village, waiting in the rain for the protest to begin. Normally, they start in the afternoon, but we had been there for hours and nothing happened. It was now getting close to one o'clock, and we hoped that we would be able to leave soon. Maybe nothing would happen, we thought, but Boaz wanted us to wait a little while longer, just to be safe.

We did not have to wait long. Ten minutes later, the streets filled with more than a hundred illegal protesters. They had lied! There was going to be a protest all along and they knew it. The protest quickly got out of control and turned into a riot. They started throwing rocks at us in mass and burning tires. With things getting quickly out of control, our sleeper cell inside the village burst out of their camouflaged hiding spot and jumped into action. Suddenly, all hell broke loose. We converged on the rioters from one side while the sleeper cell advanced on the other. The rioters scurried every which way, and it turned into a stampede.

My squad met up with the sleeper cell team just as they had captured a man. We later discovered that he was a Palestinian policeman who was supposed to help keep the peace but had joined the riot, which was illegal and could cost him his job. However, we were not allowed to bring him to our Israeli jail due to political reasons, I think. This is what we were up against: even their own police were instigating violence and unrest. You never knew whom you could trust in these villages.

While sprinting toward our comrades, I tossed a small tear gas grenade a few meters in front of our squad in front of the rioters to create a wall of smoke and confusion. I didn't have a smoke grenade, so tear gas was the next best thing.

This allowed the sleeper cell team to retreat safely with the new captive. We formed a line inside the village to establish a control point, but the rioters wouldn't relent and continued bombarding us with rocks. Equipped with a modification for my gun, I shot a few more tear gas canisters into the crowd to force them back, as they were now too close for comfort. The closer they were, the more easily they could hurl larger rocks that could kill and maim rather than just sting. Maintaining distance was important to de-escalation.

One of their rocks bounced up off the ground and smacked me in the leg, but there was too much adrenaline in my body to care. I needed to stay focused. I rushed south through a hailstorm of rocks with two other guys to take control of the southern streets of the village. We wanted to lock down the village. We were met with little resistance at first, but the further we moved into the village, the more rocks came hurling at us. I fired a few more tear gas canisters to move the rioters back and temporarily stop the rock throwing. The way clear, for the moment, we continued forward to take the road. My squad and I were at the forefront now, sprinting forward, taking land. I reloaded my tear gas gun on the go and fired several more rounds into the crowd to defend my friends.

We made our way to our red line the same beaten-up white sedan, its windshield and windows now shattered by the rock throwers. The Palestinians were still on the offense, throwing rocks and even hurling them at us with slingshots that could send a rock whipping through the air at 100 miles an hour. These were serious threats, and though we did not have permission to return lethal force (even though their rocks were plenty lethal), we were still able to keep them at bay with tear gas.

The 3 of us at Kfar Kadoom

Several Palestinian protestors took cover behind a pink two-story building about fifty meters away, close enough to keep attacking. There was a straight path to the building, obstructed only by a small blue gate. I pointed the path out to my commander, suggesting that we could sprint forward, jump the gate, move through the tear gas, and grab several of the rioters to make an arrest while we had the building as cover. We decided against that option, since our gear would have slowed us down too much to have any chance of catching someone.

Instead, we held our ground by the Toyota, avoiding the volleys of rocks and returning a few tear gas shots back and forth. Demissie, one of the Ethiopian soldiers in my squad, was at my side. The Palestinians kept shouting at him, hollering, "Nigger, nigger, nigger." They wanted to get a rise out of him with those taunts. Demissie was one of the shorter guys on our team, but also one of the toughest. He did not like being made fun of and he certainly did not like that word lobbed at him. The more they shouted it, the madder he got. I started to get angry on his behalf, and at one point I went up to the front of the line, past our red line, and dared them to come face me instead.

We eventually started to run low on tear gas, which was a problem given that they would never run out of rocks. We still had our guns, but it would have been both considered immoral and illegal to shoot them when they were "only" throwing rocks. The rocks were dangerous, though, but we had armor and shields, and would be okay. We used the car as a shield.

I got it in my head to fire a blank cartridge at the attackers in order to scare them away. I thought they might retreat if they thought we were firing live ammunition. This ended up being a bad idea. The blank didn't do anything but hurt my ears and cause them to ring. I had to take a step back until the ringing stopped and regain my composure.

Tamir took out one last tear gas grenade, the last we had on hand, gave it to me and told me to make it count. I loaded the grenade, took aim at my target, a twenty-something Palestinian man throwing rocks, and pulled the trigger. As I shot the canister, everything turned into slow motion and I could see that it looked like it was going to hit him in the head, giving us the opportunity to run up and grab him, but then it curved, hit a lamppost, and shot off to the side. Utterly disappointed, I started cursing up a storm.

As we took cover behind the car, eventually the rioters lost interest in us and turned their attention to the soldiers that were still trying to defend themselves on the main street. They had just brought in another armored truck, the same as the one in the last riot, and again used it to spray sewage water at the rioters. This is a standard part of the riot routine, which was so clockwork that it almost seemed choreographed. When the tear gas didn't work, you brought out the armored sewage trucks. The truck started spraying the crowd, sending them scurrying for cover.

Over on the southern side, we eventually started getting bored, especially as the action died down, but there were still a few men near the pink house a hundred meters in front of us. One or two were still slinging rocks and taunts, mostly at Demissie. Suddenly, he hit his breaking point, and in a burst of anger, he threw his shield to the ground and started to charge the two men. Tamir yelled for him to stand down, but Demissie ignored the orders and plowed forward. Tamir and I ran after him, trying to drag him back, but we couldn't catch up. He raced towards the men who had been calling him names, but by the time he reached their position by the house, they were long gone. Not weighed down by gear, they had darted and slipped away easily. I was thankful that they had bolted; the last thing we needed was Demissie beating up some ignorant teenagers. Tamir, Demissie and I then ran back to the cover of the car. Rocks came flying at us as we fell back, but luckily no one was hit.

More time passed and the flow of the riot carried on. When it was clear that things were not calming down, the decision was made to push further into the town and squelch the riot more aggressively. Our team pushed forward and took the pink house, this time taking and holding the building, which we did without any issues.

At that point, the protestors seemed to realize that they were not going to be able to scare us off or wait us out, and the riot finally began to cool down. Our main group made one last counter offensive, firing twenty to thirty rounds of tear gas into the village before pulling back. The other squads prepared to make an exit. However, our squad held back while the others left. The pink house was a prime position to ambush a rioter or terrorist so that we could make another arrest before heading back. After being pelted with rocks all day, we wanted at least one of them to pay. We hid and waited in ambush.

Eventually, a few Arab men walked by on the road, though they were too far away to grab quickly. Rather than advance on them, we ducked down, but just as we moved, they spotted us. We heard them calling out to others that there were still soldiers in the area. They started to gather around our squad, trying to pelt us with a barrage of rocks. We were able to dodge their rocks as we fell back and rejoined the rest of our team.

We headed back to Kadumim, the town that we had just protected, where we regrouped and discussed the riot. The mission was deemed a success. We had held our ground and kept things from getting too out of hand or spilling into another nearby village. No one got seriously injured on either side. We had captured a dirty cop, who was instigating riots, but due to the political agenda, we could only let him go and tell his commanding officers of his actions. I have a feeling that did nothing.

Our spirits lifted by the satisfaction of a job well done, we piled into our armored car and headed back to base. We reeked of tear gas so bad that our throats burned, and our eyes watered throughout the ride.

This was one of my last missions in the field as full-time military personnel. My service had come full circle and soon I would be leaving the IDF, having finished the three years of my service. I would cut my military ID card and be given my gold reservists ID.

It was often said that the real service starts once you enter the reserves. If this is true, I would have the next twenty-three years to find out.

When I first started my journey to Israel and the IDF, I was young, idealistic and driven to protect and serve the State of Israel. The fact is that Israel is the Jewish homeland and when things in the world get bad, as history has taught, there is one safe haven for us to go to, a country we can call our own. However, this philosophy, which permeated my entire being and gave me the courage to take the first step into supporting and defending the State of Israel, was not enough for me to come back year and year again always to train and be ready to defend her. No, such a commitment only comes from a more personal perspective, what I now have.

My Tzevet, my Garin, my adopted family, my cousins, and many close friends and family friends are all living their dreams in this country, and I know I could call each of them in a split second when the chips are down and they ask for help. Knowing that feeling of loyalty, deep inside me, without a second thought, those people with whom I trained and went to war, whom I call my brothers, would lift me onto their stretcher and carry me. And likewise, when the chips are down for them, who will lift the stretcher and carry them? I could never allow anyone other than myself to take on such a responsibility, such an honor. And for this reason, I return year in and year out. And although I do not currently live in the State of Israel, I know that I am currently on a journey, a journey to better myself, so when I do return, I will return with the knowledge and skills that I can use to help make the country Israel an even greater place to be.

19

COMMANDING THE GIBUSH

"The end of all our exploring will be to arrive where we started" ~ *T.S. Elliot*

It was 2 a.m. and the newest recruits were just now filing into the plugot, preparing to undertake gibush Yechatiot, as I had done just over two years ago, which now felt like a lifetime. Four of us waited for them to come and get the gear they would be working with throughout the trial. From behind our dark sunglasses, we watched them stream in, the looks on their faces fearful and hopeful, though they could not see our faces behind the dark sunglasses.

I was a Gibush Yechatiot instructor, though I wore no symbols or identification that would indicate my unit. They weren't supposed to know who was judging them, only that they were being judged, so that they would not be able to tailor their performance toward a specific person. We simply wore the dark sunglasses, black fleeces, and our special forces boots. I was quite aware, having experienced this myself, just how intimidating we looked. The sunglasses were specifically used to keep a distance between the instructors and the "kids."

Perhaps most intimidating of all, more than the dark glasses and the black fleeces, were the notepads and pens with which we would take notes. We noted every single thing they would do over the coming days. We wanted them to feel like they were under constant surveillance, not just near constant, so we often doodled in our notepads so that they would think they were being observed and documented even when they really weren't. Of course, we also took plenty of real notes, too, but the point was to never let them feel like the pressure was off.

The first activity of the day was a short march, without stretchers; just a quick hike to get their blood pumping. This was my first time being an instructor, and I struggled to keep up while taking down notes. I had to keep up physically while also making sure to write down who was doing what. We wrote down who finished first, who fell behind, and who was stuck around the middle of the pack. We noted who helped others and who did not.

After the march, we took them to these newly built sand-pits, where most of the work would be done that day. Now I was the one shouting, "Tzeh! Tzeh!" over and over again as the kids sprinted up and down the dunes and through the pits. We had them running for hours, sprinting back and forth.

There were only a few instructors from my unit with this group and we focused on assessing different things. Another person was writing down where each man placed in each sprint, which freed me up to focus on small details and the finer nuances of their performance. I noted who pushed others, who made sure to actually touch the line before doubling back, who really gave it their all every time, even if they didn't finish first, who finished with a smile versus who clearly hated every minute of it. I wrote all these things down in my notebook next to each person's number. I had no idea what their names were still, only their numbers, which is all we needed at this point and all we thought of them.

Of course, despite being just "numbers," many of them started to stand out to me. Some smiled more than others. Some worked harder than others. Some were more honest and dedicated. We made it a point to watch those specific "numbers" even more carefully, which would have been scary to them if they knew, but in fact was a good thing. Being noticed was generally a good thing, as long as you weren't being noticed for the wrong things. But not being noticed at all, and descending into mediocrity, would hurt their chances of selection into an elite unit just as badly as doing things poorly. We would rank them all, from most likely to succeed to least likely, but only the top few would make it into one of the three elite units: Maglan, Palchan Tzanhanim, Palsar Tzanhanim, of which they were being judged in this try out.

As the gibush continued, we moved on to other activities. We did crawling next, then sprinting, then Alunkah Sosiometri with the stretchers. Tzeh! Tzeh! Tzeh! We pushed them and pushed them, trying to see how much harder we could push. They were given the occasional water break, but no real rest, before being pushed again even harder.

Every physical act they did received a score and an assessment. At the end of the day, we tallied up the scores and ranked the different numbers. Everyone was divided into one of three categories based on where they ranked. But these were still just numbers, not people, and we were ranking more than just their scores. Where someone placed in each activity, their raw numbers, definitely mattered, but so did how much they chose to help teammates or the fact that they touched the line each and every time they did another lap. Many of them didn't even notice whether or not they did these things, completely uninformed on what exactly they were being judged on. Some simply practiced the behaviors as a matter of character, and that, in addition to their raw stats, was what we were screening for.

We wanted to know their subconscious habits and the nature of their characters just as much, even more actually, than how fast they could run or crawl. We took special note when someone's behavior changed based on whether they knew they were being watched at the time.

We observed everything they did, and not just when they were working out or drilling, but between exercises as well. When it was time to eat, we made note of who helped open up cans and make sandwiches. We noted who organized things. We noted who worried about the religious kid's food when they went away to pray during mealtimes.

After all the marches, sprints, crawls, drills, and other activities were done for the day, we headed back to our rooms and crunched the numbers and compared notes. After the first day, we more or less knew who were the best and the worst. They were the easiest to spot. What we didn't always see were the people in the middle. While we had no intention of taking people in the middle who performed mediocrely, many people would get better and start to shine as the gibush wore on.

On the second day, we would have more data points and we could start to see who was rising or falling within the ranks, as well as those who stayed in place. These different data points were relevant as we focused on different things, depending on the day. They basically always had to sprint and crawl and carry a stretcher, but on the second day we had them perform mental challenges, in addition to the physical trials. These were important things to know. The best soldier is not the strongest or fastest. Soldiers have to think fast, especially in Special Forces, and act on their feet. We were looking to see who was the smartest, who could think outside the box, and who were the most team oriented.

We had many different tasks that helped reveal the nuances of their characters. For example, one task involved having them dig a hole for themselves, as well as one big hole for the team. Their personal hole had to be big enough for them to fit in and the group hole had to be big enough to hold everyone's bags. We took note of who focused on their own hole without paying attention to the group hole. We paid attention to who only worked on the group hole and paid no attention to their own hole, this was also not good. In this exercise there are many qualities that can stand out, such as:

leadership, how one organizes their work, if one can find a 'creative solution,' where one focuses most of their attention, because in the time limit we gave them, it was going to be extremely difficult for the team to successfully accomplish both tasks. So, the nuts and bolts of why they chose to do what they did was very important.

We especially took note when the "numbers" displayed leadership skills, as well, as this was the sign of a potential future officer, instructor, or commander—or even just a good team player that could adapt to changing situations and take responsibility when necessary. Specifically, we took note of who naturally took charge and stepped up to make decisions and keep things organized. In addition, we took note of who delegated the workload or organized the group.

As the gibush continued, I became attached to the numbers who consistently performed well. They reminded me of myself and my friends, which made sense, as the best-performing "numbers" were the type of people that would eventually make it into the same elite units that we had. We pushed those who underperformed, trying to either break them down and make them quit, or force them to step up and prove themselves. Of course, we also challenged those that performed well just as hard, if not harder. We wanted the gibush to be as challenging as possible. We intentionally tested and toyed with the best performers, sometimes making up excuses to send them back to start over. We wanted to see how they would react to this kind of treatment, whether they would bristle against it in frustration or do what was asked of them without questioning or getting angry.

More than the physical tests, we learned about the "numbers" through how they performed on mental challenges and group exercise. There were many intellectual challenges, some as simple as taking a gun apart and putting it back together on their own, while others were complex group challenges that tested how well they worked together to solve problems. For one activity, they had to work together to tie a knot in a rope while their hands were bound together behind their backs. This allowed us to see what creative solutions they came up with to work with the rope, using their hands and teeth and each other's bodies to stabilize and manipulate the rope, it also showed us how well they worked together as a team.

Finally, we also had them speak about themselves, as we had done in our own gibushim. There was no better way to get to know our "numbers" than by letting them speak for themselves. They were asked to speak about something they cared about in front of twenty people who had been complete strangers until they entered this ordeal together only the day before, as well as a panel of commanders that were taking notes on everything they said. While they talked, we took notes on what they said, as well as on who was listening intently rather than just playing in the grass. Sometimes, we stopped and asked the audience to repeat what the speaker had said, just to be sure they were paying attention to their teammates.

As for lone soldiers, who may have been weak at Hebrew, as I was, we tested to see how resourceful they were at keeping up and understanding everything. It didn't matter necessarily that they couldn't understand everything that was said, only that they tried to keep up. I ended up quizzing the lone soldier in our group on what one kid said to make sure he had understood. I felt a sense of compassion for him, having been in the same shoes myself.

The speaking was but a small part of the gibush, of course. Afterward, we had them go back to more crawling and sprinting. Tzeh, tzeh, tzeh! These physical tests were just as much of a mental test as anything else, especially as the days wore on. We would make them run, and crawl, and sprint, and hike, and carry the loaded-down stretchers without break, for hours on end, not just to see if they could physically do it, but to see if they had the mental fortitude to maintain the same high level performance that they started with, no matter how excessive or ridiculous our requests became. We were trying to see if we could break them down, just as they had tested me. Some of them broke down and quit, which was fine—better here than on the battlefield with lives on the line.

Tzeh, Tzeh, Tzeh! We ran them harder and harder. In between the running, the mental and speaking tests had given their bodies a break, but not their minds, which allowed us to push them harder when we returned to the physical exams. We made sure to watch and see who was slowing down and who was still pushing their hardest.

We had all kinds of other mind games to test their morale. We often only took the numbers of the top performers allowed, calling out their rank in the run and their number, and then had them do a sprint, as they ran we would surreptitiously jot down other people's numbers so that they would think they had to come in near the front to get "credit" at all. We toyed with their minds and tested their confidence and resolve by encouraging them to quit. We told them we were only interested in the top three people there, and if that wasn't them, they should just leave then and stop wasting everyone's time.

About six to eight people from each group were taken into one of the three elite units, but we wanted them to think that their chances were much lower. In truth, those taken weren't necessarily the top physical performers, they might even come from the bottom, because we were judging them holistically, looking at the whole package. As commanders, we knew that teams needed many types of people. A team does not need a hundred big, brawny stupid soldiers. We need a few of those, but we also need people who can think for themselves, follow directions, rally morale, work with maps and logistics, and carry out the millions of other tasks that soldiers need to be able to do in a modern military.

Eventually night came, and we ended the physical part of the exam and sent them to bed, back to the tiny tents that they had constructed. However, before releasing them for the day, we administered a sociometry in which they would rank the performance of everyone in the group. They were allowed to add comments as well, which we took into serious consideration because we realized that there were dynamics within the group that they observed from the inside, that we might have missed as outside observers. After all, they were trying to get onto teams in which they would have to work together. They needed to get along and work well together.

The next morning, we returned and met with them. This time, we did not wear our sunglasses or the black fleeces. We wore shirts that proudly displayed the symbol of our units. We gathered them into a group and told them our names and explained who we were and what we did in the IDF. We gave them personal details about our lives inside and outside of the military. We also invited them, the "numbers" to tell us their names. These kids were no longer just numbers, but people again, and while they would not all make it into one of the units, we were proud of them for finishing the gibush. It was a strange feeling listening to them talk, seeing them as real people and not just performers to be judged.

Also strange was talking about myself. Many of them asked questions about my service, and about Tzuk Eitan, Operation Protective Edge, as they had heard some of the major stories about my unit and team. I hadn't expected these kids to know about any of these things, and it made me feel like a kind of celebrity. But that is the nature of Israel, a small and close-knit country with such a monolithic national identity.

Before letting them go, we wished them luck in the next and final phase, which was the personal interview. While we would be performing interviews, everyone interviewed candidates that were not with them during the physical exam, so there would be no preconceived notions.

The interviews ran for fifteen to thirty minutes and followed a strict format. The soldier sat in a chair before a long table where six seated commanders asked questions, listened, and took notes. This was not the easiest setting in which to give an interview, which was the whole point. We were still testing them, trying to learn about how they handled stress and pressure.

When I moved onto the group that I would be with to conduct interviews, little did I know that many of the reserve soldiers there were the same men that interviewed me two years ago. And not only that, but when I asked them about my gibush, they remembered. They must have done four gibushim since mine, but they still remembered me. It was a funny and a nice reunion, especially now sitting behind the table as equals and no longer in the solo chair facing everyone.

One of the commanders in my group started each interview the same way: "So, we know 'so-and-so' the crawler, the sprinter, and the stretcher carrier. Now we'd like to know 'so-and-so' the person."

The recruits would then tell their life stories. We would interrupt them throughout to ask them questions in order to learn about their motivations, but also to test their self-confidence. We wanted to see how they reacted to being interrupted or questioned. We tried to ask hard questions that would stump them or make them reconsider their claims. We paid attention to each little detail about how they spoke, what they said, even how they entered and exited the room. Whether or not someone closed the door behind them and how; this said something about the person's confidence, eagerness, forgetfulness, and many other traits.

At some point during the interview, we always asked about whether they drank alcohol or smoked. These were two very important questions to us. Everyone thinks they have to answer no and no, but this is not true. I was a twenty-two-year-old guy, a soldier, and would go out and party, and not long ago I, too, was an 18-19-year-old recruit. I knew very well what everyone did. We typically already knew the answer, and didn't care either way, but we wanted them to be honest. I would have loved nothing more than a funny story about something stupid they had done drunk, though I understood why they were reserved. No one wanted to seem like an alcoholic or a troublemaker during the interview.

The truth was that they were under an immense amount of pressure. They were being asked to perform harder and better than they ever had in their lives under conditions so harsh as to be comical. But this wasn't comical. They knew that this process would have huge implications about their time in the military and the shape of their careers. A huge part of the next three years of their army service was being decided over the course of four days. Their army service would also have an important impact on the rest of their lives, and it was all being determined at that very moment.

Of course, the process was even more important for us and the units. The choices we made today about who to select for each unit would decide the units' future and legacy. Our choices would decide the very composition of our units, as well as their ultimate performance and reputations. This was a great responsibility that we took very seriously. It was incumbent upon us to pick the best people, both the most obvious top performers, as well as those hidden gems that would round out the unit and make it stronger and more resilient through diversity.

In a way, this was the most important mission I had ever embarked upon. We were literally deciding the fate and future of our units, right then and there, as we selected the next generation. Hardest of all was that we would not know how well we had done at this mission, not until years later. Only time would tell if we had selected the right people that would strengthen and enrich the unit and carry the legacy forward with strength, honor and dignity.

An instructor during gibush yachatiot

EPILOGUE

OCTOBER 7TH

"Sometimes, the path we've walked has given all it can; moving forward is not giving up, but discovering new ways to make a difference." ~ *Anonymous*

Thousands of Hamas military operatives and affiliated civilians infiltrated Israel...

WHAT??!!!

I sit on my bed, in Los Angeles, at 10:30pm and begin to receive messages in my Garin group chat. Even 10 years later we are still close and message each other every day. Unfortunately, that day, the messages were of photos and videos of Hamas operatives driving down the streets of Sderot!

My mind is blown.

How can this be, what the fuck happened?

Noam, from my Garin was living next to Sderot.

He's texting our group chat about the play-by-play incidents happening outside his front door.

At this point, Noam took his pistol, locked his doors and was ready for the worst. I sit at home, pray, hope, and beg that nothing will happen to him.

As the hours go by the news begins to update the public. This was not just a singular targeted incident attack on Sderot, but a full-scale invasion from Hamas operatives on the south of Israel.

I quickly texted my adopted family on the kibbutz, Aviv and Liat, who were still living in Kibbutz Nir Oz, asking if they were ok.

I was so worried about them and all of my friends and neighbors living in Nir Oz. I paced around my room, driving myself crazy thinking about how close the kibbutz is to the Gazan city of Khan Yunis, a Hamas stronghold that I had "visited" 10 years ago.

As the hours flew by that night, I also began to check in with my army unit. For such a full-scale attack, this obviously meant war. Would we be called up?

With an instinct that was engraved in me, deep into my soul, I began to pack my army bag. If we got called up, I would be ready.

It was now 7:00 a.m., and the news had finally spread about what happened. Thousands of Hamas operatives had infiltrated the south of Israel in a surprise attack. They simultaneously came out from multiple tunnels, flew hang gliders across the morning sky, and used explosive and agricultural equipment to destroy the fence separating the borders between Israel and Gaza.

It took eight hours of fierce non-stop combat for the Israeli Dense Forces and the Israeli police to repel the attack and retake the major kibbutzim, farms, and cities that were taken over by Hamas operatives. The Israeli death count at this time was unknown, but we knew it would be high.

At this point, I came out of my room, to wash my face. I had been glued to my screen and phone for the entirety of the night, in shock and disbelief of such a horrific attack. My mom came out and I told her the news.

At the time I was staying at my parent's home for the weekend, spending time with my dad. Unfortunately, my father, Bud, was diagnosed with Parkinsons Disease and had been battling it for 5 years. At this point he was in the late stages of the disease, and I made it a point to stay at their home as often as possible so I could help around the house and spend as much time with my dad as possible.

My mom saw the door to my room was open and noticed the large, packed backpack I had received from the army many years ago. She franticly shouted, "Max, have you been called up?! What's with the bag?"

I explained to my mom that I had not been called up yet, but given what had happened it was just a matter of time. She was worried, not only for me but for the state of our family. My dad being so ill and me potentially leaving would cause great grief on him, on her, on my new girlfriend Stephanie and the rest of my family.

My heart was torn. On one hand, I had my love for Israel, my love for my brothers, my love for my friends and family in Israel, at my kibbutz that was so horrifically attacked. On the other hand, I had my life in Los Angeles, I had my father who was very ill, I had my mother who at the time was still battling stage 4 Melanoma cancer, and a new loving relationship with my wonderful girlfriend Stephanie.

And just then, I got a message from my WhatsApp. It was the team group chat. We had been called up. However, I noticed my name was not on the list. I immediately called my commander Stachi.

Ring...Ring...Ring!

Stachi, what's going on? Why isn't my name on the list?! Stachi replied, "Max you're in the US, by the time you get here we will already be at base and we cannot wait for you to make it here and even if you came, the plugot (army unit) has already gotten soldiers volunteering and coming, we're at 150% capacity. If you came, you would be sitting in Tel Aviv, waiting around for a room to open up for you."

I told Stachi, "look, I understand all that, but I cannot just sit here and watch my brothers go to war, to literally defend my home, I need to do something." Stachi said there's a lot of gear that is missing. Maybe you could help with that?

I said, "I'll look into what I can do and get back to you."

Torn between my family in Israel and my family in the US, I didn't know what to do. I'm a fighter, I'm not a logistics officer. I need to go and fight and defend our people. All I wanted to do was grab my bag, grab a plane ticket and head straight to the airport. The first flight out was at 10:00 a.m. via Turkish airlines to France and then from France to Israel. But I thought, before I do anything I need to speak to Stephanie.

I called her up and said I'm coming over; I'll see you in 15 minutes.

As I arrived at her grandmother's home, where she was staying because her home was under renovation, I ran upstairs and said shalom to her grandmother. In a frantic state, she asked if I had heard the news. Of course, I had heard and said I am thinking of going. She of course had a strong opinion on the matter. She said "Max, you can't go and leave your family here behind. You must take care of them." I spouted back, "What about my family there, what about my brothers there, who will take care of them, if not for me. I made a promise, I'm in the reserves!"

Stephanie came down to us arguing and I decided that Stephanie and I needed to go outside and talk about everything going on.

As we walked out, I asked Stephanie, "Stephanie, what should I do? My heart is torn, and I don't know what to do" She replied, "Max, I can't make this decision for you. Whatever you decide I'll support you, but this is something you need to decide on your own."

I was a little surprised, I pressed, "Would you be worried about me if I left" She answered, "Of course I would be worried, but I'm not going to be the one to stand in your way. I can't have you resent me if I told you not to go, you need to figure out what is best for you right now and stick to it."

After more thought, I said to myself, "Well both my mom and my dad are battling life threatening diseases, leaving them here alone could be devastating, and Stachi already said that there was no room for me even if I left, so with all that in mind, I said outload, "I guess I'm joining the logistics side of things this time."

And that was the beginning of what would be the next six months of my life.

October 8th

With my decision finalized on what and how I would support my team, I focused on the one big question, how am I going to send supplies to my team in Israel?

This question led to a multitude of questions, some focused-on legality, others on raising funds, and even more on what are the names of all these items in English? As you can imagine, serving in the IDF, I only spoke Hebrew, and we only described and spoke about our equipment in Hebrew and of that Hebrew, most of it was army slang. So, the only way I knew how to speak about army equipment was in Hebrew army slang. I had no idea what anything was called in English. So first, I had to quickly start googling how to describe and call the different items that may be needed, such as tactical uniforms, vests, body armor, ballistic helmets, the different brands of scopes, night vision and thermal vision binoculars, camouflage gear, and the list goes on and on and on.

After spending a couple of hours teaching myself the names of different kinds of crucial gear, I needed to figure out a system. How am I going to do this?

At first, I thought, ok the best way is to raise money, send it to Israel, and have someone in Israel buy the equipment there. Great! But how am I going to raise money here? I started to investigate Go Fund Me and other similar platforms. However, Stephanie's Safta (Grandmother) reminded me that everything needed to be run through a 501 C-3 designated charity and ideally someone with a good reputation in the community, or else it would be very hard to convince anyone to donate and to ensure the donation is legitimate. With that in mind, I looked at my Go Fund Me page and thought, anyone can make a Go Fund Me page for anything today, the money would then be going into my personal bank account in the US and from there to Israel.

Thinking as a donor, this felt too sketchy, and I didn't want any charitable funds going into my bank account. I then thought a little longer and a light bulb went off. I called the one person I knew well in fundraising for help. "Russell, can you please help me, how am I going to be able to accomplish this goal?" With a big smile that I felt burst through my phone, he said "Max, we have the platform to help you here, let me call my CFO and get you set up, from there you can use our charity to raise the funds, we promise we won't take any of it, and we will then send the funds over to Israel and help support our soldiers."

With a big sigh of relief, I thought to myself, ok one challenge completed, now to whom am I going to send the funds to in Israel? It needs to be another charitable organization to accept the funds. And then I thought, Asulin! He and Rem both started a charity, called Tzevet Paz, which was created to help the youth of Israel prepare for their army service, let's use that!

Ring Ring Ring...

"Asulin! How are you? Things are so crazy right now, are you with the team?"

"Hey Max, I know I know, I'm ok. I'm not with the team, I was placed elsewhere in reserves, but I know they are all at base getting ready to go out to the kibbutzim and search for any remaining terrorists hiding away," said Asulin.

"Oh damn, ya I had heard many were hiding away in the bushes now, waiting to ambush those that come by. I hope and pray they stay vigilant and safe. By the way I need to ask, do you still have that charity that you and Rem created a couple of months ago?" I asked.

"Ya, why? Responded Assulin."

"Well, I need help, so I am going to raise money so our

team can buy better equipment. I would like to use your charity as the receiver of funds and for you guys to buy the equipment and hand it to the Rasap's and Rasar's, logistics' officers, in the field. And from there they will quickly distribute it to the soldiers in the unit," I informed him.

Asulin replied "Max, that sounds great, let's do it!"

We both knew that the equipment in reserves was shit, purchased in the 1970's and never saw the light of day, and when going to war, I'm not going to let my brothers go with shit equipment.

So, with Asulin's permission, we now had created a charitable network where money could now be legitimately raised in the US, transferred to Israel, and used to purchase desperately needed army equipment for my boys.

Raising Money

Thankfully, my mom and dad were professional fundraisers and still had many contacts in the Jewish philanthropic community. I, too, followed in their footsteps and joined the boards of multiple charities. So, after I finished making my link, and hooked everything up to my friend's charitable organization in the US, I then began making calls.

My calls went something like this:

Ring Ring Ring

"Hi David, it's Max. How are you?"

David: I'm ok Max, with everything going on in Israel, it's been tough. Are you going over to join your team?"

Max: Yes, yes, I know it's an absolute tragedy and no I was not able to join my unit at this time. They're completely full, but I wanted to talk to you about something related. You see, the army was not prepared for this, logistically I was talking to my guys and the equipment they have is absolute dog shit. The vests are old, the scopes are old, some guys are missing bullet proof body armor, they don't have the right kinds of boots, it's an absolute mess. They are not prepared to go into battle."

David: Wait what?? Really? But Israel has one of the best armies in the world, how can they not have equipment?"

Max: Well, let's be specific, the current conscripted army is fine, they have everything they need, but Israel just called up hundreds of thousands of reserve soldiers, the most ever, and on top of that from those they called, 150% showed up. The morale in Israel, to defend our homeland, is the highest it's ever been. But these guys in the reserves need gear and they need it now.

David: Oh, I see, I see, but where is the government? Aren't they supposed to be overseeing this?

Max: Well, we can wait for the government, while soldiers go out into the field today without body armor, comfortable helmets, proper shoes, comfortable uniforms, and maybe they'll get it situated in a couple of months. Who knows, It's the Israeli government, the same place where I had to stand in line for hours to get seen by a doctor. Or you and I can start saving lives today.

David: I see, how can I help?

Max: I'm going to send you a link, please donate $10,000, and please share it with all your friends and family and ask them to donate too.

David: I'll donate $30,000, thank you for all that you're doing.

And just like that, I started raising money. He later donated another $100,000 dollars and hosted an event at their home in which we raised over $200,000 that night.

And before I knew it, with the support of my family, friends, and my girlfriend Stephanie, I was out, speaking at small engagements, explaining the situation to rooms full of people and raising hundreds of thousands of dollars.

Pivoting

Once we had raised a little bit of money, we immediately started spending it on whatever the soldiers needed. First up was Body Armor, Helmets, and Vests, these were crucial.

So, I made a call to some of the largest military vendors I knew in Israel, Agilite, Maphro, Marom Dolphin, among others. And when I spoke to them, I got the same response, I'm so sorry we're delayed on back order. It's going to be at least 4-8 weeks before we get the supplies you're asking for.

Yelling into the phone like any annoyed Israeli, I would respond: "WHAT??!! How can you not have any, there's a war going on and I need it now. I don't have 4-8 weeks to wait!!"

I would then angrily move onto the next vendor.

Eventually we realized that there was truly no equipment in Israel. Places were on back stock or only had odd sizes left over that would not fit anyone.

So, with this truth bomb hitting us and blowing up our original plans, we had to pivot. We had to start buying equipment in the US and shipping it over to Israel. What a nightmare especially considering I now needed to find an organization that would take on the risk of purchasing the equipment in the US, under their name. I began to call up friends for ideas. By this point I had met a few other people in LA who were doing the same thing. We began to share resources and help each other out. One organization was having a pretty good run of things, and they mentioned they would be willing to share their Chabad organization, which was based in the U.S. and was willing to take any risk for our soldiers. I said something I never thought I would say, "Baruch Hashem, thank G-d for Chabad"!

And from then on, anything we could not buy in Israel, we started to buy in the US and ship over to Israel. But shipping was going to have its own array of challenges.

Shipping

So, there were a few challenges. First and foremost, getting to Israel, only one airline in the world was still flying to Israel, EL AL, and thankfully they cared. So, I began messaging around, found someone who had connections there and said, let's do my first shipment together. They agreed and I ordered the necessary equipment in America. It arrived at my parent's home, express delivery within 2 days. Next, I went to the luggage store and bought as many big duffel bags as they had. I then called up some friends who came over and we began stuffing the bags. We stuffed these first bags, with tactical uniforms, body armor and helmets all of which were bought at a major discount, because America cares about defending democracy and freedom from terrorists, thank you!

Once we got the bags stuffed, I put in little Apple tracking devices and dropped them in each bag ensuring nothing could get lost. I then gave them to my newfound friend, Avi, who the next morning was going to help me get them on, at the airport. Avi lived only 10 minutes away and he had a big black pickup truck, so I brought the bags over to him to load on his car.

That morning, I woke up with so much excitement, we were going to do our first shipment, we were going to finally do something to help!

The flight was leaving at 2:00 p.m. and we needed to get there 4 hours early to be first in line to get our equipment on. There I waited for my associate Avi to come meet me with the packed bags. I got there at 10:00 a.m. excited and ready to go. There I waited for him. Waited and waited and waited. Avi was thankfully answering his phone, but he was stuck in the infamous L.A. traffic. Bumper to bumper on a true stand still on the freeway. God only knew when he was going to arrive. As the hours went by, I checked in with the air marshal he knew that he was going to "claim" our bags on the flight and bring them with him.

He was not supposed to be seen so we met in secret outside of the airport to go over the plan once again. We would bring the bags to the gate, give his name to the person on the flight that was "claiming" them, and pay / drop them off at the front desk. From there Avi knew the guys in El AL that took the bags off the planes in Israel and ours were specially marked, so they knew how to take ours off to the side. From there, they would drive them to their warehouse and from the warehouse, the logistics officer for each unit would meet, grab their bag, and head back to base bringing the much- needed equipment to the combat soldiers.

But for now, I was waiting for Avi...

An hour went by, then another, we only had two hours left until the flight took off. I was starting to panic. I had not known Avi for very long, but he seemed like a trustworthy guy. We had already waited so long getting the money raised, equipment bought, and everything packed and ready to go to my house. I called Avi again, in a panic that they would close the gate soon and we would miss our window, and more importantly, that the troops would not get this equipment in time before going full force into Gaza. He told me not to worry and that traffic was finally starting to move. Another hour went by and finally, I saw his black pick-up truck in the distance. In a rush, I jumped on the back and started throwing the twelve 100-pound bags off the truck and onto trolleys as he and I started to race back to the El Al check-in stand. Just as we got to the front, I spoke with the airline attendant who told me it was too late. There was no more room on the flight for the bags and they did not have time to get them on and they were about to close the station.

I begged him over and over, asked to speak to his boss, but his boss was not there. He had already gone to the gate. Avi was furious and started yelling at the agent, saying "don't you understand what we're doing! We're sending protective equipment to IDF soldiers. We're trying to save lives! You must let our bags on now!" The agent huffed and said "you're losing your temper and being rude. I won't speak with you anymore, go away." After getting upset, Avi stepped aside and made a phone call. He said not to worry, he knew someone high up in El Al, but time was running out!

About 25 minutes go by, and the flight will now be leaving in 30 minutes, and I'm still there pleading with the associate to please let us put something on. And then the agent's phone rings. It's his boss. His boss is now screaming at him, telling him that someone got to the pilot of the plane, who stated that he is refusing to fly the plane unless our bags get on. The agent, now red in the face, immediately opened back up the station and quickly checked all our bags and loaded them onto the plane. Avi's contact came through and 30 minutes later all our bags were on the flight and on their way to Israel!

A job well done. And after our first successful mission, it was time to scale up and scale fast.

Throughout the next few months, I created a small team of volunteers who helped with every necessity such as raising money, packing bags, driving back and forth from the airport, and now sending thousands of equipment to soldiers. And when equipment could be delivered faster from other locations such as New York or Miami, I made contacts in those cities and had them sent from there.

There were countless strangers, donors, and amazing individuals who all helped in every small way possible. It felt as if all of the diaspora and all of the people of Israel were engaged in fighting this war, in way or another.

At the end of the day, we raised over a million dollars and sent thousands of pieces of equipment, from tactical uniforms to class 3 bullet proof helmets, body armor, vests, night vision goggles, drones, camouflage kits, medical bags, and so on and so on to over 2,000 soldiers through the Israel Defense Forces. Eventually, I also returned to Israel and was back in the reserves in a logistics capacity ensuring equipment made it to the right places. But as I sit here today writing this story, the war is still waging on, and the hostages are still not free. My adopted father from my kibbutz was murdered trying to defend my kibbutz. My adopted mother, his wife, was taken hostage but she was one of the lucky ones and was released with the first wave of hostages last November. So, I beg and pray that one day soon, all our hostages will come home to us, and we will defeat our enemies and bring stability and peace back. our home. And that my little kibbutz, Nir Oz is rebuilt and brought back to life again.

Thank you to everyone for supporting Israel and supporting our soldiers, and please continue your support, as it is needed more now than ever.

DEDICATION

Although many great books about war acclaim the opportunity to ascertain glory, that does not exist, not to those who are fortunate enough to come home. For glory is reserved to those who will never be able to return, and that is a price that is too high to pay.

This book is dedicated to all those in the war in Tzuk Eitan that paid the ultimate sacrifice in defending the State of Israel. To those who obtained true glory as they bravely defended their friends, family, brothers and the rest of the Jewish people who could not lift the sword. In addition, it is dedicated to those from my unit who paid the ultimate sacrifice in the defense of the State of Israel during Operation Protective Edge (Suk Eitan). To Li Mat, Shahar Dover, Shahar Shalev, Paz Eliyahu, Yuval Heiman, and Liad Levy.

Li Mat - was the heart of our team. Constantly joking around, he lifted the intense atmosphere of the army to one where we were able to enjoy ourselves and have fun. He was always able to roll with the punches and made sure everyone felt welcomed and was having a good time despite the difficulties of being in a Special Forces unit. Li was also an incredible athlete and a humble man.

Shahar Dover – emulated excellence. He was always striving to make everything perfect. He demonstrated what it meant to be a star soldier. At times Shahar would lead the team in physical exercise. At the end of our eight-minute ab workout, he would make everyone put in an extra ten seconds. Because even when you think you are at your limit – he proved to us that when you set your mind to it, you can always accomplish more than what you thought possible.

Shahar Shalev – emanated self-sacrifice and generosity and lived with a higher standard than others. A man who did things the right way not because anyone had asked him to but because it was simply the right thing to do. When it came to his work ethic, he was always the first to sign up and the last to leave – often finishing his own tasks and helping others until the entire project was completed. Shahar had a huge heart in which everyone was always welcome. He often gave out pieces of his own candy during navigation drills so everyone would have something sweet to chew on while they navigated in the darkness all night, for twenty plus miles.

Paz Eliyahu – our commander – was the first commander to build my self-confidence and taught me that I will survive training and become a warrior of the unit. He was able to bring our team together under a singular idea – the team is more important than any single person and together we can overcome obstacles we never thought possible. Paz emanated strength, confidence, humility, and because of these traits, he commanded our respect and with it came our love. Paz not only felt like a commander but the older brother I never had.

Yuval Heiman – He was a role model for the entire team. He was the best runner, had the best endurance, was an excellent shot, simply the best at everything he set his mind to. In addition to him possessing excellent traits that made him a great soldier, he was also a kind person with an infectious smile who wanted to do good by everyone and make everyone's day a little easier. He would always be the first to volunteer when someone needed help, no matter the task.

Liad Levy - A real friend. Whether in our team or as a commander, Liad always saw directly into the hearts of those around him. As a commander he always put his soldiers' needs first and foremost, especially before himself. When he went to commanders' course, although not obligated, he made sure to come back and participate in one of the team's hardest challenges, the final Masa. No matter how difficult or painful the task, if it meant he could help out his teammates, his friends, Liad would be there. Liad was a powerful leader yet humble and quiet.

Aviv Atzili - On October 7th the world lost the kindest, gentlest lion of Zion I have had the privilege to know. Aviv was very easy-going, always had his door open to greet all with a hot cup of tea and a big hug that filled your soul with love and kindness. Aviv loved his garden, his metal workshop, and above all his friends and family. He loved the land of Israel and was a true Sabra and Zionist with all his heart. He was a great artist through his painting and sculpting which stemmed through his love of nature and his home. Through his metal working he created beautiful pieces of art about his home and his community. He was an avid traveler; I remember seeing the gorgeous photos of his time travelling throughout India with his family for over 6 months.

Aviv served in the elite special force's unit, Egoz, and served his entire reserve duty as a commander in their elite Alpanistim division. He also served as the head of the Kitat Konenut (first line of defense) for his kibbutz. On Oct 7th he grabbed his gun and started killing the terrorists that infiltrated the kibbutz. He went from home to home, space to space, switching from weapon to weapon defending and protecting his friends and family from evil terrorists that infiltrated his home. After a long fight, lasting hours, he was eventually surrounded and fell. He fought and fell defending those he loved. Aviv is survived by his wife Liat who was taken hostage and thankfully returned to Israel during a hostage deal and his amazing 3 kids, Ofri, Neta and Aya.

Tzichon Libracha – May their memories be a blessing.

ABOUT THE AUTHOR

Max Levin grew up in St. Louis, Missouri but moved to Los Angeles at 14 when his parents decided for him to continue getting a Jewish education at DeToledo High School. He then graduated and went to Young Judea year course, volunteering as a medic for Magen David Adom for 6 months. After his year, he stayed in Israel, made Aliyah (citizenship) and was drafted into the Israeli Army. During his service he joined the Special Forces Unit, Palchan Tzanhanim within the paratrooper's division and fought and was wounded in Operation Protective Edge. After a quick recovery he returned to his team and unit and finished the rest of his 3-years performing missions in the West Bank. Since finishing the Army Max returned to the United States and graduated Cum Laude from Columbia University with a degree in Financial Economics. Max currently works in private equity and commercial real estate with a focus on the energy sector.

CALL TO ACTION

Hello Everyone,

Thank you for taking the time to read my book, I hope you enjoyed it and learned something new.

If you would like to continue to support the State of Israel, there are two wonderful causes of which the proceeds of this book will be donated to.

The first is a program called Bishvil Hamachar (On the Path to Tomorrow) is a non-profit, volunteer-based organization established after the Second Lebanon War in 2009 to assist former Israel Defense Forces combat soldiers cope with difficult combat memories and adapt back to civilian life in a healthy way utilizing group outdoor activities, trekking and other physical activities in nature, combined with psychotherapeutic tools.

Please visit bshvil.org for more information and a place to donate.

The second is צוות פז - מתאחדים בזכותם.

The goal of this organization is 'to embrace one another'. Team Paz is creating a monument, in remembrance of the fallen. The monument will be built in a village for at-risk youth, close to the paratroopers' base. Team Paz will come several times a year to teach the youth of the excellence and values we gathered in the military. The emphasis is on creating a connection between the Paz team, the paratroopers and the youth village. Thanks to them we can educate a generation of excellent, young people.

If you are interested in supporting this organization please follow צוות פז - מתאחדים בזכותם on Facebook, where more information will be posted on where to donate.

Thank you again for taking the time to learn and for your support.

Am Yisrael Chai!

www.ingramcontent.com/pod-product-compliance
Lightning Source LLC
Chambersburg PA
CBHW071534120726
47907CB00014B/1791

9781637770467